Jesus Is My Vaccine

Mila Norquist

CURTISS STREET
PRESS

❀ Created with Vellum

For my brother Tom, with love

Part One

Chapter One

Amy
April, 2021

A woman jumps in front of my car. She hoists a sign that reads, "UNMASK THE KIDS." I slam my foot on the brake and yank the steering wheel. Christ! I almost hit her. Dozens of protesters clog the parking lot in front of the education department's squat red-brick building. Somebody pounds on my rear window. A cloud of placards held aloft by the angry mob blocks my view. I slowly inch forward, trying to see where there might be an empty parking spot.

Over there! I start to turn. But the crowd moves in that direction, too, as if sensing where I'm headed. Someone beats on my back right window. Jesus! What the hell? I look all around. It's a sea of signs. "I CALL MY OWN SHOTS" and "NO TO VACCINES FOR KIDS" and "VAC-

CINE MANDATES VIOLATE BODILY AUTONOMY." I swerve in the opposite direction and find an empty spot near the perimeter of the lot.

When I open my car door, a wall of noise slaps me. People in the crowd yell and whoop, jab their signs into the air as if trying to skewer low-flying birds. I witness the death of irony when a woman with an anti-abortion message on her tee-shirt shouts, "I'm not anti-vax, I'm pro choice! My body, my choice!" She tries to get a chant going with those last four words, but somebody else is having more luck with "Trust in God, not vaccines!"

Back when I first got elected to the school board in 2016, few people ever attended our meetings other than the board members. Budgets, building maintenance, and personnel issues were the usual topics. Sometimes we board members would disagree with each other. Someone might occasionally raise a voice. But there was no name-calling. There certainly weren't people in the audience telling us we should be hanged or shot.

Everything's different now. Boy, is it different. By the time I weave my way through the crowd and enter the hearing room, it's already packed with people, probably a hundred of them. I see the "Moms for Liberty" are here. There're some nasty bitches in that group, I'll tell you. I see tee-shirts and signs for other groups, too, like the 970 Alliance. Their tagline? "Uniting Conservatives for a Better America." I crane my neck to see more of the crowd. There are some "Three Percenters" out there, too. They're a self-styled militia that promotes conspiratorial views about government overreach and perceived violations of the

Constitution by government officials. All of these people look like caricatures. And they look crazy.

I'm still standing at my seat, arranging my papers on the table in front of me when Sam Levitson, our chair, pounds his gavel. He has to slam it several times before the din quiets. "The meeting will come to order." He shepherds us quickly through the approval of the agenda, the previous meeting's minutes, and the ritual recognitions of achievements by various students in the district. Things slow down when we get to the executive committee's report on the planning process for a new Mesa Vista High School. Costs are a constant concern, and we're all careful to make it clear that we're trying to balance costs and quality in our considerations. The crowd remains fairly quiet through all that.

Then Sam looks around and says, "Okay, now it's time for audience comments." The energy level in the room surges. A buzz of excitement fills the air. The temperature in the room feels like it shoots up ten degrees. "I want to remind all of you that we expect civility and politeness. We'll allot 45 minutes for comments. Anyone wishing to speak should identify yourself by name and zip code. Each speaker is allowed three minutes."

A woman in her 60s is the first to the microphone. She holds it in both hands, close to her mouth, like a lounge crooner. She says she's a physician. She's so lethargic and incoherent that the direction of her comment is at first unclear. Then I begin to get the gist of it: she feels that requiring students to wear a mask is "essentially coercing them into a medical experiment that can cause harm." She shares data from "a study" that she claims shows masks and social distancing have caused "an increase in COVID infection rates in students and staff," and that "remote learning actually caused an increase in COVID infection rates in staff." Most improbable, I think, unless being away from school left everyone with more time to hang out together and breathe in each other's faces. But dozens of people in the audience agree with her; they loudly shout their support for the claim.

The next woman, a "concerned parent," reads part of the Nuremberg Code from 1947, noting the need to get consent from individuals who are subject to medical experiments. "COVID testing and vaccines are experimental!! The Nazis paved the way for what's happening now!" Now, the crowd is on its feet, clapping, stomping feet, yelling. "No medical tyranny!" "Wake up, America!" "Jesus is my vaccine!"

Andrea Longnecker earns my appreciation by expressing her empathy for the Board in its efforts to protect students and staff. "The medical profession has been wearing masks for over 100 years and I've never heard of any of them suffering from mask usage." The crowd boos. If tar and feathers were available, I know what Andrea would soon be wearing. She looks around at the horde jeering her, obviously surprised by the vehement reaction to her benign comment. She decides not to continue and beats a hasty retreat.

I'm lost in my thoughts of sympathy for the poor woman when I hear a loud tapping. Someone raps on a microphone. "Can you hear me?" I look around. "CAN YOU HEAR ME?!" the voice shouts. I can't see where it's coming from. Then I see a large man raise a microphone a few feet on its stand. He lifts a tiny old lady onto a chair in front of the microphone. He wraps his arms around her wobbly, standing figure. He's trying to keep her steady, balanced, safe. She taps the microphone a few more times, then again shouts into it, her voice quavering with age but surprisingly loud. "Can you hear me?"

With more patience than I'd have, Sam reassures her. "Yes, ma'am, we can hear you."

"Well, I hope so, because I'm here to talk about something very important. My name is Ida Hansen, and I'm concerned about the bathroom issue!" She twists her head around like an owl, seeing if the crowd is listening. "This whole—what is it?—LJPQD thing has gone too far. My friend Yolanda told me yesterday that litter boxes have been added to school bathrooms in Mesa Vista for students who think they're cats! They call themselves *furries!*" Half the room erupts in laughter, the other half in gasps of horror.

"Yes! I'm telling you: I was just as stunned as you are. More than upset, I guess you could say. I'm furious. There is a, uh—what's the word?—oh, an 'agenda' that is being pushed on our schools. I, for one, do not think the Mesa Vista public schools should be spending money on litter boxes for students who think they're cats!"

She scowls at the five of us sitting at the dais behind a polished wood table. "What are you people? Crazy?!" Then, with the man at her side holding her tight, she turns to the crowd and yells, "When I was young and had kids in this school system, I never would have allowed this kind of insanity. You folks shouldn't either!"

The crowd erupts in some sort of delirium. Someone

starts chanting, "No Litter Boxes! No Litter Boxes!" Soon, the hysteria spreads, and two-thirds of the audience is on their feet shouting, pounding their fists into the air, transported by wild emotion.

I am simply astonished at how ready this crowd is to swallow untruths. What the hell is going on? I catch the eye of another board member. Paul raises his right eyebrow at me and lowers the other one. I immediately catch the humorous intent of his expression: he's scolding me for coddling the Furries. I burst out laughing.

Our chair waits a few moments for the fever to recede, then calmly says, "Let me be as clear as I can. There is no truth whatsoever to what Ms. Hansen has just said. There are not now, and have never been, litter boxes in the bathrooms of any Mesa Vista schools. And there won't be."

"Liar! Liar!" the old woman shouts into the microphone as her large friend starts to lift her down from the chair. Some people in the crowd echo her smear. "Liars! Liars! Liars"

"Next speaker," Sam says, his voice now betraying his weariness.

A heavy-set man wearing a blue polyester golf shirt and khaki shorts steps up to the microphone. He rants for a while about vaccines, then points at the members of the Board. "If you people require everyone to get the 'genocide jab,' you'll essentially be war criminals and should hang by the neck!" Some in the crowd shout "Hang, hang!" Sam pounds his gavel and asks for civility. When the man persists, Sam orders the AV guy to cut his mic. The man continues, calling me and my fellow board members Nazis and repeating that we should hang by the neck until dead.

The crowd is so riled up at this point that Sam, apparently fearing that things are about to get completely out of control, calls for a short recess.

When we return, the crowd seems to have thinned a bit, but those who remain share the most extreme form of zealotry. I notice one guy wearing a crown fashioned out of bullets. A tall, thin man with long hair and a scraggly beard carries a three-by-six-foot cross. His sandaled feet take him to the mic stand, where he poses, the notch of the cross resting on his shoulder. He's ready to speak as soon as Sam gives him the go-ahead, which he does.

"This here pandemic," the man says, in the tone and cadence of a Sunday preacher, "is God telling humanity to change the way we're living!" Shouts of *Amen* come from around the room. "I'm telling you folks: we are living through what the Holy Bible calls 'the end times'!" Now, the amens turn to *hallelujahs,* and two-thirds of the crowd start waving their arms above their heads.

I figure it's only a matter of time before some begin to rend their garments and speak in tongues. Pointing now at us board members, he continues, "And I am here to tell *you* that all your masks and your vaccinations and such-all are mere illusions of control over death. There is *nothing* any of us can do to make our days on earth one second longer than the Lord Jesus Christ wants them to be!" More *hallelu-jahs* all around. "We have to REPENT! We must seek God's forgiveness for the sins of quarantining, masking, getting vaccinated—trying to avoid God's gift of death!"

The man with the bullet crown shouts, "Amen, brother! Vaccines are 'Satan's Syrup'! They're the Mark of the Beast!"

Other people start shouting out: "Satan's allies want to put microchips inside us!" "They want to try to control our minds!" The cacophony grows louder and more chaotic:

"Fauci is the devil's deputy!" "They want to make it so we can't cross the gates of heaven!" "They hate Christians and want to wipe us all out!" "Vaccines make you sterile!" "Masks cause COVID!"

The din increases. I put my forehead to my hands and want to cry. I'm not sure which is causing my headache—the crowd's roar or its idiocy.

Sam Levitson hastily adjourns the meeting, prompting some in the crowd to object to being censored and shut out. I hear Sam mutter "tough shit" as he scurries past me, retreating to his office. A Mesa Vista PD officer stays around to make sure the crowd disperses and that each of us board members gets to our car safely. As I walk to mine, I watch a big hulk of a man heading to his truck. Something about him is odd—but also somehow familiar. He has a distinctive gait. And I realize I've seen him multiple times in the past couple of weeks. He seems to be everywhere I go.

Chapter Two

Marty

All of Mesa Vista's governmental bodies are problematic. It's not just the school board. The city council is a mess, too. And the county public-health department is full of tyrants. But the school board is our focus right now because of this COVID thing and because of the Nazi policies the board is imposing on the kids and school staff in our community. Social distancing, remote learning, mask requirements. Vaccinations will be next.

My team and I aren't alone in fighting against the school board. Frankly, I'm surprised and delighted at the number of people and groups in town who are energized by what's been happening. There are organizations like Moms for Liberty. Those folks don't take shit from anyone. And the members of Stand for the Constitution are equally vigorous. All these people are good at organizing, protesting, and agitating. And there's lots of 'em. That's what we need right now: large numbers. I figure the Soviets beat the Nazis in World War Two by throwing crazy numbers of troops at 'em. I like to think of all those folks at the school-board meeting as our regular troops.

By contrast, I like to think of my team as being more like Special Operations Forces. You know: the Green Berets, the Navy SEALs—the specially trained guys who carry out unconventional operations including offensive raids, demolitions, reconnaissance, search and rescue, counterterrorism.

I'm a longtime Republican activist and agitator. I used to work for Project Veritas, that group founded by James O'Keefe back in 2010. We'd use secretive recordings and edited videos to discredit mainstream media organizations and progressive groups. We were good at generating bad publicity for our targets. Working with Veritas, I honed my skills.

I moved from DC back to Mesa Vista a few years ago to care for my aging mama. But I wasn't willing to give up my interest in political agitation and mischief. After I'd been back here for about a year, I had a stroke of luck. I stumbled upon a darknet site of an organization of wealthy conservatives out here in the West intent on reconstructing this country from the ground up. Their idea was to train people to use the lens of national politics—and the playbook of seasoned activists—to shape school boards and other local offices.

My initial training occurred over a ten-day period at a

fancy private estate about ten miles outside Pinedale, Wyoming, at the western edge of the Wind River mountain range. My trainers were obviously good people with the right values and objectives. Twenty of us had been recruited and brought there to be trained in basic tactics of political disruption and activism. The general goal was to provide us with the skills to manipulate the politics of several states over the coming years—Wyoming, Colorado, and Montana. I liked that idea. I liked to think that finally I might be in a position to do something about the direction of this country. Take it back from the *true* deplorables.

In addition to learning about tactics, we also studied issues. Vaccines, for instance. This was in November, 2020. American companies recently had announced their successes with vaccination trials. Biden had seized power illegitimately and made it clear that once he took office, he would move ahead with the widespread distribution of the vaccines. My fellow trainees and I would be doing everything we could to spread chaos, encourage and radicalize anti-vaxxers, and actively oppose public officials on the wrong side of right.

I eventually found a few other people here in Mesa Vista who are true conservatives and who want to be agitators, but prefer to work in the background. They've proved to be able allies. Some people might describe us as a motley crew. As I say, I prefer to think of us as a special-ops force. There's a disabled guy in his mid-70s whom the rest of us only know by his ham-radio call sign, which he also uses as his Twitter handle—K3LVR. We pronounce it "Clever." He's rabidly opposed to vaccines and knows a lot about them. He loves using his ham radio and Twitter (the modern-day equivalent of ham radio) to spread his opinions about vaccines and governmental overreach.

Another of my confederates is a guy named Ray. He's sort of weird and a bit of a recluse. But, like K3LVR, he's good with technology and knows a helluva lot about the internet and the darknet. He's skilled at collecting information and spreading it. And, also like K3LVR, Ray has an animating issue, something he feels strongly about: race. He hates minorities (he uses the N word a lot) and anybody he perceives as trying to help them. And he sees COVID-related policies—lockdowns, masks, vaccinations— as part of larger conspiracies against White Americans.

The other member of my team is a former professional wrestler. Dwayne Fowler. He was actually in the WWE for a half-dozen years or so and did pretty well for himself. But he got hurt and had to give it up. During a televised match, "Killer Kowalski" did a flying leap off the ropes onto Dwayne. KK's own knees were supposed to absorb his falling weight, but he landed on Dwayne's hip, shattering the joint and the top of Dwayne's femur. Dwayne walks sorta funny now. But he got a nice insurance settlement from WWE and he doesn't seem unhappy with his lot in life. He's not as informed as the rest of us about politics. But the thing I really appreciate about him is that he's willing to do the grunt work, happy to get his hands dirty, if you catch my drift.

Working together, the four of us are determined to make a difference here in Mesa Vista. Our first objective is to do something about the school board and its COVID policies. The board has five members. Three of them are a problem: Amy Wilson, Paul Patton, and Sam Levitson. The other two—Tom Davis and Abbie Parish—are reliably conservative: they don't ever vote in favor of harmful policies. We need to change the balance to get a conservative majority on the board. And the easiest way to do that, we think, is to drive one of the libtards to resign and make sure that in the coming election we secure victory for a slate of conservative candidates.

We've made Amy Wilson our target. We think she's the one we can most easily rattle. And we've laid out a plan for how to do it, mostly involving personal intimidation through straightforward measures like vandalism and harassment. We think we can break her. Make her squeal like a pig.

Chapter Three

Amy

The woman in the blue T-shirt chants at my 12-year-old son Matt as he walks from his school building toward where I'm waiting for him in the pickup area. The cheap cotton material of her shirt stops several inches above her bulging navel. A thigh-sized roll of flesh spills out over the top of her spandex leggings. Half-moon sweat stains darken her armpits in testimony to the heat of the afternoon. Spittle flies from beneath her curled upper lip as she waddles along next to my son, hurling her stream of invective. "Your mother is an evil bitch. She hurts little kids." She chants it, on and on.

I recognize her from the school-board meeting the previous night. She probably slept in that shirt. She was one of dozens of women who'd shown up at the meeting, all dressed in matching blue T-shirts with "Moms for

Liberty" emblazoned across the chest. They purportedly were there to protest the board's new mandate that students wear masks in school. I say "purportedly" because who knows what their real grievance is. Really, they're just people dissatisfied with their pathetic lives. These people— and their ilk—are always exercised about something, some imagined threat to their "liberty." The "Don't Tread on Me" flags they hoisted signal their mindset: leave me the hell alone to do what I like.

When Matt reaches the safety of my car, the woman turns her attention to me. She walks around to the driver side and jabs her stubby finger at my window, leaving oily smudges. "We're comin' for you!" she bellows. "We're comin' at you like a freight train. We're gonna make you beg for mercy! If you thought January 6th was bad, wait 'til you see what we have in store for you!" Her face contorts with hatred, like the look on the faces of those segregationist who followed and jeered at the Little Rock Nine as they tried to enter Central High School in 1957.

You don't forget angry, hateful faces like that. I wouldn't forget this woman's. But I wasn't about to give her the time of day. I turn on the engine and wheel the car away from her, hoping my tires kick up gravel at her as I speed away. When I can no longer see her in my rear-view mirror, I turn to Matt, whose face is ashen. His lips and chin tremble.

I reach over to comfort him. "Oh, sweetie, I'm so sorry you had to go through that."

After a long pause, he regains enough composure to speak. "What the fuck was that all about?" A reasonable question.

"Matt, you know I don't like it when you use that word. But I understand your alarm." I pat his knee. "She's one of the crazy people we've been dealing with at our school-board meetings lately."

"She said you're evil and harm little kids. What did she mean?"

"She's upset about the remote learning and social distancing and mask mandates the school board voted to impose. She thinks they're harmful to children. And she's worried we're about to require vaccines." *She's a crazy lunatic.*

Matt removes the mask from his face and looks at it. "What's the big deal? This doesn't bother me. I don't even think about it any more."

"For these people, it's just the very idea that someone is telling them they *have* to wear it. That's what upsets them."

He thinks about that for a moment. "But life is full of things we have to do. You have to stop at that red light coming up. I have to go to school … and wear this seat belt." His facial shrug says, *that's just the way it is.*

I look over at this kid who seems to have grown up in so many ways over the past 18 months. Sandy blonde hair, longish face that had been plump not too long ago. Piercing blue eyes. "Oh, wise one. You're so right. But when these requirements get mixed up with politics, they get compli-cated—and ugly." I'm pretty impressed with myself for how calmly I'm explaining this. Smart mom. Comforting mom.

"What does politics have to do with it?"

"Well, I'm about to oversimplify it. But politics is about conflict. About people disagreeing with each other. In this case, some people—mostly Democrats—think rules like face masks and vaccines are necessary to keep the community safe and protect public health. That's an essential role of government. Others—mostly Republicans—think government should leave people alone to make their own decisions, especially when it comes to their own bodies. So, even things like seat-belt requirements were once very controversial to some people."

I saw Matt's baby blues glaze over about half way through my spiel. I should have kept it short: *Some people just love to fight.* He grunts and tunes the car's audio system to Spotify. We listen to BTS sing "Am I Wrong?" and "Not Today." Maybe Matt knows the translation of the lyrics. I don't. But I like the music anyway. And it helps take my mind off the craziness we'd just witnessed.

We drive through an unusual, tree-lined stretch of town that always makes me feel happy, lucky to live in such a place. The broad street is bordered by a tunnel of bur oaks that interlace thirty feet above it. When it's sunny, as it is today, the light drops through in mottled patterns on the street. Then, suddenly, the trees stop and you get a view of Grand Mesa, rising abruptly to 10,000 feet on the eastern end of town. Said to be the largest flat-top mountain in the world. From here in town, the sheer sandstone cliffs, deep red and grooved, look like they'd been scratched by giant bear claws. Paradise, as far as I'm concerned.

Lots of other people think so, too. Mesa Vista is a small city on the western slope of the Colorado Rockies that was once a rendezvous for mountain men and wandering buckskinners, and Ute Indians before them. In recent years, it's increasingly become a western retreat for people, many from front-range cities like Denver, who move here with the idea of escaping congestion and high prices, wanting to get their lives back into some more fundamental rhythm. An outdoors-lover's idyll, with fantastic hiking opportunities and endless sources of winter recreation.

Five minutes later, I pull the car into our driveway. Matt hops out and heads toward the side door. I hear him yell, "Holy shit! Mom!" When I join him on the sidewalk, I see the source of his distress. Someone has burned "EVIL" into our lawn with weed killer or gasoline. They'd used a fair amount of it because the legs of each letter are two feet wide.

You'd think I'd be scared. And I am. But mostly, I'm pissed. I don't really believe these people, whoever they are, would try to harm me physically. Then again, you never know what crazy people are going to do. But I know what they've *already* done, and that's enough to make my pulse speed, my muscles tense, and my teeth grind. Heat flushes through my body.

A bit later, I stand at the kitchen window, looking out at the lawn. I hear Dad coming into the kitchen behind me. The squeaky wheel on his walker hails his entrance, along with the uneven tempo of his off-kilter footfall. He pulls up next to me. I offer him a rueful smile. "They must've run out of Roundup or gasoline before they could add 'BITCH.' Otherwise, you know that'd be there, too."

"Yeah, probably. Or something harsher." He puts his arm over my shoulders and keeps it there until my muscles relax. "I'll call Tom." Tom Duffy, the chief of police, is a personal friend of ours, who has fielded frequent calls from us in recent weeks—all to no avail. The police aren't going to find who cut down the new burr oak sapling I'd planted in the front yard. No way. They wouldn't catch the lawn defiler either.

"The police won't do anything about this, Dad."

"Probably not, Amy, but they still need to know about it. Property destruction is a crime. If they ever do find out who's doing these things, they'll want to have a complete list of offenses committed." He moves to the refrigerator and removes a bottle of honey-sweetened green tea. He pours about six ounces in a glass, puts the rest back in the fridge. He smooths his silver hair straight back from his broad, tan forehead. "It's probably true that it's almost impossible to pin this sort of thing on someone."

"Yeah. I wonder who did this—and when. It must've been last night. They probably planned this after the school-board meeting and came here while we were asleep. I didn't notice anything this morning, but I guess it takes time to burn into the grass."

"Any idea who might be responsible?"

"Not really. There are so many demonstratively angry people out there. No reason to suspect one over another. But … " And then I tell him about the incident earlier outside the school—the woman who'd chanted at Matt that I'm evil and hurt little kids. She seems a likely candidate. Certainly crazy enough to have done this to my lawn. "Then again, there were a number of people at the meeting last night who hurled the word 'evil' at us. So, who knows?"

"I'm thinking we should install some of those DIY security cameras."

"Not a bad idea. Even if we don't catch someone, a security system might make us feel safer."

"I'll go over to Best Buy. I remember seeing that they have a good selection of home-security products. Then I have plans to meet up with Jack for a drink and a sandwich. So, I won't be here for dinner."

"That's fine. Say hi to my favorite uncle for me. Be careful out there."

He turns his walker on the axis of its right wheel and, with difficulty but determination, starts his slow shuffle down the hall to get his keys.

Chapter Four

Ray

Donald Trump opened my eyes. Before he came along, I didn't really pay much attention to politics or to what's going on. Oh, sure, I was painfully aware that eight years of that Black fucker Obama had driven this country into the ditch. But I had enough problems of my own, you know? I didn't have room in my life to think too much about what was ailing the nation (except the Blacks). It wasn't until Trump emerged that I saw any hope those problems might be addressed.

What I like about Trump is that he understands we need to stop the invasion of this country by immigrants. He understands that if anyone has been "left behind" in this country, it's not the coloreds. It's white guys like me. We're the ones who've been abandoned by a country that promised us a better life than we've got. Hell, I work hard.

I pay my taxes. I do what I'm supposed to do. But am I making any progress? No. I'm probably worse off than ever. I'm stuck living in a crappy trailer in a pathetic little town twenty miles outside of Mesa Vista. Meanwhile, the Mexicans and the Blacks and all the other takers of this world are doing better. It's not the way it should be. And Trump is the first politician in my lifetime who tells the truth about all that. The first one to feel the pain of people like me. Nobody but Trump is looking out for the white guy anymore.

Trump wants to help guys like me, who are sick and tired of being talked down to by the Hillary Clintons of the world who think we're "deplorable." Fuck her. *She's* deplorable. Her and the coastal elites—the Jews, the bankers, the technocrats like Bill Gates. The people who are targeting the white population, us real Americans. The people who want to take our world away from us.

So, it was thanks to Trump that in 2016 I started spending more and more time online. I hadn't really understood the appeal of the internet up until that point. But once I began to explore it, I realized it's the only real place one can find the truth. You can't believe what you see in newspapers or on television news. Except for Fox News, the media in this country are mouthpieces for liberal elites, and you're certainly not going to get the truth from them. But the internet is chock-full of people willing to tell the truth. It's amazing what you can learn on social-media networks including YouTube, Twitter, and Facebook. And with the help of people I connected with on Telegram, the messaging app, I managed to get tapped into the darknet. That was like finding a whole underground world. There's an alternate universe out there of people willing to tell you the truth and help you figure out how to use the truth to fight back.

That's how I got connected to Marty, this guy here in Mesa Vista who's smart as a whip and knows a lot about politics. He thinks this country has to be reconstructed from the ground up. He convinced me and a couple others who'd met up on a local darknet site to help him do whatever we can to seize the levers of power at the local level. Marty's right: only in that way can we—the beaten-down, the targeted—begin to rebuild our America.

The four of us talk a lot about why we need to fight against mask mandates and vaccination protocols. Through our squad, I've learned all about vaccines and how the government and the elites use vaccination programs as part of their larger conspiracies against working White Americans. Marty says if we're going to take control of the school board then we need to get conservative voters in this town more aroused. Oh sure, lots of 'em already are. You should see the size of some of these groups! But Marty says we can do more to radicalize some of those people, especially those who are anti-vaxxers.

Marty sent a message to the three of us the other day on our private Telegram channel. "It's imperative that we push anti-COVID vaccine propaganda. Why? First of all, the fewer people that get the jab, the more force it will require to mandate it. Secondly, we want to sow distrust in the system to further radicalize patriots and especially anti-vaxxers who feel increasingly threatened." As I said, Marty is smart as a whip. You can see that for yourself.

We have this disabled guy who is also part of our squad.

He seems super secretive. He goes by K3LVR. We call him Clever. I don't even know his real name. That seems kind of weird to me. Anyway, he, too, is scary smart about vaccines. He actually knows more about them than Marty, in my opinion.

Here's how K3LVR replied to Marty: "I'd ask that we refrain from calling it 'propaganda' which implies that what we're saying is misleading. I prefer the simple term 'information.' We must provide people with accurate information about vaccines. The truth will be enough to scare the pants off them and move them to action." He was referring to the health and safety risks of vaccines. That's his big thing. He really thinks vaccines are dangerous. And he's right: the truth is scary. These COVID vaccines are being rushed to production without adequate testing. Who knows what horrific problems they could cause?

Frankly, there are all sorts of reasons to be wary of vaccines. If you want to keep yourself awake at night with worry, just pay attention to some of what people are saying about them. Dwayne for example, the other member of our squad. He thinks COVID 19 vaccines will serve as a tool for the government and giant corporations to implant citizens with a microchip or similar electronic device to track all citizens' movements and hoover up all their personal information: driver's license number, social security number, banking information. I'm not exactly clear on how that second thing, the hoovering, would work. I personally think that Dwayne's theory is far-fetched, but hell, I don't know. Nothing would surprise me these days.

My own belief is that if there's a sinister purpose linked to the vaccines, it's related to the "Great Replacement" plot to systematically replace the white race in this country with non-white, minority cultures. Look, you know what's happening! Sometime in the 2040s, racial minorities will become the majority in the United States. Whites will be replaced as the dominant race. If you think that's happening accidentally or naturally, you're crazy. Changes of that magnitude don't just happen! Somebody's behind it. The government? Big corporations? Global elites? I don't know *who*. And I don't know *why*. But I believe vaccines will be used to move this replacement along. What I've read is that vaccines will contain antigens that'll impact fertility. Most white women—97 percent!—will be sterilized in this way and most white men will be injected with carcinogens that'll lead to their deaths. Anybody who agrees to be vaccinated is an idiot.

So, yeah, we can't let the school board require vaccinations. That would be catastrophic. My personal opinion? We also have to fight the school board because of critical race theory and other kinds of racist nonsense being forced down the throats of school kids all over the country.

I tell ya: this race stuff really has me amped up. I'm sick and tired of what is happening in this country. America is a white country. It's whites who founded it and whites who made it great. But the minorities think this country owes them. They argue that they've been systematically disadvantaged and "held back." Hell, that's just nonsense. If anything, whites have bent over backwards to make life easier for them. Just look at affirmative action. Colleges are full of minority kids who sit smugly in desk chairs that should be occupied by white kids who were unfairly passed over for admission.

And liberals out there whine about "structural racism" and "white privilege." They promote this "critical race theory" bullshit. They get teachers to tell kids that whites are inherently racist, oppressors by nature. This is the kind of twaddle that gives rise to Black Lives Matter protests, LGBTQ clubs in schools, "diversity training" in government agencies and organizations, and ethnic-studies curricula— all that kind of stuff that shows just how fast this country is going down the crapper. Somebody has to try to stop this, and I'm proud to be doing my part.

Chapter Five

Amy

I adore my dad. He's the sun and moon to me. My guiding light, my shining star. And having him move out here to Mesa Vista from Denver to live with us was one of the best things that's ever happened to me. But when we first talked about his doing that, it hadn't really occurred to me how much having him around might sometimes feel like I'm at work.

The thing is, I'm an occupational therapist who specializes in helping older people age productively. I spend most of my time in the homes of people who need my help to remain in their homes as they age. I develop ergonomic strategies to enable them to perform daily tasks. I help them figure out how to prevent falls, deal with poor vision, drive safely, cope with diseases like Alzheimer's, arthritis, or cancer, and recover from strokes or traumatic injuries. You get the idea.

I mentioned my Dad's walker earlier. Remember? The one with the squeaky wheel? He needs that bit of support because he has weak legs from having caught the polio virus in 1954 when he was a seven-year-old boy. And the virus left him with withered muscles in his left leg. For the most part, over the ensuing decades he overcame the obstacles that physical challenge threw his way. He could do whatever anybody else was doing—swim, ride a bike, play tennis, go for a hike. Whatever. He did it all. Sure, he did it with a gimpy leg, but he did it. Then, about twenty-five years ago, he started to feel the effects of what they now call "post-polio syndrome" or PPS. It's characterized by new weakening of what had been "good" muscles, extreme fatigue, tiredness, aches and pains, susceptibility to falls, and, in some cases, difficulty breathing.

Unfortunately, my dad is now at the point where post-polio syndrome has really impinged on the quality of his life. He's chronically in pain, and his mobility is sharply limited. He can stand, but is likely to fall over if he's not holding onto something to help him maintain balance. He has to use a walker around the house or for short jaunts, like going into the drug store. For longer walks or outdoor ventures, he has this cool, bright yellow, souped-up mobility chair that looks like something from a Marvel movie. No little red "granny scooter" for him. When he's in it, I like to hum Randy Savage's "Macho Man." It makes him laugh.

He's started to look into a versatile titanium wheelchair that would be light enough and nimble enough for him to use both inside the house and easier for him lift in and out of the car. It would increase his mobility enormously. But, as a sign of how fucked up our health-care system is, he can't just go out there and buy such a chair on his own. The company that makes them won't deal directly with individuals; it only goes through insurance companies. Dad's managed-care plan, Kaiser Permanente, is making him jump through endless hoops to get the damn chair. I hate them.

I'm exquisitely aware of his growing infirmity—not only because I love him dearly but because my professional life involves observing people cope with challenges to their quality of life. So, yeah, having him in my house is wonderful, but sometimes feels too much like my day job.

His brother—my uncle Jack—moved out here, too, about a year ago. Having him in town has been a godsend. The two of them enjoy each other's company immensely, and I no longer feel like I'm the only one my dad has to rely on. That's a big relief. And having Jack around also provides me with a sense of security that's reassuring. I know he has my back. That's huge.

This vandalism stuff has me spooked, quite frankly. I've never gone through anything like this before. I'm not used to feeling scared. And I don't like it. Not at all. My best guess is that it's coming from a person or persons unhappy with my school-board decisions. I don't really believe it has anything to do with my personal life. If, for example, it turned out to be my ex-husband, I'd be surprised. But who knows! There are a lot of fucked-up people out there.

I knew when I moved here that Mesa County is very conservative for the most part. The population is a weird mix of old retirees, young families, college students, and good ol' boys. Way more of 'em are Republicans than Democrats. But in the last couple of years, the ideological temperature has soared. Lots of Trump signs, confederate flags. I now know there are plenty of people in this town who'd burn a cross on your lawn if they find out you're a Democrat or a liberal who voted for Biden. So, I've assumed that as long as you keep your political opinions to yourself—avoid bumper stickers on your car or political signs in your yard— you're okay.

So, you may ask, why stay with this school-board gig when my decisions expose me to political blowback? Let's start with when I decided to run. It frankly didn't feel all that "political" to me. Board elections are non-partisan, meaning candidates aren't identified as being from any particular political party. That sat well with me, with my middle-of-the-road pragmatism. And I thought service on the board might be fulfilling. A way to feel I'm contributing to the community, doing my civic duty. And my job leaves me with enough flexibility in my schedule and enough bandwidth at the end of the day that I thought I could make it fit into my life. And for the most part, it's fit well and been satisfying. This is my fifth year on the board. I come up for re-election next year. I plan to run again, but honestly all this rancor and these scare tactics are making me hesitate. We'll see.

My first few years on the board were a piece of cake. We dealt with routine stuff like budgets, strategies for hiring more teachers, curriculum issues, and the like. But when COVID hit, the job went from being somewhat enjoyable to being the hardest thing I've ever done. I'm not a lover of conflict, and suddenly I was at Conflict Ground Zero. First, it was the brouhaha over school closures and remote learning. Then mask requirements and social distancing. Now vaccination policies. And each issue seemed to bring out more anger, more passion, more conflict. Now it's at the point where it's hard for me to imagine that it could get much worse. But I've thought that before. So, yeah, it could get worse.

The thing is, I'm not an ideologue. I'm a pragmatist. I'm like my dad. I believe in approaching specific situations or problems in a reasoned and logical way. My realm is facts, actions, results, consequences. What's the point of being a blindly partisan advocate or adherent of a particular ideology? I don't get it. I don't see where it gets you. It's certainly not the best way to approach problems like how to handle a pandemic virus. But look where that thinking's got me. In trouble. Possibly, in peril.

Chapter Six

Mike

I stop at the Best Buy and talk to the sales guy there about the various DIY home-security systems available. Each of them has its advantages and disadvantages, it seems. Ultimately, I settle on the SimpliSafe system, which, he says, provides an ideal balance of quality, service, ease of use, and value. This is the sort of thing I'm not good at judging, so I go with his recommendation.

While I drive from Best Buy to meet up with my brother Jack for a drink and a sandwich, I think about my daughter Amy and the harassment she's enduring. It just seems so unfair. She's not some crazy left-winger, intent on using the levers of governmental power to impose her will on others. She's a moderate, fair-minded member of the school board, making the best decisions she can with the information she has available at any point in time. Good Lord. How did we get to the point in this country that people will vandalize and terrorize a local official whose decisions they don't like?

Now, I stand inside the front door of Toby's Bar and Grille on Main Street. My brother Jack stands next to me, fondling the fronds of a nearby fern to see if it's real. He lowers his head toward it to give it a good look-see, then pushes his lower lip out in satisfaction. "The real McCoy!" He hasn't been here before, and I'm guessing his skepticism about the plant's legitimacy stems from the generally underwhelming appearance of Toby's. It looks like the previous incarnation of this building was a variety store or five-and-ten. But it's fine, in my opinion. They've spruced it up. Red-brick walls, tall potted plants. Pleasant lighting. Relatively informal. No aspirations or pretense. I like that about it.

A hostess appears, and I ask her if she has a table for two.

"Sure." She collects two menus from the hostess stand. "You gentlemen follow me. I'll get you set up on the patio."

God. The patio. All the way on the other side of the dining room! For about the hundredth time, I wish I had a hovercraft that would raise me up seven feet and whisk me over all the tables and people between the front entrance and the patio. I detest the awkward choreography of navigating this damn walker around and through all those chairs jutting out at inconvenient (perilous!) angles.

When we settle at our table and remove our face masks, I smile over at my younger brother. Six-feet tall, and still with dense musculature, he's a spry 68. I like to tease him about being a young buck. He likes to tease me about being an old cripple. It works for us.

An absolutely stunning woman approaches us. Her glossy red hair falls to her shoulders in gentle swirls. She wears a cream silk blouse, three-quarter sleeves, open at the neck, showing off a tasteful silver pendant that nestled in her deep neck dimple. Silver bracelet. Small, coiled silver earrings. Black slacks. I watch Jack taking all this in.

"Can I get you gentlemen something to drink?"

Jack says, "Oh, you're here to take our drink order. I was hoping you were coming over to say you wanted to adopt us."

A shaft of sunlight coming through the patio's pergola makes her hair glisten. She narrows her eyes and lifts the edge of her mouth ever so slightly. Looks at me. I ask for a Laphraoig, straight up. She turns to Jack with a death stare. Properly chastised, he says he wants the same, on the rocks. As she walks away, I say to him, "I don't think it's kosher to joke like that with women any more."

He allows as to how maybe that's true. "But I always hope they'll cut me some slack because of my advanced years. This salt-and-pepper hair oughta get me something!"

"Fat chance. All your advanced years get you is a negative first impression: *dirty old man*. It doesn't do you any good to then confirm it."

When our drinks arrive (delivered, I note, by a different woman), I fill him in on the latest intimidations Amy is dealing with. When I finish reporting, I sum it up editorially. "These lunatics don't understand the meaning of civil discourse. And they don't know proper limits."

"Poor Amy must be pretty frightened. Tough on her. How old is she? Forty?"

"Thirty-eight."

"God. I was still playing with my toes at thirty-eight. This sort of menacing would have made me wet myself at that age."

"Yeah. Well, I'm not too comfortable with it myself, seeing as how I don't move very fast. I feel like a sitting duck. What if one of their malicious stunts accidentally leads to a fire or something like that?"

"You wanna come stay at my place?"

"Thanks, but no. I want to be there for her."

He gives me a long, appraising look. I know that look. And I know what's coming next.

"You're having a hard time. The pain is worse, isn't it?"

"Ah, nah. It's okay."

Jack rolls his eyes at me.

"Alright. Yeah. It's not good. PPS sucks."

"Sorry, bud. It's just not fair."

"Ah, we've all got our crosses to bear."

"Don't give me that. Most of our crosses are made of tissue paper or balsa wood. Yours is made of black ironwood."

I brush off his comment with our grandfather's favorite dismissal. "Aw, gwan wid ya."

Jack stirs the ice in his glass with his index finger. "You gonna let me help out with this harassment problem?"

I know it's not an empty offer. He has plenty of time on his hands. He's one of those guys on whom the cloak of retirement doesn't settle easily. He's always itching for things to do. He'll fix things around his house that don't need fixing, just to keep busy. He'll take things apart, just to see if he can reassemble them. Plus, he was a cop back when he lived in Denver, so a little mystery like this would be just his cup of tea. His offer to help is genuine.

Plus, Jack has an advantage I decidedly lack: physical prowess. Even at his age, he's still powerfully built after decades of resistance exercises, running, and protein loading. He explained to me once that he wasn't striving for a bodybuilder look. He just wanted to be strong enough to protect himself and unnerve opponents.

"I don't know that there's much to do, Jack. I've spoken with Tom Duffy about it. He says this sort of malicious behavior tends to die out quickly. People vent their anger and frustration and then move on."

Jack snorts. "Maybe. But I think what Tom really means is he's woefully understaffed and doesn't have the personnel to devote to something like this. Even when it involves a friend. Besides, from what I can tell, most of the cops in this town are punk fascists. Going to them about these incidents will only make them laugh — or, worse yet, give them ideas. That's why you should let me help out."

"What would you do?"

"Same as them. Poke around. Talk to people. Keep my eyes open."

"Well, those are things you're good at."

"Whaddaya say?" He's eager as a dog headed to the treat bin.

"Sure. Why not. Anything that'll help put a stop to this nonsense. And you can start by helping me install the security system I bought this afternoon. How about tomorrow?"

"Free all day."

"It'll have to be after lunch. In the morning, I've got a meeting of that polio survivors' group I told you about."

"I assumed you weren't going to get involved with that. Doesn't seem like your kind of thing. I remember your reaction when I tried to talk you into going to that spousal-grief support group after Laura died." He knows I've always thought support groups smack of woe-is-me-ism.

"Yeah, well, I decided I might as well get to know some other polio survivors personally. Maybe learn from how they're coping."

Jack shrugs. "Can't hurt." He throws back the rest of his Laphroaig and signals our server for another round. "Does Amy have any ideas about who might be doing this crap?"

I tell him about the nasty fat woman at the school pick-up — and about Amy's feeling that the culprit could be any of dozens of angry people around town.

"You know," he says, "I don't know what it is about this town that seems to attract right-wing crazies. But there are more of them here than anywhere else I've ever lived."

I smile. "Jack, you spent most of your life in Denver and Boulder. Not a very representative slice of America. Hell, in Boulder, most of the people are *left-wing* crazies."

"True, but you know what I mean. This is Lunatic City. Two-thirds of voters in this city voted for that wing nut Lauren Boebert."

"Western Colorado has always been much more conservative than most of the Front-range cities. You know that."

"Not all of it. Look at Durango."

"Maybe you should've moved to Durango."

"You know damn well Durango wouldn't be a good fit for me. I'm not saying I'm sorry I moved here. I wanted to try life on the Western Slope, and figured I might as well follow your path to Mesa Vista. You've liked it here well enough these past five years. I like life here, too. It's beautiful, and the climate is great. And even though I'm much more conservative than you are, even I am sometimes put off by the political atmosphere here."

Our server brings us a second round, and each of us orders a Reuben sandwich. As we wait, our attention keeps getting diverted by a lively conversation at a table of six nearby. A big bald fellow with a ragged beard is beguiling his table-mates with a harangue against Dr. Anthony Fauci and science in general.

"The global elite has set its sights on religion, on our beliefs. They want to elevate scientists above God. But Jesus Christ is all we need. We don't need masks, ventilators, vaccines. Jesus will protect us. And if it's Christ's will that we get COVID, then we'll get COVID! I'm sick and tired of these petty public officials who think they know better than God!"

His bombast stirs a petite woman to his left to speak up. Her light gray pupils make her eyes look other-worldly. "Right! Like those petty tyrants on the school board. That Wilson woman? She sits there at those board meetings, looking all smug and proper as she delivers her communist edicts. *There will be no in-person classes until I say so! There will be masks! There will be vaccination requirements! I am Jesus Christ, the Lord of this town! Obey me!"* Enthusiastic nodding all around the table.

Jack looks at me with eyes widened. "Amy's the Lord Christ? I guess that makes you God, the Father." He holds up his water glass and says, "Could you turn this into Laphroaig for me?"

Chapter Seven

Mike

Nah. My brother's not a god, but about as close to it as most humans come. A kind, gentle soul who's good to his family, good to his friends, good to his community. Our mother sometimes said that he had quite a temper as a kid. Not surprising. He had a lot to be angry about. He got a bum deal. The remarkable thing is how, as an adult, he's managed to maintain a mantle of equanimity and good cheer that I always think of as one of his defining features.

I, on the other hand, am a bit of an asshole—and am known as such to family and friends. I don't kick dogs or light baby carriages on fire. No, I'm not evil. I'm just not very nice. A little too inclined to say things that aren't very kind. Not a people pleaser, some might say. Why? Who knows. There's never been anything obvious to explain it.

I've had nothing but a good life. No hardship, no pain, no adversity. Pretty smooth sailing. So, go figure. But my annoying manner served me well in my life as a cop. That was a perfect occupation for a guy like me. Cops are assholes. That's the way it is. So, I fit my job like OJ's hand fit that glove. C'mon. You *know* it fit!

My life here in Mesa Vista? Good enough. I don't need better. I'm 68. I have all I need: cable, a car that gets me where I need to go, and a pension that's good enough that I don't worry much about money. And this is actually a nice little city. About 50,000 people. Perfect size, as far as I'm concerned. Small enough to avoid some of the problems of larger cities (traffic congestion is a biggie for me), and large enough to offer what they call amenities. Good restaurants and bars, some up-scale, some funky. A lively downtown area with vibrant local businesses.

And that pension goes a lot further out here in Mesa County than it would if I'd stayed on the front range. Denver these days? Congested and unaffordable. Here? I have a nice, smallish one-story house with white siding, on a *cul de sac* at the end of a short street on the west edge of town. The yard has no grass, which suits me fine. My mowing days are long behind me. Instead, there's sand and stones and hardy plants that grow well in the climate out here. Somehow it manages to look well kept. I guess it's hard to fuck up a stone patch.

I like the climate here. In the winter, the weather is a lot milder than most of Colorado. It doesn't get the kind of snow they have in the higher mountains or even in Denver. In the summer it's hot, but a dry heat. Like today. For a late spring afternoon, it's ridiculously hot. But give me that over humidity any day. And it cools down the second the sun goes down, which makes it more tolerable than some hellhole like Phoenix or Las Vegas. Plus, you can always escape the heat by going up into the mountains, which are generally 10 to 20 degrees cooler.

I suppose it would be nice to have a lady friend I could snuggle up to. Some soft, giggly creature who laughs at my jokes and warms at my touch. Maybe that will happen in time. I just haven't found the right person yet.

What I personally like most about being here is that I'm near my brother Mike, his daughter Amy, and her son Matt. I never had kids, so those three are my family. It pains me to see Amy goin' through this shit people are throwin' at her. But I guess she shouldn't be surprised about what's come her way in the last eighteen months as a member of that school board. As I said to my brother, politically, this place is Lunatic City. And I say that as someone who's to the right of center himself. To these people, a moderate like Amy is dancin' out there on the far left wing with Bernie Sanders.

Do I believe there's much chance we'll be able to catch the people who are vandalizing her property? Frankly, no. Not unless we catch them in the act. And that's about as likely as catching Sinatra in Sumatra.

Chapter Eight

Matt

I'm a kid. What am I gonna do about this vandalism shit? Go out and rough somebody up? Flex my muscles at 'em and scare 'em off? Jump in my Batmobile and chase some bad guy across the top of Grand Mesa? Scour the front yard for DNA and use my grade-school chemistry set to unravel the mystery? Obvi, none of the above.

I may be not be able to do anything about the harassment aimed at my mom, but that doesn't mean I'm okay with it. I find it scary. And I don't like what it's doing to her. She's not generally the nervous sort. (I have a few friends whose moms are bat-shit crazy, so I know *my* mom is okay, for the most part.) But this stuff has rattled her. And I get it. I do. When I was in the fourth grade, a couple of kids bullied me. It was no fun at all. But at least I knew who was doing it. They weren't unknown, invisible phantoms, like these people who are bullying my mom. If they had been, I'd have shit myself. So, honestly, I think my mom is holding it together pretty well, all things considered. Still, she's shaken. As I say, I get it.

It's a good thing my grandfather is here. Pops is an amazingly calm guy. Doesn't get around too well, but he's the nicest guy ever! I mean it. Having him here is like having a warm blanket over us on the coldest day of the year. He's just the best. But, except for the fact that he's a lot smarter than I am, his chances of catching these bad guys aren't much better than mine. As I say, he doesn't get around too well.

Then there's Uncle Jack. How can I describe Jack? Well, first of all, he cracks me up. He really does. I don't know how he thinks up the funny things he says, but they just pour out of him. Also, he's a big guy. Used to be a cop. I don't picture cops being as funny as he is, but what do I know! Maybe they all are. But that's not the way most of them are on TV. And, believe me, I watch a lot of TV. As much as I can get away with. Social media, too. I'm all over Instagram and TikTok. Not Facebook. That's for old farts.

Anyway, to get back to this stuff happening to my mom. I don't tell her about it, but some of this shit has slopped over onto me, too. There are lots of kids at my school who didn't like remote learning last year. They don't like the mask mandates now. Their parents tell them my mom is one of the people responsible for all that. And they take it out on me. They push me around. Shove me into the lockers. Trip me in the cafeteria. Say nasty things about my mom. No, nobody's beaten me up. But let's just say I don't go through my days at school feeling at ease.

And the thing is, I don't know enough to say what's right. My mom thinks people should be wearing masks. She thinks people should get vaccinated, when shots are available. Pops does, too. So does Jack. But lots of people disagree with that. *Lots* of people. What do I know! I'm just a kid.

What I *do* know is that I wish my mom would get off the fucking school board. Seems like a no-brainer to me. Duh.

Chapter Nine

Mike

The fellowship hall at Grace Methodist Church looks like lots of other church meeting halls—sterile and lifeless, with a couple dozen stackable chairs, a few large folding tables, and fluorescent lighting. Just inside the door is a big square calendar on an easel, showing the meeting times of the various groups that use the room each month. I don't know whether to laugh or cry as I read through the list of support groups and the conditions for which they were formed: alcoholics, sexual-abuse survivors, gamblers, and people with eating disorders, cancer, or infertility. To name only some. Good lord. What company.

I venture into the room. There are about six other people there already gathered in a circle—more than I expected. They're all old, of course. I say "of course" because the polio vaccine largely eradicated the disease in the U.S. after 1955. So, nobody here under the age of 65.

I count three mobility scooters, two wheelchairs (one motorized), and one cane. Mine's the only walker. Half the folks look up at me with welcoming smiles. The others have vacant looks on their faces, lost either in their own thoughts or somewhere out in the ether. I find an empty chair and seat myself. One more person comes in a few minutes later. I look around and wonder if it was a good idea for me to come to this. There were good reasons I'd avoided this kind of nonsense before. Had I forsaken good sense?

My brooding over the matter is interrupted promptly at 10 o'clock, when a square-faced woman in a fuchsia polyester pantsuit speaks. "Welcome, everybody. I'm Peggy, the current coordinator of this group. I hope you all had a good summer. It's nice to have the group meet again after a hiatus." She gives us what she probably considers her thousand-watt smile, but It's only putting out about sixty. She has a Cupid's-bow mouth and thin, arching eyebrows that she must have plucked too often. She wears too much makeup. Way too much. She's plump without being actually fat.

"Three of us are returnees from last year," she says. "Glad to have you back, Dave and Minnie. The rest of you are new, and we're so glad you've decided to join us. I'll give everyone a chance to introduce themselves in a moment. First, I want to call your attention to an absence. As most of you know, our dear friend Wanda Porter died this summer. Wanda was a wonderful woman. She didn't sweat the small stuff. She saw the larger picture. She lived for the journey, not the destination. She always saw the glass as half full . . ." *Jesus Christ,* I think. *This Peggy is a Master Cliché Producer. I hope Wanda's life wasn't as trite and hackneyed as this tribute!* "We'll miss her, but her spirit will live on in the group." Peggy nods emphatically, as if to say, *By God, we will* not *forget dear Wanda.* One of the men says," Hear, hear."

And then, with a change in vocal tone that suggests all memories of Wanda are now disappearing into the empyrean domain and her name will ne'er be spoken again, Peggy slaps her knees and says, "Okay, let's introduce ourselves. As I said, I'm Peggy. I became the moderator of this group last year (my second year as a member) and decided to stay on and do it again for another round, since there were no objections to my doing so. I got polio when I was nine. I was lucky. I only lost the use of my left arm, so the effects of the acute phase of the illness were less severe for me than for most of us. But when I got hit with post-polio syndrome in the 1980s, it hit me hard—in many ways, much worse than the original virus. I don't need to go into the details now. But suffice it to say, I really need the support this kind of group offers. So, I'm glad each of you is here."

She then turns to the woman on her left and indicates we'll go clockwise around the circle, introducing ourselves. The woman's name is Sally. She has dyed light-brown hair, cut short, and Coke-bottle glasses. A timid smile comes and goes as she speaks. "I'm glad to be joining this group. I don't know why I didn't do it earlier, because frankly I've been feeling in need of support for five or six years now. This post-polio business is the pits.

Much worse, in my opinion, than the polio itself, which seemed manageable, somehow. What I mean is that once the acute phase of the virus was over and I finally got out of the hospital a few months later, I felt it was just a matter of trying to get on with life and try each day to work toward improvement. And that's what I did. For decades. And it was okay.

"But this post-polio stuff ... there's no getting better with this, no building toward improvement. It's hard." A rueful look overtakes her as she seems to go someplace else in her head, then return. "Oh well, you folks don't need to listen to all that. You already know it. So, I guess all I want to say now is that I look forward to getting to know you and learning from you how to cope with this."

I'm next, and I figure I can't improve on what Sally said, so I say pretty much the same thing. But then I add something else I've been thinking a lot about recently. "I don't know about the rest of you, but I find it fascinating to watch how our society is dealing with this whole COVID epidemic. It's made me think a lot about the 1950s and how differently American society responded then to the polio epidemic. I don't know whether you all ever talk about that. I hope so."

"We do, Mike. And we look forward to hearing your thoughts," Peggy says. "Thank you."

Next, we hear from David, a returnee, who hasn't much to say by way of self-introduction. So, I decide to latch onto his appearance as a way to remember him. David wears a Vietnam veterans cap that indicates he was with the 101st Airborne. He strikes me as the kind of guy who wears that hat everywhere and only removes it at home. And I'm guessing, because of his polio, he must have been part of the 101st's support staff back at Fort Campbell, Kentucky.

David yields to a handsome fellow named Steve, who sits in a snazzy motorized wheelchair. He looks dapper in a blue buttoned-down Oxford shirt and gray slacks. His voice is a rich baritone. "I decided to join this group because I'm one of those people who has gone his whole life not talking about polio or its effects on me. When I was a kid, I couldn't talk to my family about polio or my emotions. If I brought up the subject, my family would change the topic. It made me feel as if I had done something that embarrassed them. So, I learned to behave as if my physical challenges and emotional traumas didn't exist. I never talked about it. If someone asked me a question about my experience with polio, I'd wave off the question and do what my family did—change the subject. Well, I'm no genius, but I'm just smart enough to know that a lifetime of such behavior hasn't been good for me. And I hope this will be a forum where I can learn to talk about polio and how it has affected my life."

Peggy says, "I hope you'll find it is, Steve. Thanks for joining us."

A beautiful woman with salt-and-pepper hair swept into a French bun speaks next. "My name is Sofia, with an *f*, not *ph*. The Italian spelling, not Greek. I grew up in the North End of Boston in the 1950s." She turns to her right and looks at Steve. "It's interesting, though not surprising, how strongly our family's attitudes about polio affected us. I contracted polio when I was eight. My father visited me at my hospital bedside, my mother apparently found it impossible to do so. And when I finally got home, my mother never once made any effort to help me. It's easy to see how I got the impression that I had finally done something really bad to warrant such punishment. Fortunately, my father had no compunctions at all about helping me when I really needed it. My mother and I —"

She stops suddenly and sits quietly for a moment, looking down at hands folded in her lap. When she finally looks up, she says, "Yes, I think each of us bears the legacy of how our individual family dealt with our contracting polio. But it also fascinates me to think about the cultural expectations surrounding polio in the 1950s and how those affected each of us. You all know the polio mantra was, and always would be: Do it by yourself, no matter how hard, no matter how long it takes. And, yes, as Steve said, the other part was: For god's sake, don't talk about it. Don't sulk, don't whine, don't feel sorry for yourself.

"'Fight! Fight! Fight! was, and would always be, the polio theme song. There was no such thing as feeling sorry for yourself, crying, or saying 'it hurts.' Unless you wanted to be a 'helpless cripple,' synonymous with 'hateful devil,' you fought, you fell, you climbed, you stretched, you kept working. You consciously or subconsciously repressed feelings of anger, rage, self-pity and grief in order to move forward and lead successful lives."

Again she pauses. And everyone waits for more. "And, now, here we are, polio survivors who are dealing, much later in life, with symptoms of post-polio syndrome, which can't be conquered by hard work, grit, and determination— and which have stirred up long repressed or forgotten fears and anxieties. And most of us have never dealt with the emotional reality of having had polio over sixty years ago.

So, we're easily done in by the emotional impact of dealing with our post-polio problems."

I find myself stunned by Sofia's cogent summation of our collective situation. She painted the picture of what we face about as clearly as anyone could. The hear-a-pin-drop silence in the room suggests that everyone else is equally struck by her words.

A mouselike woman next to Sofia clears her throat. She says her name is Minnie. I almost laugh out loud when she says that because she is tiny, with a sharp, pointy nose, close-set eyes, and ears that stick out like jug handles. Her voice is high and squeaky. I quickly hold all this against her, thinking that whatever she'll have to say won't possibly be as insightful as Sofia's comments. Maybe not, but Minnie surprises me. She looks at Sofia and says, "So, like the rest of us, you were indoctrinated with the idea that you could do *anything*, miraculous things, but that you'd never achieve the physical mobility you wanted unless you pushed harder, fought harder, than anyone else *in the world!* Right? And you felt that if you didn't reach your goal, it meant that you hadn't worked hard enough, tried your best. Right?"

Sofia nods.

Minnie continues. "I developed polio at the age of three in September, 1954, in Hamilton, New York. As I was growing up, my mother frequently read me *The Little Engine That Could* with its repeated refrain: 'I think I can. I think I can.'" She stops, and a smirk takes over her face. "I hate people who believe it's okay to burn books, but I would happily make an exception for *The Little Engine That Could*." This gets a big laugh from everyone in the room. "What a lie we were fed—the notion that determination would conquer all. I hate the psychic damage that lie caused!"

"It wasn't true that I could do anything I set my mind to. I knew it, my mother knew it, the physical therapists knew it, the doctors knew it. God, I hated being told to try. I had tried and tried and tried and tried and tried and tried and tried. Until I was thirty, I believed that if I just tried harder, I would get better. What nonsense it was! My family desperately wanted me to come through the ordeal of polio unwounded, capable, competent, and independent. To satisfy them and make them happy, I simply walled off everything within me that was wounded, frail, needy. No wonder I've dealt with depression my whole adult life. The cultural expectations Sofia spoke of, along with the try-harder mantra, left me a mess psychologically." Now Minnie takes a pause, then adds, with a wry smile, "I'm trying my hardest to deal with it. And that's why I'm returning for a second year of these group meetings."

I wouldn't be surprised if my jaw has been hanging open for the past ten minutes. It's not as if I'm unaware that women are good at talking about their experiences and reflecting on them, sharing their emotions. But one doesn't often get such a pointed illustration of that as we've just had. These women are astonishingly reflective. It's clear to me that this group really might be helpful to me in thinking about my own struggles.

Now, Peggy gestures to a heavy, bald fellow seated on a scooter to her right. The only one left to hear from. He's wearing a green-and-white checked shirt that hangs over the mass of his stomach. Bright red-white-and-blue suspenders clash with the shirt in an interesting fashion statement. The white name tag stuck to his shirt says "EARL" in bold block letters. "Earl," Peggy says, "please tell us a little about yourself."

After considerable throat-clearing, the man starts. "I'm Earl. I suspect my story is a little different from the rest of yours. Most of you probably don't know how you caught the virus. That's the typical case. Like Sally here, most of you were probably just going about your business as kids, and then suddenly, out of the blue, got whacked by this horrible virus. You have no idea how it happened. But, I'm a rare instance of someone who knows *exactly* how he caught polio! In my case, it was from the Salk vaccine itself!" He peers around at us as if daring anyone to challenge him.

"There were only about two hundred of us in the whole country who got polio that way, most of us out here in the West. Oh, there were something like 40,000 children who developed headaches, neck stiffness, some temporary muscle weakness and fever from the vaccine. For them, those symptoms were temporary." He pauses, then clears his throat again. "But, as I say, about two hundred of us were permanently paralyzed. Still, I guess we were better off than the ten who died from the vaccine."

He looks down at the mottled hands that rest on his lap, his withered limbs barely discernible inside his pant legs. He lets out a snort that conveys both frustration and indignation. "Anyway, I'm in the same boat as the rest of you now, but how I got onboard is a little different. To be honest, I'm pretty bitter about it. And it makes me mighty sympathetic to all the folks out there now who are resistant to the COVID vaccine." He stops and looks directly at me, I guess because of my earlier remark about society's response to COVID. "I don't think the government should be pushing people to get it if they don't want to. Damn vaccines aren't as safe as the companies and the government say." He crosses his arms and looks around the circle with a scowl.

I can't let that comment pass unanswered. "Actually, the vaccines are incredibly safe and effective. The data show—"

"You don't know that! We don't know what's going to happen to all these vaccinated people a year from now, three years from now—"

Peggy interrupts him. "Let's please not get into that now. We have lots to talk about today, and we can return to this topic in future meetings." I give Earl a conciliatory nod and a thin smile. He offers an icy glower in return. *Okay, there's one asshole I don't care to know.*

For the next 75 minutes, the group turns to other topics. Near the end, a fellow named Hal goes on for a while about how polio survivors can benefit from palliative care. "It's not the same as hospice. People think that, but it's not. It's about making the most of life with a serious illness, whether the disease is terminal or not. It can be for people like us—not bedridden, still living at home, and wanting a better life. They may be severely affected by pain, for instance, or chronic weakness or stress—survivors using ventilators or those losing more muscle mass; others additionally affected by complications of aging. Palliative care offers a holistic approach to things like pain management, whether it's emotional pain or a nagging rotator cuff." He pats his own right shoulder to indicate he knows whereof he speaks. "It can really offer an amazingly helpful layer of support."

Peggy finally gently cuts him off, suggesting that any of us who want to know more about palliative-care programs should talk with Hal after the meeting. She closes things out by calling our attention to a book she'd come across called *Access Anything: Colorado—Adventuring with Disabilities*. She holds up a copy. The cover art clashes with the brassy hue of her hair. "It's really wonderful, the only handicap-accessible guidebook to Colorado that I know of. If anyone wants to borrow my copy, let me know."

Most of us linger for a few minutes, greeting each other and exchanging pleasantries. I notice that Earl seems to have no interest in that. He promptly aimed his scooter for the exit doors and was out of there like a shot. *Typical of his ilk. Angry assholes are all alike.* Since our brief exchange about vaccines, I'd been building quite a case for not liking the man. But then it struck me: I know almost nothing about him except that he's a bitter person. He'd said so himself. But that didn't necessarily mean he's an asshole. Probably I was being unfair. I remembered a little plaque my grandmother used to have hanging in her kitchen: *Presume Goodwill.* If she were here, she'd tell me that would be a better place to start in my dealings with Earl.

By the time I get out to the parking lot, Earl somehow had wrangled his scooter into his van and is already heading out the drive. The Trump sticker on his rear bumper taxes my new forbearance toward him.

Chapter Ten

Jack

I have all the components of the home-security system unboxed and laid out on the dining table when Mike gets home from his meeting with the polio support group.

He looks it over. "Christ. Maybe I went overboard. It's not like we're trying to secure Fort Knox."

"It's alright. You did good. There's not that much, and it's all basic stuff. Nothing over the top. Just window and door sensors. Glass-break sensors. Two outdoor cameras. Two indoor cameras. It'll only take an hour or two to install this." The outdoor cameras take the longest to put up because we have to figure out the most advantageous positions and angles for them. We configure the system to Amy's wifi and then test every element to make sure each works.

By 3:00, we're done and have retired to Amy's comfortable flagstone patio with a couple of beers. I ask Mike how the support-group meeting was.

"It was about what you'd expect. A bunch of us old cripples, as you like to say, sitting around in a circle staring at one another's clunky shoes. But there were several people who were amazingly insightful and articulate about their experiences. So, I'll definitely give it a go for a while and hope that it meets its potential."

"Nice people?"

"I think so, for the most part. And there were a couple of folks I could imagine being friends with. But there was one guy who seems pretty much an asshole. He —"

Mike is interrupted by Amy, who comes bursting through the door, swearing up and down. Matt walks in behind her, gawking at his mother's eruption. "Goddamnit, I'm getting tired of this shit!" she yells, her voice heavy with rage. Her blue irises telegraph her anger. When she notices me, her volume drops thirty decibels. "Oh, hi, Jack. Sorry."

I smile and tip the neck of my beer bottle toward her. "Hi, Amy. What's up?"

She hurls her purse at an empty chair and collapses on another beside it. Her shiny dark hair bounces up, then settles back to her shoulders. "I went to pick Matt up at school and had to run inside to leave some paperwork. When I came out to wait for him, I found that somebody had keyed the car. Both sides! Big, nasty scrapes."

"Do you know that it happened while you were in the school building?" Mike asks.

"Well, I think so. I didn't notice it when I got into the

car here at home or got out at the school. But I suppose the scratches could have been there before."

I consider this. "Doesn't really matter *when*, does it? What matters is that someone did that to your car."

"Right."

"Did you notice if there are security cameras anywhere around there?" I ask.

"There are up at the school, but I parked down near the athletic field to make myself get in more steps. I haven't hit 10,000 a single day this week! Anyway, there aren't any cameras down by the field. I looked."

"Were there other people around? Anybody who might have seen it happen?"

"Not down that far."

"Do you have a few minutes to talk about this? I told your dad I'd help look into this nonsense. To get started, it would be useful to see if we can generate a list of people who might be doing this."

"Sure. How can I help?"

I pull a pen and a small tablet of paper from my pocket.

My brother laughs. "Ever the detective! You should have a deerstalker hat and an Inverness cape."

I flip him the bird. "Old habits die hard." I turn to Amy. "Do you know the name of the woman who accosted you and Matt outside the school yesterday?"

"I'm pretty sure her name is Becky Dubrovsky."

I write it down. "Know anything about her?"

"Nope."

"Ever had previous encounters with her?"

"Not other than seeing her in the crowd at board meetings."

"Okay. We'll look into this Becky. How about others? Can you think of any specific people who might be angry enough at you that they'd do these things?"

Amy pushes back a lock of hair that had fallen across her face. "Oh, I don't know, Jack. I have a hard time understanding how anybody gets this angry at school-board members who are just trying to keep kids and teachers safe. It just doesn't make sense to me. I've tried to think whether there's any other reason someone might be mad at me. The only thing I can come up with is Danny."

Mike and I look at each other, then back at Amy. "Your ex?" I ask.

"Yeah. Even though the divorce was three years ago, Danny's still really bitter about it. He sends me angry emails from time to time, claiming that I ruined his life, left him destitute, am a bad mother, blah, blah, blah. And on the rare occasions when we have to see each other, his face radiates hatred. Plus, people tell me he's one of a group of teachers at the high school who vocally oppose school-board policies related to COVID."

"Do you keep his emails?"

"Yup."

"Good. Don't delete them. If you don't mind, we might want to take a look at them at some point." I flip my notebook closed and raise my eyebrows at her and my brother. "Okay. Two people we can look into. That's not a bad start."

Chapter Eleven

Mike

The virus that invaded me when I was seven years old is 5,000 times smaller than the width of a human hair. Tiny but potent. The early symptoms of its presence resemble the flu: fatigue, fever, aches and pains, vomiting, and stiff neck. But, those symptoms can quickly change within a matter of hours to an inability to breathe without mechanical assistance, paralysis or lifelong distortion of limbs, even death.

When I got struck with polio in the mid-1950s, the US had endured almost forty years of yearly polio epidemics that left thousands dead and thousands more disabled. The first of those horrific epidemics, whose epicenter in 1916 was traced to an immigrant section of Brooklyn called "Pigtown," infected 27,363 children across 26 states. Six thousand children — most under five years old — died that terrible summer and early fall.

That was horrific. But then each year the epidemics worsened. Public health officials were baffled by the mercurial properties of polio: one year, a community would experience many cases; the next year, few cases would be reported. No one could explain the unpredictable nature of the disease. Pregnant women were found to be especially susceptible to the virus. Boys were more apt to be paralyzed than girls. The age of polio's victims was also getting older. By the 1940s, the average age of victims was between 5 and 9 years. All of this was incredibly baffling to public health officials.

In 1952, the United States experienced its worst polio year with 57,879 reported cases. An estimated 600,000 were reported worldwide that same year. Parents lived in fear of warm weather. They adhered to all public health recommendations and warnings: avoid large public gatherings, never allow children to swim in public swimming pools, and insist upon frequent hand washing. Some mothers forbad their children from eating peaches in the summer for fear that the virus could flourish in the "peach fuzz." Others kept their children away from church services during the summer months.

My brother and I were too young to appreciate our parents' terror. For us, "polio weather" was a terrible annoyance. Every time we turned around, our parents seemed to be curtailing our activities. They did their best to protect us. But the polio virus found its way to me anyway. It caught me mere months before the Salk polio vaccine would be approved and widely distributed, effectively leading to the eventual eradication of wild-virus polio in the United States.

Polio still is not eradicated worldwide, although the global case count has been dramatically reduced. The public health community believes that polio can be eradicated, but time is running out. If eradication is not soon realized, it is now estimated that over 10 million more children will be paralyzed by mid-century. There is no known cure for polio. Vaccination is the only prevention for the killer and crippler that prefers children as its victims.

As I grew from boyhood to adolescence to early adulthood, I watched as the polio vaccine reduced the scourge of polio. I saw other vaccines came along for other diseases such as diphtheria, tetanus, measles, rubella, and pertussis. I marveled as scientific research and epidemiological studies led to declines in death from smoking and heart disease, to new screenings for the early detection of cancer and to treatments for for many kinds of tumors. These and other public-health achievements led me to want a career that would bring the benefits of such advances to the public.

And that's what happened. I spent my whole career in public health, the last eight years as the executive director of the Colorado Department of Public Health and Environment. For the twenty years before that, I held various positions in the department's Disease Control and Public Health Response Division, which is responsible for making sure that the state of Colorado is prepared to respond rapidly and effectively to public health concerns and emergencies.

I'm proud of the work I did over the course of my

career. Those of us in the field of public health work to assure the conditions in which people can be healthy. That can mean vaccinating children and adults to prevent the spread of disease. Tracking disease outbreaks. Educating people about the risks of alcohol and tobacco. Setting safety standards to protect workers, developing school-nutrition programs to make sure kids have access to healthy food. It's all about conducting scientific research and data analysis in order to give science-based solutions to problems.

Why am I going on about all this? To explain that contracting polio was the formative event of my life and was responsible for my career choice. But also to say that the science of public health, while not perfect by any means, is pretty damn good. Miraculous, in many ways. Consider vaccines. They're amazingly effective tools for reducing or eliminating the chances that people will contract certain diseases. It breaks my heart that so many people are skeptical of them, distrust them, refuse them. Truly, it's heartbreaking.

I'm appalled (and more than a little worried) that so many people doubt or dismiss the amazing science that has led to the coming COVID vaccines. My best guess at this point is that roughly a million Americans will die of COVID. That's horrific. What few are paying attention to is that public health experts and medical professionals are now talking about the alarming incidence of what they're calling long-COVID — that is, the persistence of symptoms long after the acute illness with the virus has passed. This scares me because we know that viruses linger in the human body and sometimes "come back" with very unfortunate consequences. A familiar example is the chicken pox virus that often resurrects itself late in life to cause a painful bout of shingles in older adults.

An even better example is what I'm dealing with now — post-polio syndrome. I spent years thinking that my polio was a static disorder that had plateaued at a level of stability that would last more or less indefinitely. But then, in the 1980s, I began to experience perplexing symptoms: fatigue, muscle pain, joint pain, and—most alarmingly—new muscle weakness. Around that time, the medical community began to take note of the accumulating reports of similar things from people who had suffered through a bout of paralytic polio and they coined the term "post-polio syndrome."

The same sort of thing is happening to some of the people who've contracted COVID. Some time after they've recovered from the initial bout of illness (roughly six weeks later seems common), they notice that they suffer from unresolved pain or tiredness, shortness of breath, and/or cognitive problems—thinking, reasoning, and remembering —or what people sometimes describe as 'mental fog.' The symptoms can come and go, but have an impact on the person's everyday functioning, and cannot be explained by another health problem.

I've seen frequent references to the cognitive problems, which seem to have a severe impact on a person's life. Long-haul COVID patients may experience changes in the way they think, concentrate, speak and remember, and these symptoms can affect their ability to work or even maintain activities of daily living. All of that increases a person's risk of experiencing depression and anxiety. That's on top of all the other mental-health issues they may be experiencing: long periods of isolation, stress from job loss and financial difficulties, and grief from the loss of good health or even grief from the death of loved ones lost to COVID.

It will be a while, of course, before scientists can tell us whether the vaccines will provide any protection against long-COVID. They might. In any case, there's no reason — no reason at all—to believe the vaccines do any harm to people. By contrast, the anti-vaxxers are doing such egregious harm. It makes me sick.

Chapter Twelve

Jack

For us to get underway with our "investigation," I had to do some initial spadework. I'd decided we'd start with Fat Becky. She's our number one suspect at this point. After all, she actually accosted Amy and Matt outside the school. So, yes, she's Numero Uno in my book.

While Mike and I wait for a pot of coffee to brew in Amy's kitchen, I pull out my laptop and sit next to him at the breakfast table. I flip it open, wait for it to link to Amy's wifi, and then open Safari. "Have you ever been on Facebook?" I ask my brother.

"No, thank God."

"I get you, Kemosabe. No reasonable person should. Judging from what I've read over the years, it's a horrible, detestable platform—depending on one's predilections, either a sewer of hatred and misinformation or a shiny vortex of vacation photos and puppy videos. But for purposes of finding out about someone like Fat Becky, it's perfect."

"Are you ... what's the word? A member?"

"I think the word is *user*. And no, I wasn't. Until late last week. Now I am. Consider me modern! You'll find me in Hillary's 'basket of deplorables.'"

I turn the laptop so Mike can see what I'm doing. I log in, then navigate to the Facebook group for Mesa Vista's chapter of Moms for Liberty. Next to the group logo, it reads, "Moms for Liberty—Mesa County, CO. Private Group, 91 members. Moms for Liberty is dedicated to fighting for the survival of America by unifying, educating, and empowering parents to defend their parental rights at all levels of government."

"I don't really understand what I'm looking at here."

"Within Facebook, people can join affinity groups of all sorts. There's everything under the sun. You name it. Suppose you're interested in crafting. Or motorcycles. Or home brewing. There are groups for almost everything. Most groups are open membership, meaning that anybody can join and see the members and posts of the group. Others, like Moms for Liberty, are closed groups, which are more exclusive. To join a closed group you have to be approved by an administrator or invited by a current member. In this case, I got approval from a Marni Reynolds, one of the group administrators. So, we're in."

"Just like that?"

"Well, I had to tell a few fibs—not exactly the first time someone's done that on Facebook, I'm sure. I said I'm the grandfather of a kid at Chatfield Elementary School and another at Grand Mesa Middle School and that I'm angry as hell about the way the District 51 school board has handled the COVID epidemic."

"They let old men into the moms' group?"

"Yup." I point at the screen. "Says right here under *About Us*: "We're not just Moms. We are Moms, Dads, Grands, Aunts, Uncles, Friends." Basically, they'll accept anybody who increases their numbers and buys into their agenda. Or, as in my case, claims to."

"And our Miss Becky is on here?"

I scroll down the membership roster and slow when I get to the Ds. Becky Dubrovsky. Her mug looks out at us. Sad to see double chins on a woman her age. "Her kids, Angela and Simon, go to Pomona Elementary and Grand Mesa Middle School, respectively. No mention of a husband. Apparently, she works at the IHOP over by Highway 6 and Rt. 50. She posts a lot of vitriol about the school board and the county board of supervisors. No specific mention of Amy that I could find."

"Okay. So, what do we do with this information?"

"We treat ourselves to a stack of buttermilk pancakes!" I open a bag I'd stowed behind my chair and pull out two blue T-shirts, each emblazoned with *Grandpas for Liberty*. "First, we gotta make sure we look the part!"

Chapter Thirteen

Mike

I have to hand it to my brother. When he undertakes a mission, he goes into it whole hog. These T-shirts are a perfect example. His attitude is, *Let's give this thing everything we've got.* I like that about him. But as I've often told him, the word "excessive" isn't part of his vocabulary. I reminded him of that again when he asked me also to don a bright red TRUMP cap.

"Nope. I won't do it. You can, if you want. But I'm not wearing that thing. The T-shirt is enough!"

Maybe I was miffed because the T-shirt, though a clever and well-intentioned purchase, was, to me, an instrument of torture. I mostly wear button-up shirts because putting on a pull-over shirt is hard for me. I have pain in my damn shoulders. Decades of leg weakness has meant that I've had to rely more on my arms and shoulders to get up from a sitting position and perform other normal activities. And as each shoulder has lost normal muscle strength in recent years, the ball simply doesn't move normally within the socket, meaning that other muscles get overused and the whole area is subject to problems such as arthritis, bursitis, and tendinitis. Damn painful.

So, putting on that T-shirt was no picnic, and when Jack handed me the red cap, I was in a bad mood.

"C'mon," he said, "the hat completes the look!"

I barked back at him more ferociously than I intended. "I said no, Jack. Drop it."

He raised his eyebrows and his palms. "Okay, okay. Just trying to make us look legit."

"You always go overboard!" That stung him.

"I don't *always* do anything! But, fine. Leave the hat." He snatched his keys from the table and said, "Let's go."

So, now we're driving in silence along Rt. 6, which doesn't exactly show Mesa Vista to best advantage. A visitor who only traveled through town on this road would think he'd stumbled into the Seventh Circle of Hell and would keep on going, never to return. It's a plastic canyon of dollar stores, gas stations, supermarkets, fast-food joints, car washes, pawn shops, hair salons, discount-tire stores, vape shops, used-car dealerships, doughnut shops, trailer parks, sleazy motels, liquor stores, nail salons, pizza shops, and establishments selling storm doors, stockade fencing, skimobiles, auto accessories, seat-covers, marijuana, and sex toys. Lots of corrugated plastic and galvanized-metal sheeting. Signs with missing letters. Litter-strewn side-walks and gutters. Every few blocks, a vacant lot.

In defense of Mesa Vista, I want to say that some residential parts of town are lovely, and there are more than enough really good restaurants, bars, and cultural amenities to satisfy most people's needs and wants. But every time I find myself traveling Rt. 6 through town, I feel a little bit of my soul withering away. In fact, there goes some of it right now.

We reach the IHOP, which is nestled between a Buffalo Wild Wings and an Olive Garden. Across the street there's a "Soulful Cajun" food truck. This is a real Culinary Row. Hard to tell it apart from Paris's *Rue des Martyrs*. The parking lot's in sad condition, the pavement cracked and split over the years by frost, a gnarled and rusty chainlink fence surrounding it.

As Jack retrieves my walker from the trunk of his Toyota, I watch a thin old man with a goatee. He's walking a small old dog on a leash. Even from thirty yards away I can see the leash is old, too. It's been mended multiple times with what looks like adhesive tape. Good thing the dog isn't bigger or that leash wouldn't do its job. The dog sniffs the hard-packed dirt of the verge and then positions itself into a curved-back posture to unload a dump, which the man inspects and then generously leaves behind as a gift to the community. Classy. He and the dog continue down the street.

We negotiate the two sets of glass doors at the IHOP entrance (not easy with a walker) and stand next to the sign that orders us to wait to be seated. One glance around tells me there's only one other set of patrons in there at the moment. An old woman with crepe-paper skin appears with two menus and guides us to a booth looking out on Rt. 6. "Your server Becky will be with you in a moment."

I spy Becky leaning against the counter at the servers' station, reading a copy of *National Enquirer*. When the old woman says something to her, Becky glances our way with a hint of annoyance, then folds her source of news down between a coffeemaker and a toaster oven. Dear Becky probably has never met a work ethic she didn't loath. She picks up a coffee pot and heads our way.

"Coffee for you fellas?" Her meaty body is stuffed into black pants made from some stretchy spandex-like material that allows us to see every slight dimple on Becky's cellulite-coated thighs, every crease of flesh. She wears a red, short-sleeve shirt. A black name tag perches above her pillowy right breast.

"That would be great," Jack says, sliding his eye up her shirt, "uh, Miss Becky."

She pours our coffee. "Grandpas for Liberty, eh? I'm a Mom for Liberty!"

"Really!" Jack says with feigned surprise.

"Yup. One of the charter members of our Mesa Vista group."

"Well, ain't that sumpthin!" He looks across at me and picks up his mug in a toast. "We're in mighty fine company, Mike! This here gal's one of us! Another patriot!" I wonder at the inspiration for his new vernacular. I consider adopting it for myself, too. But, he's doing such a convincing job that I decide not to join in, lest I goof up and accidentally break the spell he's casting. I just smile and raise my mug toward the two of them.

"You fellas know what you want or should I give you a minute?"

"Aw, hell, Becky. I think we know what we want. I'll take

a short stack of buttermilk pancakes and a side of link sausages. My little buddy here will have —"

I speak for myself. "Eggs over medium, crisp bacon, and whole-wheat toast, please."

"Comin' right up." She waddles off toward the kitchen.

I look at Jack. "Where you from, pardner?"

He laughs. "In the Facebook profile I made up for myself, I said I'd moved here after decades in Texas. I figured I'd better furnish myself with a veneer of authenticity."

"Well, let's hope you can sustain it."

"I suspect ol' Becky is no Henry Higgins when it comes to detecting fraudulent accents. I could probably talk like Daffy Duck and not raise her suspicions."

Becky comes back a few minutes later, coffee pot again in hand. "Top that off for ya?"

Jack holds up his mug. "I'd wrassle the devil himself for another cup of that coal oil."

She fills his mug and puts the pot on the table behind her. She crosses her arms and looks at us. "Nice of you fellas to lend your support to Moms for Liberty."

"Hell, honey, there ain't nothin' 'nice' about it! This here country's hitched its wagon to a falling star. We're goin' down the crapper under this Biden fella, and we's all obliged to do what we can to fight against those who stand in the way of our freedoms—there in Washington, DC, like them patriots did on January 6th; and right here in Mesa Vista, too. That's the way I see it, anyhow."

Becky's head pumps up and down like one of those drinking-bird toys.

Jack continues. "Why, you take this local school board, for instance. Three of them five are libtard wackos. That Amy Wilson! Well, to my way of thinkin', she's the devil incarnate. If she had her way, we'd all be wearing astronaut suits around town and we'd be hooked up to IVs 24/7 so the gummint could pour whatever chemicals it wants into our veins whenever it wants!"

I smile with new regard for my brother's talents. And Miss Becky is looking at him like she wants to have his babies.

"You are exactly, one-hundred percent correct, mister. That woman is just plain evil."

Jack and I shoot each other a glance at the word "evil."

She's picking up steam. "So is them other two on that board! I swear, we're gonna have to do whatever it takes to get them off o' there. *Whatever it takes!*"

The short-order cook dings the bell at the kitchen counter, so Becky disappears for a bit, then reappears with our food. She puts our plates in front of us, then pulls up a chair. "You don't mind if I set a spell, do ya? I don't have any other tables."

Jack puts a look on his face like he's Sylvester and has just managed to catch Tweety Bird. He takes off his red cap and smooths his hair back. "Why, honey, nothin' would please us more!" Then he gives her a long, hard look. "Say, do you have a kid at Grand Mesa Middle School?"

"Yes, I do. My son Simon is in the seventh grade there."

Jack snaps his fingers, then slaps the table. "I thought I'd seen you before! 'Course, a pretty lady like you is hard to forget! I remember seeing you outside the school a week or so ago. You was angry, yellin' at some woman in a car. You had a Moms for Liberty T-shirt on, and you was really givin' that woman hell. I couldn't see who it was, but she won't soon be forgettin' the tongue lashin' you gave her!"

Becky leans her ample upper body forward and beams with pride. "Yes! That was me! And that woman in the car was Amy Wilson!"

"No!"

"Yes, sir, it was!"

"You took the fight straight to the devil herself?"

"I did!"

"Well, Miss Becky, I am right proud of you. Not everybody has the guts to confront these people directly. Some folk talk the talk, but they won't walk the walk. You know what I mean? Then there are folk like you who aren't afraid to walk right up to the beast!"

Now, Becky beams. "Oh, that weren't nothin'. I just gave her a piece of my mind, that's all."

"Don't you understate what that's worth, my pretty friend. Why, that's golden!" Here, he pauses, and points his fork at what remains of his pancakes. "These here are just the finest flapjacks around. Mmm, mmm!" He takes another bite and then shoots a look up at Becky like he's just seen the risen Lord. "Oh, my! I just thought of sumpthin. I heard that somebody cut down a young tree at that Wilson woman's house and burned 'EVIL' into her lawn with chemicals." He looks up at Becky with unalloyed admiration. "I'm now guessin' that might have been you, lovely lady! Not many other folks around here would have the gumption to do that! I salute you, Miss Becky. You're a Patriot!"

Becky giggles. And when Becky giggles, all of Becky jiggles. When the ripples and undulations of flesh slow, she shakes her head. "I wish I could take credit for that. But I can't. I heard about it, though." She giggles and jiggles again.

"Well, my gosh! If it wasn't you, who could it have been?! I've only been in this town for a while, but you're the first person I've met with true courage. So, if not you, who?"

Becky blushes. You could almost feel the heat from the blood rushing to her body's surface. She swats Jack's compliment away. "Aw, I'm not that courageous. And, honestly, I don't believe in damaging another person's property, no matter how angry you are at 'em. I have a sister who fired a pellet gun at every window in her boyfriend's house when she found out he was cheating on her. I told her I thought that's just wrong. I draw the line at that kind of thing."

"So, you wouldn't do that, eh?"

"Nope."

Now, I'm not a great lie detector, but I have no trouble saying Becky's being truthful. I'm starting to think she's not our culprit.

"Do you know who did it?"

She shakes her head. "I don't."

Jack gives her a conspiratorial look. "Well, I'm a good-ol' country boy with few scruples. Any idea who I might connect with around here if I wanted to cause some ... trouble ... for heavy-handed gummint officials like that Wilson woman?"

Becky actually looks up and points her index finger

under her chins, as if this pose is the time-proven way to summon a name. "I can't say for sure, but maybe a fella named Marty Stauffer. He often shows up at meetings of local public boards and makes a ruckus. He likes to shout and hurl insults. I don't know if he's into vandalism, but I wouldn't be surprised." Here, she finally looks over at me. "You're pretty quiet. You lookin' to cause some damage, too?"

I smile. "No, ma'am. I'm more the mild type. I'm like you. I don't like those liberals. Not one bit. But destroying someone's property is goin' a step too far. Just wrong, in my opinion."

"Pussy!" Jack mutters.

"Besides, I'm not exactly fleet of foot these days"—I gesture toward my walker—"so I'd probably just get my lame ass caught if I did something bad."

She laughs and stands up. "Well, I wish you both well. Maybe I'll see you at a Moms for Liberty meeting. What are your names, fellas?"

Jack offers his hand for a shake. "I'm Jack, Miss Becky. And this here is my brother Mike. It's a real pleasure to meet you. We'll make a point of stopping into IHOP again, now that we know we have a friend here. A pretty friend. Why, you're pretty enough to make a cowboy forget his horse, Miss Becky."

"Aw. And you're a flirt, Jack. Do be sure to come back." She places the check on the table before heading off to check on a newly seated party.

Jack leaves cash on the table, including a healthy tip.

"Jesus!" I say, when we got outside. "She was a real

asshole to Matt and Amy! You shouldn't have given her a big tip!"

"We want her on our side. She's got loose lips."

"*All* of her is loose! But as obnoxious as she was to Amy, I don't figure her for the vandalism."

"Nope. Me neither. We'll have to keep looking. And we'll have to check out this Marty Stauffer fella."

Chapter Fourteen

Amy

My new OT assignment takes me to the Valley View neighborhood of Mesa Vista. Spacious lots with older homes. Agnes Moore's house looks like it was built in the 1930s. Light yellow clapboard with dark green shutters and a hip roof shingled with green-gray asphalt tiles. A-shaped dormers here and there, suggesting a third floor that's more than an attic. A brick walk leads up to a green front door with sidelights. Nice place.

I ring the doorbell and wait. And wait some more. Finally, I hear several locks being turned and one security chain being unlatched. A small woman cracks the door open a couple inches. A second security chain prevents it from opening wider. "Yes? What is it?" Her breath wheezes out at me like it's escaping from under a seat cushion. It smells like soiled kitty litter. Maybe damp bath towels that have been sitting in a hamper for a week. I can't quite place it. I step back about ten inches.

"Mrs. Moore, I'm Amy Wilson, an occupational therapist. I have an appointment with you this morning."

She turns her head so that there's just one beady eye peering out at me. "Are you from the government?"

"No, as I say, I'm an occupational therapist. A health-care worker. Your doctor arranged for me to come see you."

"I'm not sick."

"No, but he says you've fallen twice in the past month and he wants me to help you figure out how to stay safe so you can maintain your independence and continue to live at home."

"Damn meddlers," she mutters as she unhooks the door chain and steps aside to let me in. As I walk by her, I am hit by an onslaught of odors that remind me of sewer gas or stagnant water in a flower vase. I'm grateful that I'm wearing a face mask, but disappointed it's not doing much to protect me from this olfactory assault. I follow Agnes as she nudges her walker over multiple dirty throw rugs that litter the path to the living room. I see a dark stain on the back of her skirt. I don't want to think about its origin. She seats herself in a huge, gaudily upholstered chair, pulls a blanket over her lap, and firmly folds her arms across her chest. I sit across from her, about ten or twelve feet away.

Her deep, close-set eyes fix on me from her skeletal, triangular face. "Tell me again what this is all about."

The stench is less severe now that I'm farther away from her. I repeat the doctor's concern about her falls and his worry that it may no longer be safe for her to be living alone at home.

She tells me she's 84 years old. Her husband died ten years ago, her daughter and grandchildren have moved to New Jersey, and her son lives in the small town of Loma, about 20 minutes away from Mesa Vista. She says her daughter and son-in-law had begged her to move east to live with them or to let them pay for her to move to Mesa Vista's finest continuing-care retirement community. "Nope. Not gonna do that. I plan to remain in my own home as I grow older. And nobody's gonna talk me out of that."

"Agnes, let me be clear. I'm not here to try to persuade you to move or do anything else you don't want to do. I'm here to help you figure out how to remain in your home — or whatever you decide you want."

She stares at me. I'm wondering if she heard what I said. Finally, she says, "I'm glad they didn't send no black person out here to help me. I wouldn'ta liked that at all."

I'm so taken aback by this comment that I have no idea how to respond. I glare back at her. "I'm going to work with you to come up with ideas that fit with your wants and needs, as well as your budget and this specific home environment." Dear God. I have to get out of here. I can't stand another minute of this stench—literal or moral. "Today, I'm mostly here to introduce myself and give you some things to think about before I return next week. Okay?"

Her implacability lifts just enough to allow a nod. Then she starts to cough and can't seem to stop. She picks up a water glass from the table next to her, but it's empty. She holds it out to me with a beseeching look. I take the glass and go to the kitchen, where I expect to find an overflowing trash can and food rotting in the sink. But I don't. I fill the glass and take it back to her, thinking now that the odors are coming from her person only, not from household sources as well. She sips the water and eventually is able to clear her throat.

"You okay?"

She nods.

"Good. So, over the next few days, I want you to think honestly about those things you're having trouble with. Could be anything. Changing light bulbs in hard-to-reach places, fixing meals, opening jars or doorknobs, climbing the stairs, driving to the store." I pause and think of what I should be saying instead: *bathing, changing your clothes. . .* I look around the densely appointed living room. "I'd also like you to think about how we can trim the number of objects in each of the rooms where you spend time so we can reduce your risk of tripping or falling. I'm thinking of unnecessary throw rugs, chairs, electrical cords."

I gesture toward the blanket on her lap. "That blanket looks cozy. I bet you love it. But I wonder if you might get by with one that's much smaller but equally pretty. A little lap blanket. That one is so big that it must be hard to get it completely out of your way as you stand up and move away from the chair. It could easily snag your foot and topple you over."

She seems a bit miffed by that comment and looks at me like she's just caught me trying to steal her jewelry. But I don't care. That damn blanket is a genuine hazard. I reach into my tote bag and pull out some tip sheets that I can leave with her to jog her thinking. "We'll make this work for you, so you can continue to live independently. Okay?"

She nods.

I stand and give her my business card. "Call me if you have any questions. Now, you stay there. No need to get up. I'll let myself out and I'll see you next week."

Outside, I whip my mask off and take in big gulps of fresh air. I sniff my shirt sleeve to see if the miasma has permeated my clothing. Seems okay. Good thing, because I'm meeting my boyfriend for lunch.

As I drive, I think about how common it is to encounter old people with, um, odor problems. Sometimes it's a result of depression or boredom. Every day's the same for them, and there's nothing special to get gussied up for. Sometimes it's a matter of the bathroom being a scary place for older people. It has slippery, hard surfaces. The perfect setting for a fall. So, taking a bath or a shower, once a regular part of their routine, is now a basic act that carries significant risks. The possibility of a bruised ego, a broken hip, or even a permanent change in mobility is enough to deter anyone from stepping into a tub or a shower.

Discomfort is another common culprit. Old people get cold much more easily, so getting undressed may be unpleasant. And changing clothes can itself be a real hassle because of joint pain and lower energy levels. They may tire out quickly and no longer have the sense of balance and range of motion they once had.

And the problem can be exacerbated by people nagging at them. As people get older, they often feel as if they're losing control over their lives. One thing that some old people try to keep a tight grip on for as long as possible is their own personal hygiene. Caregivers and family members can nag all they want, but the more you pester them about something, the more they tend to resist. If left to work through it on their own, often they change their own behavior.

Exiting Agnes's neighborhood, I see a woman walking with a boy about Matty's age, and I think about how it's not just old people who respond poorly to nagging. Last year, I was having a hard time getting Matty to do his homework. I was at wits end about it. I'd harangue him and nag him endlessly. Finally, his teacher suggested I stop doing that. "Get off his back," she said. So, I did. And, amazingly, after a couple weeks, it worked. He started doing his homework on his own, with no badgering from me.

Yeah, there's a lesson in all this. And it's not lost on me. I get it. People generally don't like to be told what to do. They don't want to be told to wear masks, stay six feet apart, get vaccinated. Even if it's for their own good and the good of others. In fact, many will just double-down on their resistance. But what am I supposed to do as a public official? Just say, *Aw, fuck it. Let everybody do what they want. Public safety be damned.* No, and we all know that the people who resist public-health measures aren't going to magically change their minds on the matter if we leave them alone. The whole thing makes my head ache. I can't wait to get a drink.

Five minutes later, I swing my car into a parking lot off 5th Street. I'm meeting Will for lunch at our favorite restaurant, Bin 707. His Kia Nero pulls in next to me. A shaft of light pierces his sunroof and illuminates his dark hair, its textured spikes reminding me of curved meringue peaks on a pie. We hug, then head directly to the patio with its cheerful turquoise chairs. There are trees growing up around the patio and plants along the railing. There's no roof. The effect is of dining in a private treehouse in a lush garden, although we're no more than twenty feet away from a poorly paved parking lot.

Kelly, our favorite server, comes to our table within ninety seconds. She has two frozen margaritas in hand, the one with salt for Will, the one without for me. "You want to see a menu?" She knows we don't. Although we vary our selections widely when we're here for dinner (there are *so* many good choices!), at lunch we always get the same thing— he seared salmon BLT for me, the pork "Katsu" sando for Will. "No, just the usual, please."

The eye roll Kelly throws our way is part of the routine. She's the kind of server who's affection for her customers is expressed in feigned disdain: the greater the apparent scorn, the greater her fondness. "You guys are in a rut." She starts to walk away.

Will winks at me, then calls to her. "Hey, smart ass! Please ask Tony to put a dollop of that plum tapenade on the side for me." Clearly, Will has adapted himself to Kelly's style. He signals his pride in himself over this comment by exhaling on his bent knuckles and polishing them on his shirt. "How's that for breaking out of the mold, getting out of the rut?"

Kelly lowers her sunglasses and gazes at him over their top. "'Smart ass,' eh? Well, we'll see what you get on the side. I might hock a loogie into your ta-pe-NAD!" She sashays her ass away from the table. We toast with our margarita glasses.

"How was your morning," I ask. He's a graphic designer. What I selfishly like about his job is that he has the same sort of flexibility in his schedule that I have, so we can easily do things like meet for lunch—or go for a hike on a beautiful fall afternoon, if we want.

"Good. I met with the people from St. Mary's Hospital about the new brochure for their mammography center. They seemed pleased with my ideas. Then I worked on the menu for Kannah Creek. It's not easy because their offerings are really too extensive for the size and layout they want. But I'll figure it out."

I squeeze his hand. His long, slender fingers would be the envy of many women I know. "You always do." I take another sip of the margarita. I tell him about my appointment with Agnes Moore, summing it up succinctly. "So, the woman is a racist, and she stinks."

"Ah, you're being redundant." Now, *he* squeezes *my* hand and says, "Sounds like she's going to be a challenge. Sorry, Amy. It seems like you almost always have at least one patient who's problematic."

"True. Why do you suppose that is?"

"Statistical probability. The world's full of assholes. Like the vandals you're dealing with. Speaking of which, how are your dad and Matt coping with all that?"

"They seem okay. Dad's solid as a rock and Matt's quiet as one."

He laughs. We're silent for a couple of moments. I watch him lick some salt from the rim of his glass and take a gulp of his margarita.

Kelly shows up with our food. When she leaves, I lift the toasted bread off the top of my sandwich, cut off a third of the salmon, and put it aside on a bread plate. "I'll bring that home for Annabelle. She likes salmon."

"I wish you'd let yourself live a little. Have salt with your margarita. Eat all the salmon. Have a root-beer float for dessert. Eat pizza in bed. You know, throw caution to the wind! "

I ignore his ribbing and reach over to pinch his cheek. "I threw caution to the wind when I took up with you."

He smiles. "Ah! I hadn't considered that." He slathers some plum tapenade on his sandwich and then carefully works his way around its perimeter. He rarely gets away from lunch here without some of the katsu sauce falling on his shirt. This time, he has the tapenade to contend with, too. I fear a sartorial disaster. I watch as he eats it like it's an ice-cream cone. He's calculating where the dripping and slippage is likely to occur next, and he twists the sando around quickly to deal with each impending peril. Eventually, the inevitable occurs, and he gets a reddish-brown glob on his crisp blue shirt.

"Hey there, piggy. Oink, oink."

He laughs. "It's possible that adding the tapenade was an unforced error."

"Just goes to show that you follow your own advice: throw caution to the wind."

Chapter Fifteen

Mike

It's my second meeting of the post-polio support group. We've been listening for twenty minutes to a soft-spoken gentleman from the Area Agency on Aging. He's a dead-ringer for Wally Cox. He's informing us about the programs and long-term support services the agency provides to older adults, focusing on disability resources. "We provide vouchers to help pay for all kinds of *things* you might need, from hearing aids to personal emergency-response systems. Or *people* you might need, such as someone to help you with chores. We also provide legal services, Medicare counseling, nutritions programs, and transportation services."

The guy's well-intentioned, but I'm miffed that we're sitting here listening to him. He hasn't said anything we couldn't have learned from a brochure—in fact, from the very pamphlet he handed out to us at the start of his talk. If I'm going to spend my time at a support group of polio survivors, then dammit, I want to hear from them, not from this modern-day Mr. Peepers.

Now, Peggy rises to thank him, then addresses the rest of us. "As I hope you remember, I asked at the last minute that each of you be prepared today to tell the group about your hobby or interest of choice. Hobbies are good for us. They keep our minds engaged, they can encourage movement and social interaction. They can add to our personal development and combat depression. In all these ways, hobbies are good for our health. And that's what post-polio support groups are all about–promoting health and wellness among its members. So, who wants to start?"

A little woman on a red scooter timidly raises her hand as if doing so risks a dog attack, the wrath of the group, or a smiting from the Lord.

Peggy says, "Wonderful. Go ahead, Minnie."

Minnie swallows hard, then brings her hand to her throat. "Goodness. I'm just so excited to tell you about this." She rocks back and forth in her chair with obvious excitement. "My passion is calligraphy. Do you all know what that is?" Affirmative nods all around. I'm relieved. If these people have lived this long and somehow don't know what calligraphy is, then I don't think I want to hear from them. "Well, when I was a little girl, my dad did calligraphy, and I thought it was so cool. I soon found myself begging for lead pencils and fancy gel pens. Before I knew it, my dad was giving me calligraphy lessons at our dining room table.

"Some of you might assume calligraphy is obsolete."

She slowly looks around the circle as if to identify who among us might be guilty of such a thought. "Oh, no! It's certainly not. It's still very popular. What I love about it is it helps my brain." She taps her right temple with a pale, attenuated index finger. "When I practice calligraphy, I feel myself entering a more focused state that instantly banishes my anxiety and—like Peggy said—makes me feel less depressed. Besides the mental benefits, it's satisfying to create something beautiful and tangible. Plus, there's money to be made! Why, I've made lots of money over the years, doing things like addressing wedding invitations or transcribing love poems." She nods vigorously, as if perhaps we wouldn't believe that. "If you'd like to try your hand at this art form, you can take a class at Mesa Community College." She passes around several samples of her work, which—I must say—are impressive.

Then David Hawkins, who never takes off the Vietnam veterans cap that indicates he was with the 101st Airborne, tells us about his passion for building models of military items—everything from Bradley tanks to B-1 bombers, warships to anti-aircraft weapons. "I just love it! Keeps me in constant mind of my days with the Screaming Eagles." He practically foams at the mouth. "It's just so damn satisfying when I finish one of my models. Any of you want to come by my house sometime and see my arsenal, I'd be proud to show it to you!"

Sofia smooths her carefully coiffed hair and says, "My hobby is genealogy. You know: figuring out family trees, lines of descent. I started out doing it with my own family tree. I was able to trace both sides of my family back more than three hundred years. Now, I mostly do the research for friends who are interested in knowing more about their own families. Or, for fun, I just pick people out of the news —like a mayor or a county commissioner—and see what I can find out about their family history.

"Yesterday, I decided to do some research on Anthony Fauci. His maternal grandfather, Giovanni Abys, was an artist who painted landscapes and portraits. He also designed labels for products like cans of olive oil, and he did illustrations for Italian magazines. His paternal grand-father, Antonino Fauci, was from a family in Sicily that ran a hot-springs spa. Now, I don't know why I find that inter-esting; I just do. With the help of Google and the internet and genealogical sites, you can find out so much about people. I tell you, it's fun. Keeps me busy. And it's less fattening than my other hobby — cooking!"

We hear from Steve about his vinyl-record collection and from Sally about macrame. I begin to think I might throw in the towel on this damn group. Apart from one reference to polio by the man from the aging council, the word hadn't been mentioned in the hour we'd been there. What the hell was I wasting my time for?

When it's my turn, I say "Well, I admire all you folks for your good hobbies. I don't know what it says about me, but I've never had a hobby. Neither of my parents did, and I guess I followed in their footsteps. So, you might wonder, how do I spend my time? Well, I do a lot of reading—"

Minnie chimes in, "Reading's a hobby!" She bobs her head up and down. "It certainly is!"

I ignore her. "—mostly news. I've gotta keep up on what's happening out there. Politics and that sort of thing. ... And I nap." Lots of laughter at that, presumably inspired by self-recognition. "And I enjoy time with my daughter and my grandson. Throw in a little television, and my days are pretty full. I don't know how I'd fit in pole dancing, shuffleboard, or beekeeping." I'm about to add more. Then, realizing my last sentence probably came off a bit snarky, think better of it. I signal to Peggy that I'm done.

"Well, thank you, Mike," Peggy says. "*À chacun ses goûts,* I guess." She giggles. "I should have added that I also dabble in French." Another giggle. "*Un petit passe-temps.*" She beams with self-satisfaction. I want to dabble her face in a tub of hot water to rid it of a pound or two of makeup. She turns to her right. "And last, but not least, Earl!"

This guy just oozes bad temper. His posture and his face radiate sore-headedness. "Those are *hobbies* you all are talking about. Mine's not a hobby. It's a service. And a passion. I run a ham radio station and maintain a substantial presence on social media. My wife views my work as a mistress that takes my time and affection. Some of you people may know about ham radio." You could tell he didn't think it was likely with this bunch.

"Well, I use the small-frequency bands to keep my audience informed about politics and about the people in government who are trying to take away our freedoms. Same on social media. It's good to stay informed—and inform others." He looks at me, the self-pronounced news consumer. "But people also need help knowin' *what* to think. Like about face masks or these vaccines. I help 'em see what's wrong with public officials and their misguided policies. We've ceded too much control to government. People need to know how to challenge officials. I give them ideas about what to do. I'm sort of a modern-day Thomas

Paine. But I'm not a pamphleteer. My parchment is the airwaves and the internet." He crosses his arm and leans back in his chair. The look on his face reads, *I guess I just topped all you motherfuckers.*

Peggy says, "Well, that's certainly an interesting hobby, Earl. I'm sure there are many people out there grateful for your help in knowing what to think." I can't tell if she's being earnest or sarcastic. I hope the latter, but I don't think so.

"Now, I thought we might spend some time talking about how we each experienced the onset of post-polio syndrome. How it started, how you noticed it. As always, I want everyone to feel free to talk—or not!—as you like. I'll begin.

"As I said last time, polio affected my left arm, leaving it pretty much useless. But I found ways to overcome most of the obstacles that presented for me—just as the rest of you did, I assume. I got on with life, eventually marrying and having kids. I first noticed the toll that overexertion and bravado had taken on my polio-affected muscles when my children were small. At one point, I could carry a heavy suitcase for a mile with my right arm, if I had to, through sheer determination. But when my children arrived, I discovered I couldn't carry my two-year old to a neighbor's house three blocks away, no matter how hard I tried. Carrying my children up steps became simply impossible for me. And I began to notice that other people were picking up my children and carrying them around for me. That was all pretty shocking and disappointing to me as a mother, and it was then that I had to admit that something new was happening to me."

David, who'd been nodding as Peggy spoke, says, "Yeah, it's interesting how it's those normal, everyday activities that are often the first real sign of a new problem. In my case, I first noticed my new weakness when I was in the garden. My wife and I had always enjoyed gardening together. And I'd have no trouble getting down to do planting or weeding, but it gradually became so difficult for me to get up that I had to give up completely on helping my wife with the gardening." He allows a wry smile to cross his face. "It's always bothered me that the garden's appearance hasn't suffered from the loss of my ministrations." Several of us laugh in appreciation of his self-deprecatory humor.

We all sit quietly, waiting for someone else to speak. It reminds me of a Quaker service or meeting I once attended. It was of the unprogrammed kind, where, after someone has been moved to speak, there's a silence of several minutes (to me, intolerably uncomfortable) for everyone to allow that person's message to sink in.

Now, thank god, Steve speaks. "Well, you know, I think it's pretty common for us polio survivors to be in denial when we notice the onset of post-polio syndrome. We don't want to admit that the new problems might be permanent or that they represent a new stage in our relationship with impairment. Sure, maybe we tire more easily, or we can't walk as far as we once could, or our muscles seem weaker, or perhaps a leg collapses occasionally, or our breathing is more labored. But all of us spent decades experiencing daily fluctuations in our energy and strength, and it was natural for most of us to rely on the lessons we learned so long ago — push ahead in spite of the new fatigue or weakness; do more; don't give in to one's body. Following the injunction "use it or lose it" had always worked for us previously, and we didn't want to dwell on the possibility that these new problems were somehow related to our original polio.

"I remember I'd go through these periods where I'd drop into total denial. I'd tell myself that it just couldn't be true, that it had to be a lie. After all, the medical people had told us that we weren't going to get worse—that one of the good things about polio was that our condition was stable! So, what kind of sick joke was this to change their minds?!"

Minnie excitedly says, "I had that same thought many times. It just didn't seem fair or right. Surely someone was wrong about this!"

After a poignant silence, Peggy looks at her watch, then speaks. "Well, I think we have time to hear from one more person, if anyone else feels like talking." Minnie and Earl are both shaking their heads. And I'm not going to talk, at least not today. But Sofia raises her hand, signaling that she'll speak. Again, she looks elegant. A hip-length gray cashmere sweater, her hair pulled back again, twisted higher on her head this time than last. She's wearing thin horn-rimmed glasses that accentuate the intelligence of the eyes behind them.

"My post-polio symptoms emerged over a number of years, but I steadfastly resisted the implication that these new problems required any major changes in my life or in my way of dealing with polio's legacies. The changes began when I was in my late thirties. At first, it was merely a matter of fatigue. I found it increasingly difficult to stand for more than a few minutes, even with these." Here, she knocks on the braces underneath her wool pants.

"But the real problem all along had been falls. When I was a young girl learning to walk with crutches and long leg braces, I learned to fall safely so as not to hurt myself when the inevitable happened. Equally important, of course, was learning how to raise myself to a standing position once again. As long as I could pick myself up and stand on my own two feet—brace-bound and crutch-propped though I was—a fall was an opportunity to show my ability to overcome physical challenges. Besides, that was the polio mantra, as I said last time we met: 'Do it by yourself, no matter how hard, no matter how long it takes.'"

Minnie excitedly interjects. "Damn that 'little engine that could.' Damn it to hell!" Everyone chuckles.

"Yes," Sofia smiles empathetically. "Damn it to hell. Because there comes a time when the little engine simply *can't* do it. I knew the day would come when I simply would no longer be able to get myself up." She pauses, sighs, and presses her flat palms down against her thighs. "Oh, what the hell. I'll tell you what happened. One rainy night in 1984, some thirty years after I came down with polio, while walking with friends to dinner in Brooklyn, my left crutch slipped and I fell to the sidewalk, as I had so many times before. But when I turned over and tried to use one crutch to boost myself to my feet, I discovered I couldn't do it. The strange thing is that I don't think it was even a matter of strength. Rather, it had to do with a subtle, mysterious change in my own sense of rhythm and balance. My friends finally had to help me up."

"That must have been hard for you—to accept that help, to let go of the polio mantra," I say.

"It was. But it was even harder to accept that I might never again get to my feet on my own; to accept that a part of my life had ended; to accept that my body had decided—and decided autonomously, on its own—that the moment had come for me to face up to my limitations."

Another long silence prevails. I assume everyone is doing what I am—thinking how hard, but how necessary, it is to accept limitations.

Peggy ends the quietude. "What wonderful contributions we heard today. Thanks to each of you who spoke for sharing with us. At the next meeting, let's talk some more about the symptoms we're experiencing and what, if anything, we're finding helps alleviate them. See you all then."

On the way out the door, Earl and I find ourselves performing a comical Alphonse and Gaston routine. I gesture for him to motor through first. He insists I go ahead. I demur. He insists more firmly. I again sweep my arm forward, urging him through the door. Neither of us budges. Then we both move forward simultaneously. His scooter crashes into my walker and I tumble to the floor. Others hurry over (such as they can) to see if I'm okay. Two of the more able-bodied folk help me up and brush off my clothes. Earl stands up from his scooter and looks genuinely abashed. "I'm sorry, Mike. Are you okay?"

I slap him on the shoulder. "Fit as a fiddle, Earl. Not your fault at all. Just part of the continuing joy of polio. Vaccinated people miss out on so much fun in life!" I exit, certain that I'd left Earl trying to figure out if I'd insulted him or simply made a joke.

Chapter Sixteen

Marty

The four members of my squad talk as a group at least once a week. One-on-one discussions occur as needed. For our group calls, the squad uses Signal, not Zoom. Signal employs end-to-end encryption for calls and for all account information. The company can't read your messages or listen to your calls, and no one else can either. The app is careful about asking for permission to use both your microphone and your video camera. Both K3LVR and Ray are very sophisticated about technology, communications, the internet, and the like. They believe that Signal is our most secure video-conferencing option, so that's why we use it.

We had a group call last night. To me, they're always fun and lively. These guys are endlessly entertaining. Dwayne cracks me up. He really does. I've never known anybody as eager to get out there and cause mischief as Dwayne. He's not afraid of anything. I guess all those years as a wrestler toughened him up pretty well. If we were to give him the go-ahead, he'd break bones, smash skulls, set fires. Anything. His basic instinct leans toward mayhem. We're always having to rein him in. The rest of us don't see any need to indulge Dwayne's appetites. There's plenty of trouble we can cause for people like Amy Wilson without breaking any bones.

And I have to say, K3LVR is a pretty passionate guy, too, in his own way. He's not able to get out there and do any of the physical dirty work we need to have done, but I have no doubt he would if he could. You can tell from the passion in his voice. He gets pretty amped up when we talk about vaccines, masking requirements, government mandates. Even more worked up than the rest of us. I'm not really sure what's behind his intensity, his vehemence, but he can really work himself into a blind rage in a couple of minutes.

The four of us talked last night about the need to ramp up the pressure on Wilson and what we could do to accomplish that. We started by reviewing what we'd done so far and agreed that cutting down the new sapling that she planted in the spring was probably too subtle. Any juvenile delinquent in her neighborhood might've done that. The same thing for keying her car—fairly standard, although that seemed more menacing. And, I'm proud to say, I did that myself. I'm a big believer in the adage that "Opportunity knocks, but it won't do your dishes." You gotta act when you can in order to achieve your goals. So, when I saw Wilson's car that day near the school, I took out my key. Did the dishes.

Dwayne's idea a couple weeks ago to burn "EVIL" into her lawn was a good one. That was a substantial step up. But so far, Wilson hasn't made any statements to the *Daily Sentinel* about the kind of harassment she's receiving. We thought she'd start whining to the press about it right away. And we're not the only source of pressure on her. Dwayne has been stalking her, and he reported that he saw Wilson being harassed outside her son's school by some fat woman from "Mom's for Liberty." His description of it made us all laugh. Ray joked about deputizing that woman to our squad.

We threw around some ideas for next steps. Dwayne, of course, thought we should accost Wilson directly. "Approach her in a parking lot and threaten her," he said.

I tried to cool Dwayne's jets. "Dwayne, that's a crime in Colorado. Of course, we're—well, *you're*—already commit-ting a crime by stalking her and harassing her. But it wouldn't be wise to confront her directly for another reason: she'd see your face and be able to identify you." I didn't add that Dwayne has a distinctive and memorable appearance, with his big head, bent nose, cauliflower ear, and tall, big-bear shape. Plus, the peculiar stride.

Dwayne grunted.

K3LVR argued in favor of escalated vandalism as the next step.

"What do you have in mind?" I asked.

"I don't know," K3LVR acknowledged. He paused a bit, then continued. "Do I recall correctly, Dwayne, that you said her house has white siding? Maybe we paint some-thing on the side of her house in bright red paint. Or on the garage door. 'Bitch' or 'Stop the Masks' or "Fuck You" or 'No Vax.'"

We all thought a moment. Ray spoke up. "How about putting 'Wilson' inside a cancel circle. You know, a big diagonal slant across her name."

"Oh, I like that," K3LVR said.

We all agreed that should be our next escalation. Dwayne said he'd execute the plan forthwith. Actually, he said, "I'll get to it before you can say *knife*," which struck me as an odd expression.

I raised a topic we hadn't discussed in a while — extending our efforts to the Mesa County Health Department. We'd talked about that early on, but so far hadn't taken any concrete steps. As time has passed, K3LVR and I have become more agitated about Diana Tarrant, the Deputy Director of the health department. We regard her as the driving force behind the county's oppressive COVID policies. I really believe it's time to take her on. "Let's crack her like an egg," I said, making Dwayne guffaw. We agreed that each of us would work on some ideas for how we might achieve that. K3LVR said, "I don't think we need to reinvent the wheel here. We can use a lot of the same tactics we're using against Wilson."

Good point. There's nothing wrong with our tactics. We just need to give them time to work.

Chapter Seventeen

Jack

Doing this sort of thing is old hat to me. But Mike's aghast. "You trespassed?"

"I just had a little look around."

"But you entered someone's property without their knowledge or consent."

"Well, if you put it that way . . ."

"How else would you put it?"

"I. Had. A. Little. Look. Around. But I repeat myself."

"Look, we're trying to catch a malefactor, not become ones ourselves."

"Oh, dear naive brother. If only you knew how little difference there is between criminals and cops. Malefactors all! Anyway, nobody saw me. It's as if I was never there!"

He sighs. "Okay. What did you find?"

"Well, I don't know if you've seen the place your former

son-in-law has landed in, but it's a real dump. An old, dilapidated wood-frame house with an unattached garage roofed with corrugated metal. I didn't go in the house. It was the garage I was interested in. I wanted to see if there were any saws, a gas can, or any containers of weed killer."

"And?"

"None of the above. I hoped there might be a saw with some fresh wood in the teeth. No such luck. And I didn't see anything at all that could have been used to burn Amy's grass. Nothing of the sort in his trash cans, either."

"That doesn't mean Danny didn't do it."

"Right. It just means I didn't see instruments that could have been used to do it."

"So, where does that leave us?"

"Well, I don't know about you, but it leaves me wanting to pay Danny a visit."

Mike thinks about this. "If it's all the same to you, I'll sit this one out. I don't feel like seeing him. And you'll be just as effective without me. Maybe more so."

I smile. "Maybe." I flex my biceps in a bodybuilder pose. "And if I have to rough him up a little, it'd probably be best not to have any witnesses to it."

"Jesus. Don't rough him up. Besides, he's a little twerp. A dink. He'll fold the second you curl your lip at him."

I look at my watch. "No time like the present. He's probably home from work now."

———

THE SUN IS low in the sky when I pull up again in front of Danny's house. The houses here are far apart, not because the lots are big, but because few people apparently had ever wanted to build a place out in this godforsaken corner of town. A couple of dogs bark in the distance when I get out of the car. I can smell wood burning somewhere.

Danny answers the door wearing a pair of sweatpants and a soiled T-shirt. "Yes? Can I help you?" A skinny guy. Long nose, small dark eyes, jutting brow, a thin droopy mustache. Greasy hair worn medium length over the ears. About 5'9", maybe 150 pounds. He looks like his years apart from Amy have been unkind to him.

"Yeah. I'm selling subscriptions to *Architectural Digest*. Judging from your attire, I gather you're the proprietor of this elegant property. I'm guessing you might be interested in a subscription."

He gives me the once-over and what I suspect is his most intimidating look. A one-eyed Barbie doll would have frightened me more. "Take a hike," he says, and starts to close the door.

I stick my foot inside the door frame, then use my shoulder to shove the door open. He stumbles back a bit, and I enter.

"What the hell? Who are you? What do you want?"

"I want to have a little chat, Danny. Do I look at all familiar to you?" We'd met before. I suppose I'm egotistical, but I like to think people remember me. He shakes his head. That hurts my feelings. I'm a sensitive guy. "I'm Amy's uncle. I was at your wedding ceremony."

A glimmer of recognition passes across his otherwise vacuous face. "Uh, okay. Again, what do you want?"

"As I said: to chat. You see, Danny boy, my wonderful niece has been experiencing some trouble from some low-life hooligans. And you know what? When I asked Amy to come up with the names of people who might be doing this stuff, she mentioned you. Apparently you're pretty abusive toward her in emails and text messages. Not nice, Danny."

"What kind of 'stuff'?"

"Huh?"

"What's this trouble she's experiencing?"

"Vandalism. But I suspect you already know that."

"Look, I don't know anything about it." He tries to usher me back out the door. But let's just say he has difficulty moving me. Apparently, he thinks all us old guys are pushovers.

"I'm betting you *do* know something about it."

"Listen, there're a lot of people out there who dislike Amy. They don't like the way she goes around ordering students and teachers to wear masks, get vaccinated, and all that shit. Who does she think she is? The Queen of England? She drives around town in that fancy Audi. Wears her fancy clothes. Hangs out at ritzy restaurants with that pretty-boy Will Warren. Hell, half the town would show up and cheer if someone said they were going to hang that bitch by the neck."

I slam him up against the wall, almost pushing him through the cheap wallboard. I press my forearm against his throat. "Don't you dare call my niece a bitch or I'll break your thumbs. And don't think I wouldn't, you little shit." I press harder. "Now, tell me what you know!"

His eyes bug out with what looks like genuine fear. He tries to speak, but can't. I let up a bit on the pressure. He croaks. "I'm telling you, I didn't do anything and I don't know anything!"

I drop my arm. He takes in big gulps of air.

I snarl in his face. "If I find out otherwise, I'm going to come back here again. And our next chat will be less friendly." I start to go, then turn back to him. "And I don't want to hear about Amy receiving any more abusive emails and texts. Got it?"

He looks at me, but makes no sign of having heard me.

I grab his arm and twist it. "I said, *'Got it?'*"

He grunts. "Yeah. I got it."

I fling him against the wall and leave Chez Danny. Glamorous as it is, I hope not to return.

I FILL my brother in on my enchanting conversation with his former son-in-law. Then, sipping the scotch Mike has poured me, I say, "What a little weasel he is! How did you stand him all those years?"

"Fortunately, I seldom had to see him. But I'll tell ya, I was never so happy as when Amy told me she was divorcing him."

"I can understand that." Then I mention the thought that had nagged at me as I drove back from Danny's dump. "His comment about Amy's Audi. He said it with palpable envy. No wonder. I saw the crappy old VW he drives. I think the disparity makes him crazy. Enough to make him want to key Amy's car. He envies her that car, her obviously higher economic order." I take another gulp of scotch. "I'll bet you a bottle of this scotch he's the one who keyed the car. But I don't know how I'm going to prove it. Damn, it kills me that I didn't have the presence of mind to demand to see his keys."

"Why? What would you have done with his keys?"

"See if there's any dark blue paint in the grooves of any of them."

"Would there be?"

"If he used one of the keys to do it, sure. They call it 'keying a car' because that's what most people who commit the act use. A key. Most people don't carry around a screwdriver or an awl in case they want to scratch someone's car. They use what they have available. A key."

Chapter Eighteen

Amy

I push my cart up and down the aisles at the Sprouts Farmers Market on Independence Avenue. There's no Whole Foods in Mesa Vista. Sprouts is the next best thing. Not as expensive as Whole Foods, but also not as good. Still, better than the alternatives. I'm doing the shopping for my dad's birthday dinner tonight.

Jack will be there. My son Matt, too, of course. And Dad's former long-time colleague at the state's Public Health Department, Hannah Matthews. She and my dad think the world of one another. When I called her last week to invite her to come out and celebrate Dad's 70th with us, she said wild horses couldn't keep her from coming. Sweet lady. It's a four-hour drive from Denver, so not a trivial effort. To make it worth her while, I asked her if she would stay with us for a few days.

"Do I get to sleep in the same bed with your dad?" Hannah asked, with unmasked glee. I knew she was joking. Well, probably joking.

"I guess that's up to you two."

"Not solely my decision?"

"Probably not."

"Damn." A long pause. "Well, let's see if this ol' gal still has it. Whaddaya think? A red teddy? Black camisole and tap pants?"

This cracked me up. I'm sorry, but this was just too funny. "Whatever happens, Hannah, I know he will be absolutely delighted to have you here. He loves you to the moon and back." I sincerely doubt my dad has slept with a woman in the eight years since Mom died. But if he were going to do so, I'd hope it would be with Hannah.

"Yeah? Let the old codger show it!"

As I reach for a bag of Santitas chips to go along with the salsa and guac already in my cart, the memory of that phone conversation makes me laugh again. This would be a fun few days.

I pick Matt up at school on my way home from the market.

"Good day?" I ask, trying to take in his mood.

"Sucked."

"How so?"

"I got a C on Tuesday's math test."

I reach over and rub his shoulder. I look at that sweet face. "I know it's bad parenting to say this, but not since my own math classes have I ever had to calculate the area of a cylinder. So, I think you're just fine, bud. You can add, subtract, multiply, and divide. Beyond that, don't worry too much about it. You'll learn what you need to know, when you need it."

He smiles. "Sheesh. This, from a school-board member? Maybe I should alert the media to your thinking."

"Good idea. I don't have enough problems!"

I pull into the driveway. We carry the groceries into the house, and I start in on the evening's meal, Dad's favorite: caesar salad, beef bourguignon, and key lime pie for dessert. Usually, I'd make the bourguignon in the slow cooker, but I hadn't got my act together earlier enough today to do that. Fortunately, I have just enough time to follow Julia Child's stovetop directions. But it'll be tight. I work assiduously, frying the bacon, sautéing the carrots and diced onions, adding the minced garlic, pearled onions, wine, and tomato paste.

I'm transferring the red enameled pot to the oven when the doorbell rings. It must be Hannah. It's a little too early for Jack my to show up. I throw open the door. Hannah steps in, holding a large, beautifully wrapped package. "Christ! Let me put this down before my arms fail me!" She lowers the box toward the floor, then drops it the last 8 inches. "Shit. Well, it's not breakable. So WTF." She hugs me tight, then pulls back and smiles. It's a stunner of a smile. There's something in it. A kind of mischief. It's always there in her smile. I've seen it for years. Something that seems to be saying, *You know what would be fun to do?*

"Damn, it's good to see you," I say. "You don't look a day older than the last time I saw you! How do you do that?"

She laughs. "Sweetie, there's nothing here but artifice. Everything's pushed up, pulled in, tucked around, pressed down, wrangled here and there. If I sneeze, all hell's gonna break loose."

"Well, so be it. You look great." I pull her farther into the foyer to give her a hug. As I do, I also give her a closer look. Her make-up is expert. Eye liner, eye shadow, color on the cheekbones, lipstick. She probably looks better at sixty-five than she did at forty-five. There are small lines at the outside edge of her eyes, and permanent suggestions of a smile at the corners of her mouth that add to her face, give it pattern, and meaning. God, I envy her. "Welcome, dear lady."

"Thank you. It's so good to be here." She gives me another tight hug, the sort of hug that says, *I really mean this. It's good to be with you.* "Where's the birthday boy?"

We hear little vinyl wheels rolling toward us and we both look down the hallway. There's Dad, his longish silver hair, swept back from his forehead. His brown eyes big and full of intelligence. Light-gray cashmere cardigan sweater over a pale blue shirt. Fancy jeans. He looks great. "Hi, ya," he says, with his smiling eyes and a grin that stretches from here to Mars. He rolls on until he reaches us, pushes his walker aside, then pulls Hannah into a tight hug. I'm not party to it, but I can see it's the same kind of hug she'd just given me. Holy cow. Fancy lingerie, be damned.

"Well!" she says, pushing her silvery blonde hair away from a face that has flushed bright pink. "It's good to be here. Helluva drive! I almost hit a deer coming through Glenwood Springs. I thought they were only a hazard at night!"

Dad says, "Only slightly less hazardous than drunk drivers around Vail. Glad you're okay. It's so nice of you to come! Welcome, welcome, welcome." He hugs her again, and I wish I could make myself disappear.

Instead, Dad and Hannah disappear, presumably getting her settled in the guest room and catching up. I continue working on the dinner. After about an hour, Jack arrives and the festivities kick into higher gear. Maybe it's the onset of drinking, not Jack's arrival, that accounts for the elevated spirits. That's a chicken-or-egg kind of question.

It's a beautiful early evening. We've moved out to the patio. Jack is throwing a ball for Annabelle, my rescue dog, part Great Pyrenees, part Border Collie. This is a more complicated operation than one would think, because Belle has mastered the part about chasing the ball and picking it up. But she doesn't get the part about bringing it back and giving it to you. She wants you to chase her and pry it loose from her jaws. Not a very restful game for the human participant.

"She could be taught," Jack says.

"Nah. What's the fun in that?" I reply. "Annabelle's fine. Aren't you, my sweet BellieBelle?" She looks at me with those almond-shaped brown eyes that sparkle with affection. Then she comes over to me with the yellow tennis ball chomped in one side of her mouth. I pat her head. She pushes her nose under my other forearm, which causes some of my drink to slop from the glass onto my jeans. I put the glass down and reach for the ball. She turns her head away, making me miss it. The look in her eyes dares me to try that again.

"What an adorable dog," Hannah says.

I feint with my right and grab at the ball with my left. Belle moves her head a quarter inch, and I miss again. Jack then lunges for her, but Annabelle does a fast 180-degree spin and evades his grasp.

"You two are being outsmarted by a dog," Matt says, laughing. "No wonder you're having a hard time catching the vandal."

"Vandal?" Hannah asks.

Jack grabs Matt in a headlock and says "Okay, smart ass. If you think you could do a better job, we'd be glad to deputize you onto our investigative squad." Before releasing Matt, Jack gives him a noogie.

I take a cheap shot. "Yeah, Matt. Maybe some of your mathematical skills would come in handy in sussing out our perp."

Suddenly sheepish, Matt inspects his shoes. "Touché."

Hannah looks around, as if pleading for *someone* to answer her. "Vandal? Perp?"

Dad explains to Hannah the various damages to my property the past few weeks, concluding with, "… and we're not having a lot of luck identifying our culprit." As if empathizing with Dad, Annabelle comes over and rests her head in his lap. She looks up at him, her eyes outlined in black. Her broad white shoulders push against his legs and her well-furred tail sweeps back and forth with sweet affability. But then she hears a squirrel moving along the fence. She spins around, spots it, and tears after it. Half way down the yard, the squirrel does a quick about face and runs back the other way. Belle's momentum carries her a few yards forward before she's able to pull off a course correction. Now advantaged, the squirrel makes it safely to the neighbor's tree that overhangs our fence. The wily rodent chatters noisily down at poor Belle, amplifying the dog's humiliation. Matt, feeling sorry for Belle, asks her if she'd like a treat, and Belle bounds toward the patio door. We all take the opportunity to move the party inside.

"Oh, my god, that smells so good," Hannah says, reacting to the aroma of stew coming from the kitchen.

I smile at her. "If you need to freshen up before dinner, now's a good time. This should be ready in about ten minutes." I busy myself adding the mushrooms for the final few minutes of cooking time. I cheat with the mashed potatoes, microwaving store-bought mashed rather than making my own.

Over dinner, the conversation inevitably touches on COVID. Hannah tells us about her cousin, who's been suffering from continuing symptoms of the virus. "Her doctors are saying she's one of the unfortunate people who have 'long-COVID.'"

Jack says, "I'm sorry, Hannah. I'm just an uninformed ex-cop. Would you tell a wretched ignoramus like me what that means?"

Hannah laughs. "You're lucky you're so good looking, Jack. Otherwise, I'd leave you wallowing in your ignorance."

Matt snorts. Jack sneers at Hannah.

Hannah says, "It just means long-lingering effects like severe fatigue, pain, shortness of breath, and cognitive problems."

I ask, "Was your cousin intubated, Hannah?"

"Yup. She was in the hospital's intensive-care unit and on a ventilator for two weeks. She'd developed pneumonia that had led to acute respiratory distress syndrome. So, she needed a ventilator. I've read that for patients with COVID and ARDS, ending up on a ventilator for a couple of weeks is not uncommon."

"And, from what I hear, that's a problem," Dad says. "If a patient is on a ventilator for a short time, they tend to do pretty well. But the longer a patient is on one, the lower the chance of a good outcome. In order to be intubated, a patient has to be sedated. And if you're on a ventilator for a couple of weeks, the sedative medications tend to build up in the body and cause all kinds of side effects." Here, he gestures toward Hannah. "Just like your cousin's—pain or tiredness, shortness of breath, and cognitive problems."

I've seen so many older patients with these issues, so I find this topic fascinating. I say, "Long-COVID can't be diagnosed. Right? I mean there's no test for it. If you've had COVID and then have various continuing symptoms after your initial sickness, you're assumed to have long-COVID. In that sense, it's sort of like post-polio syndrome. There's no test for it, right? A key part of the diagnosis is that one had an earlier polio infection. Right?" I look at Dad. He nods in affirmation.

"Okay. So what's interesting to me is how complicated all this is. Have you heard of something called post-intensive-care syndrome, or PICS?"

Hannah shakes her head. Jack and Matt look confused. Dad nods and says, "Yup.

It's a collection of physical, mental, and emotional symptoms that continue to persist after a patient leaves an intensive care unit."

"Exactly! Well, it's actually quite interesting. It turns out that people who end up in an ICU for whatever reason —an accident, a stroke, complications from surgery, a virus, whatever — often develop a set of symptoms that start after the critical illness and persist after discharge from the ICU. The symptoms can last for weeks, months, and even years."

Dad smiles, knowing where I'm headed with this. He says, "And they're just like a lot of the PPS and post-COVID symptoms, right?"

"Right. Cognitive symptoms such as decreased memory and thinking problems, difficulty talking, forgetfulness, poor concentration, trouble organizing and problem solving. Emotional symptoms such as anxiety, depression, decreased motivation, and things we associate with PTSD, like nightmares and unwanted memories. Finally, there are physical symptoms like muscle weakness and fatigue, tiredness, decreased mobility, difficulty breathing, and insomnia."

"What causes all this?" Hannah asks.

"It's a combination of factors," I answer, with more confidence than I should be showing, given the complexity of the topic. "Obviously, care in the ICU can be intense, as the name suggests, due to the serious medical conditions patients face, such as respiratory failure or sepsis. So, in the ICU, the caregivers may be using life-sustaining equipment such endotracheal tubes or mechanical ventilators. And, as Dad was saying a minute ago, the longer a person is on a ventilator, the worse the outcome. *Many* people who spend a prolonged time in an ICU get delirium. The strange surroundings, multiple mind-altering medications, isolation and loss of control can leave patients with lasting and recurrent sensations of terror or dread, including post-traumatic stress disorder (PTSD)."

Hannah jumps in, suddenly animated by something I said. "That's my cousin. Exactly!She was so disoriented because of the sedatives that she didn't really know what was going on. She had hallucinations where she believed the doctors and nurses were trying to harm her. Like when the nurses would turn her or reposition her so she wouldn't get bedsores, she felt pain or discomfort and thought people were trying to hurt her or attack her."

"That's so sad," I say. "And I've heard that from so many people over the years."

"Think about what it means from a physical stand-point," Hannah says. "Once you have a tube down your throat, you can't eat anymore. You can't go to the bath-room. You can't bathe yourself. Every single day that you lie in bed, the weakness you feel keeps increasing."

"Yup," I say. "I have an OT patient right now who told me she couldn't hold her head up when she came out of intubation. She couldn't grip or squeeze things because she was so weak. She had tight muscles in her ankles from lying in bed for so long, making it impossible for her to stand."

"Terrible," Dad says.

"I've had ICU nurses tell me all that's pretty common. Even if you're only intubated for a week, you're still going to struggle to stand up and walk. You're going to need equipment, like a walker or wheelchair, to help you get around. You're going to need a specialized physical-therapy team to help you recover. And you look like hell, older and frailer. You might go into the ICU looking young and healthy but you come out looking like you've aged 10 or 20 years. Patients have bruises from all the IVs. They may have injuries from catheters."

Jack says, "God. This sounds awful. I hope I never end up in an ICU."

Hannah interjects. "Exactly. I have a provision in my living will that says I don't ever

"Yeah," I say. "Being in an ICU can be ruinous to your health. People may be so weak from intubation that they start having nerve pain. Many people say it feels like their body is on fire. Months later, people can still be struggling with breathing, muscle weakness and fatigue, tiredness, and foggy thinking. Patients who've survived the ICU often tell me that they feel like they're not the same person they were before they got sick. Recovered patients often can't return to work. And depending on their former job, they may feel like the person they were before they got sick no longer exists. You can work on helping a patient regain strength and movement, but helping them feel like the person they were before they got sick is a hard thing to do."

I see Dad and Hannah looking at each other and smiling. He says, "Ivan Illich."

She says, "Iatrogenic disease." She tries to high-five Dad. But I know that raising his arm that high would be painful, so I'm not surprised when he simply gives her a thumbs-up.

Out of boredom or hunger or both, Jack and Matt get up and go to the stove, where they help themselves to some more beef bourguignon. When they're seated again, the conversation turns to President Biden's problems getting his major agenda items passed through Congress. Although

I suppose it's inevitable that the subject would come up at some point, I wish it hadn't because Jack's more conservative than my dad on lots of matters, and I know from experience that this topic could easily lead to conflict. As I've said, I'm not big on conflict, even when I'm only an observer of it. It just makes me uneasy. Fortunately, on this occasion, the brothers bicker, but manage not to have a full-out row. Maybe it's the calming influence of Hannah's presence. Or maybe it's my well-timed presentation of the key-lime pie. In any case, comity prevails.

Unfortunately, that doesn't mean the rest of the evening is calm. As I clear the table with help from Jack and Matt, Hannah and my dad head to the living room. Annabelle, hearing a neighbor's dog barking, excitedly bolts from the kitchen toward the patio door like an eighty-pound torpedo, clipping the backs of my dad's legs and sending him into a fall. He hits the side of his head on the coffee table, and blood immediately starts to pour from just above his left ear. Even minor head wounds can bleed profusely because the scalp and face have many blood vessels close to the surface of the skin. But this looks worse than a minor gash.

We decide to hurry him to the emergency room ourselves rather than wait for an ambulance to get here. While Hannah and I get dad into Jack's car, he arms the security system and tells Matty to stay inside until we get back. It only takes ten minutes to get Dad to the hospital, and they take him right in. The ER doc decides to admit him and keep him overnight, so they can monitor him for signs of a concussion or a cranial hematoma. That seems wise to all of us.

Jack and I say goodbye to Dad and leave the room so he and Hannah can say goodnight without us around. When she eventually joins us in the waiting room, she's smiling. "That guy is just remarkable. He refuses to let things get him down. He kept making jokes about falls being par for the course for an old cripple. I pointed out that any one of us could have had a nasty fall if Annabelle had clipped us. He said, 'Yeah, but Belle is especially fond of taking me down. She knows she can do it. I suspect she was frustrated at not getting that squirrel, so decided to go for an easier target. *Topple the crip!* That's Belle's motto.'"

As we walk to the car, I feel for Hannah. She must be worried about Dad — and disappointed not to have the evening with him that she'd been looking forward to. I put my arm around her shoulder. "I'm sorry you got cheated out of time tonight with Dad. Would you be willing to consider staying on longer than you planned?" .

She brightens. "Of course! If you hadn't suggested it, I'd have had to ask. Thank you!"

My phone dings. A text message. It's from Matty. *"The alarm system says there's somebody in our yard!!"*

Jack drives us home like a bat outta hell.

Chapter Nineteen

Jack

W e don't get there in time. I'd hoped that because we were only ten minutes away (or seven, with my pedal to the metal), we'd get there fast enough to catch someone in the yard or driving away. I'd been prepared to throw my car into a slide to block the road if there was a vehicle exiting Amy's cul-de-sac. No such luck.

Matt sees us pull up and opens the front door to us when we step on the porch. His mother rushes in and hugs him. "I'm sorry we left you alone, honey. Are you okay?"

He shrugs. "Yeah. Fine." But I can see he's shook up. It's natural to be spooked in a situation like this.

"Did you actually see anybody?" I ask him.

Matt shakes his head. "When the alarm sounded, I wasn't sure what was happening at first. And I guess I was more concerned with making sure the doors were locked and the windows were closed. So, I checked around, then turned on all the outside lights. I didn't see anything."

"Any car pulling away?"

"Not that I saw."

"Okay. Good man." I grab a flashlight from the counter in Amy's mud room and go outside to look around. It's been so dry here lately that there aren't any shoe prints visible. Crickets chirp, and I can smell some grass clippings from a neighbor's pile of yard waste. When I come around from the side of the yard to the driveway, the odor of the clippings yields to the smell of wet paint. On the white garage door there's a big circle in red paint. A "cancel" sign. Inside the circle, "WILSON." A red slash across the name from one edge of the circle to its diametrically opposite edge. I loop around the rest of the house to see if there's anything else. Nothing.

Back inside, I tell the three of them about the cancel symbol. Amy's hand goes to her forehead. I feel for her. I really do. This is getting old. She takes a few steps back and forth, her hands clenched into tight fists. She looks up at the ceiling and screams, "God DAMN it!" Matt stands still, obviously unnerved. Hannah pulls Amy into a hug. Annabelle pushes her head between Hannah and Amy, trying to horn in on the embrace.

Pointing to the dog, I turn to Matt. "Did Annabelle bark at any point?"

"No. She was asleep next to me on the couch. The TV was on. She didn't leap up until the alarm sounded."

I ask Amy if I may use her laptop. She brings me the MacBook and I sit at the kitchen table and pull up the website of the security company. I navigate to the account

Mike and I had set up, and soon am looking at video recorded by one of the outdoor cameras. The angle wasn't great, but it caught the moving image of a person carrying a small can, moving away from the garage and then out of view. I hoped one of the other cameras might've caught the person coming onto the property. No such luck. Still, at least we have something.

The person wore dark clothing, including watch cap and gloves. A big person. Almost certainly male, judging from the upper body. Too heavy to be Danny. A distinctive gait — not quite a limp, but some bodily deference to an old injury, I guess. I show Amy the video, just in case anything about the person seems familiar.

"Yes!" she shouts. "I've seen that person before. His stride is weird; that's why I remember him. In fact, I've seen him a number of times in the past few weeks, including going to his car after the last school-board meeting. He seems to be all over town."

Oh, that's not good. "Look, Amy, I don't want to scare you, but it sounds like he might be stalking you. I want you to be very careful. Always try to park near other people. Keep your eyes open. Be aware of who's around you. If you see him again, be cautious, but see if you can find out what he's driving."

"He was walking to a truck. White, I think."

"Well, keep an eye out for it. See if you can get a license plate number."

She's made Hannah and herself some chamomile tea. Amy says, "It's just as well Dad's not here. He'd really be upset by this." I nod, and pour myself a glass of Red Label. She watches me, then gets up, splashes her tea into the sink and pours herself a glass of scotch, too. She holds it up and says, "Hannah? One for you too?"

Hannah looks at her mug of tea, then says, "Christ, yes."

We talk a while longer, and then I take my leave, promising to be back early in the morning. "Call me if anything concerns you. Anything at all." Amy walks me to the door. I hug her. "We'll find out who's doing this. I promise we will."

She looks up at me. "What makes you so sure?"

"'Cuz these people aren't as smart as they think they are."

Chapter Twenty

Amy

I get Matty off to school, then make bacon and eggs for Hannah and me. After we've eaten, we take our coffee into the living room. Hannah opens the digital *New York Times* on her iPad, and I make a couple of phone calls, cancelling some of my appointments for the day. I keep one scheduled for late afternoon, figuring that by then we'll either have Dad home from the hospital or know he'll be there for another night.

It turns out to be the former. When I phone the nurses' station at Mesa Valley Hospital, a perky-voiced nurse named Cindy tells me that Dad seems fine. The doctor had just been in to see him and was inclined to let him go home. She told me to check back at about 11 AM, when she'd have a better idea about the timing of his discharge.

Hannah has been listening to my end of the conversation. When I hang up, she says, "Sounds like he's going to get to come home?" I nod. "Good. He'll be more comfortable here, and we'll keep a close eye on him." She pauses to take a sip of her coffee, then continues. "To be honest, I wasn't really prepared for how much weaker he seems since I saw him last a couple years ago. This post-polio stuff is just ravaging that poor body of his."

"It's horrible. It really is. Some days, I don't know how he goes on. In fact, I'm sure there are some days he doesn't *want* to go on." I wonder if I'd disclosed too much, saying more than she had the emotional strength to bear. I soften the message. "But your arrival yesterday showed just how much he can rally. He hasn't been so chipper in months. You're just the tonic he needs."

She smiles. "You're sweet to say that, Amy. I love the old goat, and I'm sorry to see him suffering."

A characteristic knock at the front door signals Jack's arrival. He never uses the doorbell and is partial to a loud rap. I guess it doesn't bother his thick knuckles. He lets himself in and enters the living room carrying new sponges, a big jug of white vinegar, and a bottle of lemon juice. "Captain Clean, reporting for duty, ma'am." He wears faded, stained dungarees and a ratty old blue chambray shirt that has holes at the elbows and a blotch of dried green paint on the left sleeve.

"Aw, Jack, you don't have to do this!"

"Well, I read that there's a better chance of getting it all off if you tackle it within the first 24 hours, before it takes hold. I'm gonna try an environmentally friendly approach first." He hoists the vinegar and lemon juice. "If that doesn't work, I'll bring out heavier weaponry."

"Thank you."

"Hear anything about Mikey?"

"Looks like they're going to let him come home. Probably early afternoon."

"Good. If I get right to work, I can probably be done before he gets home."

Hannah and I watch him leave through the door to the garage. We hear the motor raise the door, then lower it. "You're lucky to have Jack here in town," Hannah says.

"Don't I know it. He raises Mike's spirits. And especially now, with all this crap happening, I feel slightly less vulnerable with Jack around."

She removes the glasses she's been wearing to read on her tablet. "Amy, why do you want to stay on the school board? I understand that you'd not want to give in to this intimidation, but really, is it worth it?"

I give it a moment before I answer. "I'm struggling with this. I am. And, hell, I'm starting to wonder if I shouldn't just pack it in. But, yeah, I don't want to let these assholes drive me from the board. I've liked the work—up until all this started. And I really believe we've been making the smartest, most rational decisions for the community during COVID, even if there are a lot of people out there who feel otherwise. I dunno, Hannah. *Somebody's* gotta do it. And maybe I sound arrogant saying it, but I figure better me than some Trumpian dickwad. Anyway, the community will ultimately decide who they want."

"True. But you know better than I that turnout for elections like school-board or county supervisor is horrid. So, the advantage goes to whichever side is more organized, and that's usually whoever's angrier. And we know who that is right now. Why not just let the air out of their balloon? Announce you're not running for re-election and defuse the situation?"

She has a point. "Yeah, maybe you're right. I'll think about it."

She smiles. "I'm not trying to talk you out of public service. Lord knows I believe in it. I spent my life at it. But, as Kenny Rogers advised, 'you gotta know when to fold 'em.'"

I laugh. "Not my favorite singer, but good advice, none-theless."

She stands. "Well, if you don't mind, I'm going to go take a shower. I didn't get to try to seduce your dad last night, but hope springs eternal, and it's a new day!"

Four hours later, she and I are driving Dad home from the hospital. His hairline has been shaved up above the gash, putting the six stitches on stark display. The whole area around the wound is discolored, but he claims it doesn't hurt too much. Probably because his multiple pains elsewhere in his body are more noticeable. We tell him about the events of the previous evening, and Hannah was right: he finds the whole thing very upsetting.

Fortunately, by the time we pull into the driveway, Jack has eliminated most traces of the red cancel symbol. There's still a ghostly outline of it, but he says he's opti-mistic that a product he intends to buy at Ace Hardware will remove even that, obviating any need to repaint the door. "But we'll see," he says. He comes over to help Dad out of the car and gives him a hug. "Glad you're home, bro. Hard to keep a tough man down!"

Dad laughs. "Maybe so. But not hard to knock him down in the first place. Just ask Annabelle."

Chapter Twenty-One

Mike

Amy has gone out to an OT appointment. Hannah sits on the sofa next to the big easy chair that she and Amy planted me in when I got home. Hannah's been so solicitous. Making sure I'm comfortable. Getting me whatever I want to drink. Fetching reading material. We've been reminiscing for a while. Talking about mutual friends and colleagues, recalling favorite projects we worked on together. That sort of thing. Gradually, she steers the conversation to my condition and how I cope with it. Not a topic I'm predisposed to talk about. But she's always been good at drawing me out on personal matters.

"Obviously, getting clipped by Annabelle isn't a regular occurrence, but has falling become a problem for you?"

I laugh. "Actually, Annabelle *is* a menace, a constant threat looming in the house. She doesn't regularly knock me over, no, but she has a few times, and I've grown wary of her. She's big enough and heavy enough that just brushing against me can topple me. But the bigger risk factors for falls are things PPS has saddled me with, like greater weakness, poor balance and bad reflexes, worsening arthritis."

"I can see that those things would make you more prone to falling."

"Well, not only more prone to falling, but harder to fall *well*. Meaning, able to reposition my body as I'm starting to fall to protect myself and minimize the damage. The consequences of a fall for me are likely to be more severe than for someone who never had polio. And I worry about breaking a wrist or an arm or—God forbid—a leg."

Hannah grimaces as she nods. "Yeah, that would be horrific. … You mentioned greater weakness. Is that mostly in your legs?"

"No. It's generalized weakening of the muscles. I hate it. I feel like my body is constantly flashing signs to the world in bright neon: *This guy's body is weak!* Things like needing the walker or sometimes a mobility chair. Or not being able to do the outdoor grilling anymore because my arms aren't strong enough to lift the heavy lid of the gas grill! That's a tiny thing, I know—by itself, unimportant. But it's one of those things that overlaps with other little things to suddenly have weight, consequence, meaning. It's not easy to accept that now I have a hard time lifting a casserole dish to wash it, or raising a stack of clean plates to an upper cupboard. Frankly, that's tough to take, psychologically or emotionally. It makes me feel like a wimp. I guess what I'm saying is that now there's this disturbing element of humiliation to my weakness that I hadn't experienced before. It's hard."

She reaches across the space between the sofa and my chair. She squeezes my hand. "Nobody thinks you're a wimp. In fact, everyone admires your spirit. But, I'm sorry about how it makes you feel, Mike. I'm sure it's incredibly challenging—and exhausting."

Now she's really touched on something important. The exhaustion. The constant muscular fatigue, for sure. But worse is the mental exhaustion that comes from being slightly depressed and from the constant mental vigilance that this damn post-polio syndrome forces on me. I mention the latter.

"What do you mean, 'mental vigilance'?"

How to explain it? "I just mean that whenever I have to go anywhere or do anything outside the house, I find myself totally preoccupied in advance, worrying about whether I can get there, how far away I'll have to park, will there be stairs I can't climb, will the walking surface be smooth and clear of things that could easily trip me, will there be chairs that aren't too low and that have firm arms at a height that will let me push myself up from sitting. The list goes on and on.

"And it's not just the physical environment, but the human element, too. How many people will I have to talk to? How long will I have to stand to talk with them? If the only chair that's good for me is off by itself, will people think I'm being antisocial if I sit in it? I mean, I find all of it absolutely exhausting. It makes it hard for me to want to do anything, go anywhere, be with anyone. So it's not just mentally draining; it's also isolating."

She gets up and comes around behind my chair. She leans over, runs her hands down my chest, and rests her chin on the top of my head. "God. How awful. I knew things had gotten worse for you. But I see now how little of it I'd even imagined." She kisses the crown of my head. Then she moves around and kneels beside me. "And I bet you don't talk about any of that with Amy and Jack, so they don't know any of that."

"Oh, they know about the weakness. And they know that I worry about going places and don't like being in a group of people. But they don't know the extent of my feelings about all that, no."

"Thank you for sharing it with me. I wish there were something I could do, but I know there isn't."

"Just having you here helps. Thanks for coming. It means a lot to me."

"Well, how about if I stay longer? Amy suggested that I do so, but I want to check with you and make sure that's okay with you."

"Are you kidding? That would be wonderful."

"I'm going to make a drink. Do you suppose you can have Scotch even though you're taking a pain killer?"

"Try to stop me."

Chapter Twenty-Two

Amy

I look out at the sea of angry faces. The board finished its usual business half an hour ago, and Sam Levitson, the chair, had opened the meeting to public comments. We'd been listening to irate citizens who'd paraded to the microphone to unload their venom at us. Now, we watch as a tiny, kindly-looking elderly woman takes the mic. She introduces herself as a concerned citizen and grandmother. I'm beguiled by her appearance and think, *Ah, at last. Someone who'll say something nice!* But soon her benign mien is overshadowed by her nasty manner. She jabs her finger in the direction of those of us up on the dais. "You people have allowed the schools in this District to indoctrinate students with ways of thinking that are contrary to Christian and patriotic beliefs. Teaching all this garbage about diversity and inclusion. Force-feeding your ideologies about race and gender. Glorifying homosexuality."

She looks around at the crowd behind her. They murmur their approval and encouragement. Gathering strength from them, she raises her voice. "You're shaming students into believing they're homophobic or racist for having normal American opinions or beliefs. You're interfering with parents' responsibility to raise their children in the fear and admonition of the Lord, according to the Bible." She raises her fist in the air and thrusts it forward, as if she's a first lieutenant urging her troops to break out of the trench and storm enemy lines. "You ought to be ashamed of yourselves for bringing this division to our midst!" The crowd doesn't charge at us, but they're certainly riled up now, thanks to this chameleon. One minute she was Andy Griffith's Aunt Bee; the next, she was Joan of Arc.

The next couple of speakers pound on the same theme. A man quoting the Bible points at us board members and urges the crowd to "dump hot coals on their heads" in retribution for our "evil decisions." A young woman with a baby on her hip says, "Our schools should focus on reading, writing, and arithmetic. All this diversity and equity crap has nothin' to do with them basics. It's your job to get our schools back to the basics. You don't have the right to indoctrinate our kids the way you're doin'." The crowd roars.

A woman who says she's a police officer in town complains about an essay assignment in an English class at R-5 High School. She says it involved an excerpt from *The Hate U Give*, a book about a Black teenage girl who witnesses a white police officer fatally shoot her Black friend. "That essay assignment was inappropriate and one-sided! This Board needs to unmask our kids and stop dividing us with all this critical race theory crap!" she says, drawing more cheers from the crowd. "Crap" seems to be the preferred word of the evening.

The time clock brings an end to the comments, though not to the desire to make them or hear them. This audience would gladly go on longer if the chair would allow it. Fortunately, Sam Levitson gavels the meeting to a close.

I'd arranged in advance with two of my board colleagues — Paul and Sam— to go out for drinks after the board meeting. We hadn't socialized in a while and we agreed it would be good to get together. We'd decided to hang around in the board office for a half hour or so after the meeting, with the expectation that by then the crowd would've gone home and the parking log would be mostly empty. We were wrong. It was still full of people, many carrying signs that read "My Body, My Choice" and "Masks = Child Abuse." Women waved Trump flags. Two young children, urged on by their parents, shouted into megaphones, "Don't touch me, pedophiles!" That particularly mystified me. Groups of adults chanted "Shame on you!" Each of us managed to get out of there physically unscathed.

Now, we're seated at a high-top table in the bar area of the Goat and Clover Tavern. Paul is talking about how ridiculous things have gotten. "The crazy thing is, Critical Race Theory isn't taught anywhere in the District 51 system! Nowhere! Not a single classroom! But you'd never be able to convince those people of that."

"Right," Sam says. "They think anything having to do with race — like the essay assignment the cop mentioned — is CRT. They haven't the faintest idea what CRT is, so they're scared. They think their kids are being taught to hate themselves. As for 'the glorification of homosexuality'? I don't know where that woman gets that idea? But attitudes about gay people are evolving across all of society, and it's not happening because of teachings in the classroom. But the change scares them, and the schools are the first place they can think to blame."

For some reason, what comes to my mind is the woman a few weeks ago who raised the alarm about "furries" who allegedly want litter boxes in school bathrooms. I start to laugh, then laugh harder, until I'm having to grab handfuls of cocktail napkins to wipe the tears from my eyes. Paul and Sam are smiling at me, waiting for my explanation. I squeal, "furries!" and again dissolve in laughter. Soon, both of them are in convulsions, too.

"Oh, god!" I shriek. "I'm about to pee myself. I need a litter box." More hooting and guffawing.

When we all settle down, Paul says, "I spent some time looking into that whole topic after that night's meeting. It turns out, that same rumor or canard—maybe I should say that same poop—has made its way around school-board circles in Maine, Iowa, Michigan, Pennsylvania and other states. There's no truth to it anywhere, of course. What happens is that some rightwing group takes a kernel of truth about something and twists it into something diabolical they try to pin on liberals."

"So, there *is* a kernel of truth to that story?" Sam asks.

"Only that there is a sub-culture of young people out

there who craft alter-egos as anthropomorphized animals. A 'furry' might draw himself as a cartoon tiger, or dress up as a dragon at a convention for fellow enthusiasts. It's apparently a decades-old thing. And, relative to lots of other crazy American subcultures, it's fairly benign."

I ask, "So this nonsense about schools accommodating furries is happening because—"

Paul jumps in. "Because right-wing groups have incorporated it into their effort to discredit public education and to demand further control over the schools. Convince gullible people that educators are giving special treatment to students who 'identify as cats,' and you've captured their hearts and minds."

As he tries to capture our server's attention, Sam says to us, "Second round?" We nod.

Paul laughs, then says, "I'm chuckling because I just remembered another funny thing. After the 'litter box' story went viral when a woman raised it at a school-board meeting in Michigan, variations of it started appearing elsewhere. In Texas, a member of "Moms for Liberty" was running for a school board there. She started spreading baseless claims on Twitter and Facebook that furries were getting special privileges. She alleged that the height of cafeteria tables was being lowered in some of the district's middle and high schools to allow furries to more easily eat without utensils or their hands — in other words, like a dog or cat eats from a bowl."

"Oh, good Lord," I say, laughing. Sam chortles, too.

Paul nods and smiles. "True! And I read that in Iowa, some right-wing blog claimed that furry students were being allowed to dress up at school like animals and bark and growl at the teachers. It also claimed they were being excused from doing homework because they said they couldn't grip a pen or pencil with their paws! I mean, who is stupid enough to believe this shit?"

Sam is now laughing so hard he's holding his stomach. "Okay, enough, enough! I can't take any more."

Our server removes our empty glasses and replaces them with full ones. We've now settled down. Paul says, "Here's the serious part. All this nonsense isn't just happening organically. It's inspired, pushed, orchestrated by right-wing groups with deep pockets and long arms. All this activity around school boards across the country is the work of national influencers and activists intent on stirring the pot of community politics. There are teams of them around the country."

Sam twirls his beer in the glass. "Yeah, and they're inciting harassment that's driving lots of school-board members across the U.S. to quit."

I weigh whether to tell them about the harassment campaign against me. Finally, I decide to do so. Better to have them know what's happening. "So, guys, I have something to tell you ..."

Needless to say, we're at that hightop table well into the night.

Chapter Twenty-Three

Mike

Amy gets up to bring the bowl of green beans around to me. She knows I don't have the strength to take it with an extended arm—and if I tried, it would be painful. She scoops some onto my plate. "More?"

"No. That's enough. Thanks, sweetie."

Earlier, as we enjoyed the crudités platter Hannah had prepared, Amy had told us all about the craziness at the school-board meeting the previous evening. Jack now brings us back to the same general topic, but with a different focus. "It's not just at public meetings. It seems to be happening everywhere. I read in this morning's *Sentinel* that at the Mesa Center last week, an elderly volunteer usher got pushed to the floor when she told a theater patron he would have to keep his mask on throughout the performance, per current Mesa

County Public health orders. Another got called a Nazi for doing the same thing. People have lost their freakin' minds!"

Hannah nods. "When I was at Sprouts on Sunday, I watched an older woman blow her top over—get this!—the *shape* of one of the breads! She stood there yelling that the store's resident baker should be fired. I just couldn't believe what I was seeing!"

The conversation makes me glad that I no longer venture out into the world as frequently as I once did. Sounds like a jungle out there. I say, "Seems like civility is dead. Rampant boorish behavior is becoming normalized the longer COVID has its finger pressed on our collective buttons." Hannah pats my hand, which I'm sure is a well-intentioned gesture but makes me feel like a good dog that's being congratulated for speaking on demand or bringing his human the newspaper.

Jack says, "Judging from what I read, one's chances of taking an airplane flight anywhere without some sort of incident on board are about zero. Passengers yelling at flight attendants, throwing things, getting in fights. Last week, some goofball on a Delta flight mooned the flight attendant and fellow passengers after refusing to wear a mask."

Matty laughs at this just after taking a swig of milk, which now spurts out his nose and sprays on his pasta bolognese. Now, I'm laughing, too. Strangely, I find that the further I get into my 70s, the more my mind works like a 12-year-old's. If anyone at the table farted, I'd probably dissolve in hysterics.

Hannah raises her wine glass. "Amy, this is delicious.

Thanks so much for going to the trouble of making this meal. I appreciate it."

Jack, his mouth full, points to his plate with his fork, and makes his eyebrows dance with delight. "Mmmmm, mmmmm!" He throws in a thumbs-up for good measure.

Having regained my composure, I steer the conversation to a topic I'd thought about a lot. "You know, it wasn't like this in the 1950s when the country was fighting the polio epidemic. People were united then in their desire to eliminate polio. Now, they can't agree on anything about COVID. Some people even think the whole thing's a hoax. They think COVID doesn't exist!"

"Yeah," Jack says. "Well, those folks are gonna die from it. That's not a bad thing, as far as I'm concerned. Cull the herd. Unfortunately, their stupidity is killing other people, too."

Amy gets up to get more butter for the French bread. Annabelle springs to her feet and scurries to her side. I swear, that dog could hear a refrigerator door open from three miles away.

Hannah, who long labored with me at the Colorado department of public health, knows the whole problem well. "Lots of people just don't trust government any more. At any level—federal, state, or local. That trust has been declining for decades. Since the 1960s. But it's at an all-time low now."

I scoop some bolognese sauce onto a wedge of bread. "Right. In the current political environment, with the country as divided as it is, no presidential administration is equipped to establish trust. Any effort by a president — or his people — to persuade the public of the safety and efficacy of a rapidly developed vaccine is going to fail."

Bitterness palpable in her voice, Hannah says, "Trump didn't even try! Oh, he praised himself for how fast a vaccine was developed. 'They tell me nobody's ever seen anything like this before in history!' But then he made no effort to sell the public on the vaccine. In fact, he did the opposite."

Amy nods. "His totally dismissive attitude from the very beginning of the pandemic really undermined every effort of public-health agencies to deal with it."

"Right. It just fed the anti-science posture of most of his supporters."

Matt asks, "Why are people anti-science?"

"Oh, I don't know, Matt. It's a good question," I say. "Some people resist things they can't understand. They hear scientists talk. And to them, it all sounds like mumbo-jumbo. Also, some people who are religious are afraid of science. Lots of evangelical Christians think scientists are on a mission to undermine and destroy peoples' faith in God."

A bit of bolognese drips from my fork to my shirt. I pride myself on my tidiness, so this is disappointing. My effort to deal with the debacle is further disappointing. Dipping my napkin in my water and dabbing at the spot doesn't produce the miracle I'd hoped for.

Hannah has been watching my faltering efforts. Perhaps to shift attention from me, she speaks up. "You know, what the country had in the 1950s—and what's badly needed now—is a group of non-partisan truth-tellers outside the government who could be *the authoritative voice* on things like vaccinations, the wisdom of masks, social distancing, and what not."

"Right," I say. "A credible, non-partisan, and nationally renowned non-governmental organization to manage the pro-vaccine campaign. It worked in the 1950s with the March of Dimes."

Matty looks up at this. Naturally, he would find this a weird phrase. *March of Dimes?* I imagine him picturing a long parade of ten-cent coins.

I say to him "It was an organization whose original name was the National Foundation for Infantile Paralysis. It worked to fund the race to develop a vaccine against polio. Families and schools saved coins to contribute to the March of Dimes to fund the anti-polio efforts. It organized the largest clinical trial in U.S. history, with 1.8 million children. It was all funded by a concerned nation, one dime at a time."

Jack joins in. "And when it was announced in the spring of 1955 that a safe and effective vaccine had been developed, there was a huge national celebration. People really got on the bandwagon to get vaccinated. All around the country. Unfortunately, it came a year too late for your granddad."

Matt pats my arm. "Sorry, Pops."

I smile at him. "It's okay, kiddo. Made me tough as nails."

I think Matt is realizing he's never really heard me talk about my experience with polio. He looks up at me from under long, thick eye lashes that must drive the seventh-grade girls crazy. "What was the worst part of it?"

All heads turn toward me. "Oh, gosh, I don't know,

Matty. I suppose at first it was being in the hospital with my mom and dad unable to come into my room. They had to stand outside my door in robes and masks. And no one told me much. It was scary to be alone, laying flat on my back and not knowing what was happening.

"And I learned many years later that doctors in those days barely understood the disease. Nor did they have effective treatments for dealing with it. Except for iron lungs. Those were for kids who got polio in their lungs." I explain to Matt about the big metal cylinders that kids would be put in to help them breathe.

"But for kids like me, who had it in the legs—or kids who had it in their arms—the standard treatment was bedrest, immobilizing the affected limbs with splints or bulky plaster casts to keep the muscles from stretching. That was pretty hard."

The four of them watch me. I decide to press on. "And there was this one treatment that was just horrific. Atrocious. I hated it. Nurses would come in and wrap my leg in scalding hot towels. They were called hot packs, and they smelled horrible. Actually I think they were made of wool army blankets. I remember I could see the nurse on our ward reach into a tub of boiling water with a stick and run the steaming wool blanket through a wringer before wrapping it around my leg. Too hot for her to touch with her bare hands, but apparently not too hot for my 7-year-old leg!"

Matt's eyes are big. He's trying to picture this whole thing. "How long were you in the hospital?"

"Several months. After I finally got home, I had physical therapy for a long time. A nurse would come and massage my leg and exercise it, trying to keep the muscles active. When she stopped coming, my own grandfather—we called *him* Pops, too—would come almost every day and do the same thing. He'd stretch me out on a towel on the living-room carpet and get to work on my leg, massaging it and bending it." I'd been talking a long time. "Good lord. I'm sorry. I've turned this into a pity party. Let's talk about something else."

"*Aw, pshaw!*" Jack says, employing another of our grand-father's favorite phrases. "There's never been a moment in your life when you were self-pitying. At least, not aloud to others. But who knows what thoughts rumble around unspoken in that head of yours."

Trying to diffuse the built-up tension, I say, "Mostly, I think about which superhero I'm like." That gets the laugh I aimed for.

"And? Who would that be?" Hannah asks, her smile electric. "Captain Marvel?"

"In my earlier years, I was Superman, the 'Man of Steel.' Polio was my Kryptonite. But now, in my dotage, I'm more like Spider-man, clinging to walls—or anything else that'll keep me from falling." Now Hannah pats my hand. *Poor puppy.* Sheesh.

Annabelle came to the table when the laughter started. She probably thought dinner had ended and leftovers were imminent. Now she lifts my forearm with her snout, looking for a handout from the table.

"And here's Underdog! Best known for knocking down old cripples," I say.

Matty laughs. "No! A crime fighter!" Then, with surprising alacrity, he breaks into song:

"When criminals in this world appear,
And break the laws that they should fear,
And frighten all who see or hear,
The cry goes up both far and near for
Underdog,
Underdog,
UNDERDOG!"

WE APPLAUD MATT'S RENDITION. Jack says, "Good lord, Matty. How do you know that theme song? That show was on TV in ..." He looks around. "When? The late 60s and early 70s?"

Hannah says, "Sounds about right."

Matt says, "There's this new thing called cable tv, Uncle Jack, where everything lives forever."

Jack lunges at Matty and snaps him into a headlock.

Amy pats Annabelle's head. "Boys, boys! Settle down! As for UnderBelle here, maybe she should spend less time searching for calories and more time catching criminals!"

Jack loosens his grip on Matty and looks at me. "Speaking of which, I was thinking we still haven't checked out that Marty Stauffer our IHOP server mentioned. Seems like we should. See if he's our Green Goblin."

"We? *We?*" I hold up my right forearm and press down with my middle and ring fingers toward my palm. "I got nuthin. My spinnerets ain't working, bub! No spider silk. See? You're all on your own."

Matt, apparently loving all this superhero talk, looks up at Jack with wide eyes. "Which superhero are you, Uncle Jack?"

"Little buddy, I am Captain America. Honest, up-front, loyal, noble, dependable. And the best-looking avenger, for sure." He turns his face from side to side and tilts it up so we can better appreciate his profile. "I have no super powers, but I don't need 'em. I've taken down countless bad guys without 'em."

I put my head in my hands. "Jesus Christ!"

"Not a bad comparison, Mike! Like Christ, I'm an all-around good guy!"

Chapter Twenty-Four

Jack

Marty Stauffer sits behind a gray metal desk in a shabby little office on Route 6. The low, flat building houses three businesses—a nail salon and a dry cleaner, with Stauffer's Insurance Agency sandwiched in between them. When I enter, he stands and extends his hand. "Marty Stauffer. What can I do for ya, friend?"

He's a short, slim, sandy-haired guy with a fine lacework of broken veins on his cheeks that seem to give him a healthy look if you aren't too observant. He has a widow's peak with the hair receding substantially on either side of the peak, and his hair is cut short without sideburns. His clothes are Western — boots, dark blue jeans, and a plaid shirt, unbuttoned at the top. A wide, hand-tooled leather belt with silver mountings. Looks silly on a fella pushin' paper in a one-man insurance agency.

"Name's Jack Franklin. I'm here to talk with you about property vandalism." I watch him to see if he flinches. I don't detect anything.

He gestures for me to sit. "Do you already have a homeowner's policy, Mr. Franklin?"

"I do."

"Well, almost every homeowner policy covers damage from vandalism. But I'd be happy to talk with you about your current coverage and see what else we might be able to do for you."

"I'm not concerned about my own property, Marty. Nobody's been messing with it."

"Then whose property are we talking about?"

"My niece's."

He picks up a pen. "Where's her home located?"

"Paradise Hills."

He scribbles then looks up. "Nice area."

"It is."

"What's your niece's name?" He prepares to write again.

"Amy Wilson."

He looks like he's just bitten his tongue. "The woman from the school board?"

"You know of her?"

"Everybody knows of her."

"You know of anyone who'd want to damage her property?"

He allows himself to smirk. He shouldn't have. It predisposes me to want to knock out his teeth. "I imagine lots of people would."

I stand and lean over the desk. "How about you, Marty?"

"How about me what?"

"Don't get smart with me, Marty. Did you vandalize my niece's property?"

Now he looks shaken. "I certainly did not."

"You know anything about who did? You hear anything about it?"

"No." He tries to look me in the eye when he says this. I can tell the effort isn't easy.

I turn and look out the dull, cloudy plate-glass window. Only two cars occupy any of the angled parking spaces. Coming in, I'd noticed that the faded blue VW Jetta was laden with stickers proclaiming Marty's support for Trump, guns, and other sources of evil. "That your VW, Marty?"

"Yeah. Why?"

"I'd like to have a look in the trunk."

He laughs. "What would make you think I'd let you look in the trunk of my car?"

I turn back to him, letting my wind breaker fall open at the zipper to reveal the

Glock 43 tucked into my belt. "Just a hunch, Marty. Just a hunch. I'm a former cop. I know how to handle this gun if I need to. So, just keep your hands where I can see them, and let's go take a look in your car."

His eyes shift back and forth as he appears to weigh his options. Finally, he gets up, comes around his desk, and heads out the door. He opens the trunk and steps back to let me look. I gesture for him to move over to the side where I can see him. The trunk looks empty except for

3'x3' white placard that reads "No Masks! No Vax!" I lift it to see what might be under it. Just the compact spare tire. No saws, no Roundup or gasoline, no can of red paint. Not even any dirt. Disappointingly tidy trunk.

"Let me look inside the car."

He glares at me. I smile and pat my Glock. With a sigh, he unlocks the front passenger door. Nothing of note there either. A crumpled pack of Marlboros on the passenger seat.

I already knew that Marty lives in an apartment on North 12th street. No garages there. So, unless he has a storage unit somewhere, this shit-heap of a car is where I'd probably see some sign of his involvement in the vandalism. I close the car door.

Marty says, "I don't know what you're looking for. And I don't know when this vandalism took place. But I've been in Texas for the past six weeks. Just got back the day before yesterday. So, I haven't been in town. I didn't damage your niece's property. And I don't know who did."

"Why were you in Texas?"

"My mother was in the hospital. She died last Wednesday." He excavates his phone from the pocket of his jeans and pulls up a web page showing me an obituary for a Miriam Stauffer."

"What did she die of, Marty? COVID?"

He nods.

"She vaccinated?"

He shakes his head.

"That change your mind at all about the wisdom of vaccinations?"

"Not at all."

"Well, Marty, that convinces me you're stupid enough to be a vandal. And if I come up with evidence that you are, you and I'll be meeting again. And that little visit won't go well for you."

He watches as I drive away. I give him a cordial toot.

Chapter Twenty-Five

Hannah

I know that all this turmoil surrounding Amy causes Mike more concern than he's showing. How could it not? His only child, being horribly harassed by unknown, unseen assholes? It must be awful for him. But, look: this is not a man who's easily rattled. Think about what he's been through— the polio itself, now the post-polio syndrome. The death of his wife. And in all the years I've known him, he's never complained. Never whined. Never adopted a woe-is-me attitude. Never wondered (at least, not aloud) *Why me?* I love that about him. But it's not what originally attracted me to him. No. He's also devilishly handsome and charming. Gallant. Funny. Smart as all get-out.

We met about twenty years ago. I enrolled in a public-policy course he was teaching at the University of Denver. At that time, he was the widely respected head of the Disease Control and Public Health Response Division in the state's department of public health. The focus of his course was broader than public health. It was about decision-making in local communities—about navigating conflicts over schools, public health, airports, parks, roads and highways, and other surprisingly incendiary topics. He was brilliant. He walked us through case studies he'd written himself. Teased out nuances that most of us doofuses—myself included—never would have caught.

I don't believe I did a very good job of hiding my attraction to him. In fact, I was a bit shameless in my flirting. I admit it. He can't have failed to notice my interest. But he was a gentleman. A professional. Plus, he was married. I knew he wouldn't let himself get involved with one of his students. But that didn't stop me from wishing he would.

Two years after the course ended, I saw that Mike was the keynote speaker at the annual meeting of the National Association of County and City Health Officials. The convention happened to be in Denver. I signed up as a nonmember guest attendee. After his speech, I waited until he'd worked through the crowd of people wanting to have a word with him, hoping for a moment of his attention.

To my delight, he recognized me immediately. "Hannah! How good to see you! I didn't know you're a NACCHO member."

"I'm not," I admitted, allowing a coy smile to cross my face. "I heard you were speaking today and I came to hear you. To see you."

"Well, that's kind of you. How are you?"

"Good, thanks. It would be great to catch up. Are you by any chance free to have a drink—or dinner?"

Was it my imagination that his face fell a bit? "I'm not. I'm sorry. I have to get home. My wife and I are taking our daughter out to dinner to celebrate her 21st birthday."

I laughed and decided to tease him. "Just how every young woman wants to celebrate her 21st birthday! Dinner with her parents!"

Fortunately, he laughed at my joke. "She's going out afterwards. So, we'll only cramp her style temporarily." He paused, then continued. "But how about lunch tomorrow. Would you be able to meet me somewhere downtown?"

Well, that lunch turned out to be pivotal for me. I'd made a mid-career change from public housing to public health and had just completed a masters degree in public health. Mike told me about an open position in the division he headed at the state's public-health department and encouraged me to apply for it. I got that job, and over the coming fifteen years, Mike and I became close colleagues and good friends. Our relationship is one I've cherished for years now.

Anyway, I was saying that I figure he must be pretty shaken by what's happening to Amy, even though it's not evident in the way he comports himself. But then, he's always been that way. I remember when Laura died. She and Mike had been happily married for twenty-seven years. One evening as they were watching television, she got up from the living-room couch to head to the bathroom. Halfway across the room, she dropped to the floor. A brain aneurysm. Dead in thirty seconds.

I can't even imagine how traumatic that must have been for him. Although he mourned her death and wasn't quite himself for a long time, he never gave himself over to despair or self-pity. At work, he was always the consummate professional—sharp, focused, all-in. I don't know how he did it. I really don't.

There were many times in the years since then that I hoped—and a few occasions when I actually was convinced —that Mike and I might find ourselves together. We went out for countless dinners, sometimes traveled together for work, enjoyed drinks at the end of a stressful day, occasionally took turns cooking for each other. That sort of thing. But it never became romantic (much less sexual), although I admit to having tried, every now and then, to use my feminine wiles to lure him in that direction. Alas.

Then a few years ago, he moved out here to Mesa Vista to live with Amy and Matty. I have to tell you: that broke my heart. Absolutely crushed it. This man who was so important to me just up and left Denver. This happened a year or so after he retired. I'd been thinking maybe I'd retire, too, and he and I could travel the world together, keep one another company in our later years. But then he left. The thing is, I don't know whether he gave me even a moment's thought when he was making that decision. He never said.

The only way I could cope with the heartache was to keep working. So, here I am at sixty-five. Still not retired. Still at the public health department. Still pining away for Mike.

And although I'm thrilled to have this chance to be out here with him and his family for a while, it's not easy.

There's a lot between us that's unspoken—and may never be spoken. Plus, I'd give anything for him to let me try to bring comfort to that aching body of his.

Chapter Twenty-Six

Marty

I gotta say: that shook me up. I've been confronted before by people I've messed with, but never by someone packing heat. And this guy—this Jack Franklin— didn't look like he kids around. I believed he'd use that Glock if I gave him any reason to.

When he said his niece is Amy Wilson, I about spit my teeth out. His presence in my office couldn't just have been a coincidence. He must've somehow found out about our squad's operation. But how? Did that idiot Dwayne leave behind a clue somewhere that led this guy to us?

I'm lucky I had that PDF of my aunt's obituary on my phone—and that I was quick enough to think to use it to back up my lie about being in Texas the past six weeks. I made the calculated bet that he hadn't seen me before and didn't know I hadn't been out of town. And I don't know what he was looking for in my trunk, but I'm damn glad he didn't find it. Close call. That guy's scary.

The whole thing shook me up enough that I convened an emergency group call of the squad on Signal. I explained what had happened. Naturally, everybody seemed a bit rattled by the news. Like me, Ray thought Dwayne was probably the one who'd fucked up somehow.

"Look, I don't think so," Dwayne said. "I haven't been near Amy Wilson or her house since late last week. That's the night I painted the red cancel sign on her garage door. It was a dark night and there were no outdoor lights on. I did notice that since the previous time I'd been to the house, somebody had installed a few outdoor security cameras. But I was dressed in dark clothes and had a mask on my face. My truck was parked a hundred yards away. I don't see how anybody could have identified me. And even if they did, how would they link me to you, Marty? That makes no sense."

I grumbled, but Ray ultimately agreed with Dwayne that something—or someone—else must've led the uncle to me.

K3LVR said, "I think it's time we find out more about Amy Wilson's family. History and background. We know she has a son, but the appearance of this uncle is unsettling. Who is he? Where does he live? What's his background? You say he claimed to be a former cop, Marty?"

"That's what he said."

"Maybe it's true. Or maybe he just said it to rattle you. In any case, we should find out. And we should know if Wilson has other relatives who might cause us concern."

"How are we gonna find all that out?" Dwayne asked.

K3LVR said, "I know someone who's an amateur genealogist. I'll talk with her about which are the most productive ancestry sites to explore. Shouldn't be very hard."

"Good," I said. "Well, get on that right away, if you can."

"Copy. Roger that, Marty."

I said, "So, what's our next step, if any?"

This question was greeted with silence. I prodded. "Anybody? Any ideas?"

Ray cleared his throat. "I was thinking we should call Child Services on her. Accuse her of child abuse." He laughed. "I've done that to other people. Causes them no end of grief! I'll be glad to take care of that."

"Can a claim be filed anonymously?"

"You bet."

"Well, it would still be smart to use a phone that can't be traced back to you."

"I know."

"How about the rest of you? Any ideas?"

K3LVR said, "We haven't even done one of the most basic things yet. Let's dox her."

"Docks?" Dwayne asked. "I don't understand."

"*Dox*. It means to take someone's personal information — name, address, job, phone numbers, email addresses, home address, and other identifying data—and expose it publicly, usually on the internet."

"What does that accomplish?" Dwayne asked.

Jesus Christ! This guy is so stupid he doesn't realize how miserable he should be. I'm glad we're not meeting in person, so he can't see the look of incredulity on my face. I decide not to answer, lest my voice betray my revulsion at his ignorance. I try to remind myself that we brought him in precisely because of his dull-headedness (and his brawn). He's too cretinous to understand that every task he undertakes for the squad puts him in legal jeopardy.

K3LVR, who has more patience with Dwayne's vacuousness than I do, answered him. "Well, to put it simply, Dwayne, it's a way of getting more people involved in harassing her. With her contact information, people who are angry with her will make her life miserable. Some people will do relatively trivial things like order pizza deliveries or magazine subscriptions using her name and address. Others will ramp it up—harass her family, make threats, cyberbully her, maybe vandalize. Who knows? But we know at the very least it will result in a flood of angry messages to her. And, if we're lucky, it will rattle her. Make her fear for her safety."

"Oh. Okay. But I'm not sure I would know how to go about doing that."

I jumped in. "Nobody's suggesting that you do it, Dwayne." You can barely find your ass in the dark. "Who's gonna take on this task?"

K3LVR said, "It's my suggestion. I'll do it."

"Good," I said. "Thanks. How about you, Ray? What do you have up your sleeve?"

"Dwayne and I've been talking. We think it would be a good idea to buy a GPS tracker to put on Wilson's car. That way, we can know where she is most of the time. That'll come in handy as we ramp up our harassment."

"Do you have a particular one in mind?" I asked.

"I've checked out several of them. They vary in purchase

price and in the monthly data-subscription fee. But, all in, it wouldn't cost us more than about three hundred dollars, I'd guess."

"That sounds good. Why don't you consult with K3LVR to decide on the best one for our needs. Then go ahead and buy one and hide it in her car. Good idea. We probably should have done that sooner. Anything else?"

Ray hemmed and hawed for a bit, then said, "I have a weird coincidence to report," then said that new occupational therapist sent to his mother's house is none other than Amy Wilson! The others hooted.

"Jesus Christ!," I said. "What are the chances of that! One in a million?"

"Pretty weird, right? When you combine that with Wilson's uncle showing up at Marty's office out of the blue, it's all a little unsettling. Do you think they're somehow on to us?"

K3LVR said, "I don't see how. I think the two things have to be unrelated."

Ray said, "Naturally, I'll insist that my mother get rid of her and find a replacement. I don't want that Wilson woman anywhere near my mother."

I thought about that for a bit. "Maybe it might be a good idea to keep Wilson on. Your mother could be a spy for us. She could talk to Wilson, find out what she's thinking. That sort of thing."

"That's not a bad idea, but honestly, I don't think my mother is sharp enough to pull that off. I wish she could."

K3LVR said, "But *you* could do that, Ray. It would be totally normal for you to be there at your mother's house. Wilson would have no reason to suspect you. You could hang around there, talk with her. We might be able to learn some things. You could at least try it for a while, and if it's not yielding anything, you can send her packing."

"I'll think about it. You're right: it might be useful."

Dwayne started to laugh, then said. "Pizza deliveries. I love that. I'm gonna do that to her. Order five large pepperoni pizzas. That'll be fabulous."

Jesus Christ.

Chapter Twenty-Seven

Mike

I'm reluctant to go to this morning's PPS support-group meeting. It seems rude to leave Hannah home alone. But she talks me into it. "Go, go! It'll be good for you. I have plenty to keep me busy here." We're standing at the patio door, looking out at the rain—the first significant waterfall we've had in weeks. The sky has been pregnant with it for the past few days. Earlier this morning, the clouds' waters broke. It's coming in from the West. "But let me drive you over there. I can drop you off right up close to the door. Otherwise, you're going to get soaked crossing the parking lot."

"I'll be fine."

"Of course, you'll be *fine*. That's not the point. I'm taking you."

At about a quarter to ten, we head in Hannah's car to

Grace Lutheran. The rain beats hard and steady, staying slightly ahead of the wipers. The oncoming traffic seems a mirage through the sheeted rain water. I say, "My theory is that the particular configuration of hills and valleys in the area around here acts like a funnel, steering storms like this right over town."

"Any support for that theory?"

"No, but I stick to it anyway."

We're now heading into the higher outskirts of town. As the hills steepen, the water in the gutters tumbles twigs and early-fallen leaves along before it. Where the hills ease, the gutters clog, and deep puddles overflow onto the sidewalks.

True to her word, Hannah gets me close to the door, nosing the front of her car under the little portico that shelters the church's side doors to the meeting rooms.

"Thanks very much. I'll see you about 11:30?"

"You sure will."

Inside, the air's thick with the smell of wet wool. Everybody looks a little frayed. I notice our ranks are thinner this morning—not a surprise, in light of the deluge. Steve, the vinyl-record collector, clears his throat. "Peggy can't be here today, so she asked me to moderate our session in her absence. If I remember correctly, we were talking about how each of us has been coping with PPS. Mike, we haven't heard from you at all on this, so why don't you start us off, if you would."

"Sure. I, uh, I suppose first I ought to address the obvious question of what the hell happened to my head. You're right if you're thinking it was a fall, but it wasn't just my weakness or clumsiness responsible for it. And this time, not Earl's scooter either." That gets a laugh, even from Earl. "No, I got clipped by my daughter's 70-pound dog and hit my head on a table on the way down. So, I might as well start there—with falling. That's something I do more and more frequently now, and something that I worry more about. I suspect most of us in this room, especially those of us with lower-extremity weakness, have always had to worry about falls and try to mitigate the risk of them."

I let my gaze make a survey of the faces around me. "How many of you have fallen in the past month?" All but one raises a hand. "How many of you have fallen more frequently in the past year than you did the previous year?" Everybody raises a hand. "Okay. So, falls are a problem. And, as much as I dislike this wound on my head, I know that breaking a wrist, an arm, or a femur would be much worse. So, yeah, I worry about falls, the way all you do.

"Then there's the growing weakness. You'd think that I'd have adjusted to it gradually. After all, it didn't come on suddenly, out of nowhere. When I was still working, I had a very long walk down the hallway from the elevators to my corner office. It was a couple hundred yards. That was fine in the early years, but eventually, making that walk became something I dreaded. It just got harder and harder as I got weaker. Still, that was something I understood and accepted. But I find it's not as easy now to accept that I have a hard time, say, lifting a pot off the stove or putting clean dishes onto an upper shelf. For some reason that's harder to take, psychologically or emotionally."

Minnie jumps in. "I know just what you mean, Mike. It's when the damn weakness begins to affect even the most pedestrian activities of everyday life that it takes its heaviest emotional toll."

I nod and then sit quietly for a moment, not sure I want to continue. I certainly don't feel like talking about the disturbing element of humiliation to my weakness—or about the exhaustion brought on by the constant mental vigilance PPS requires. I felt okay discussing all that with Hannah, but I don't want to do it with these folks I don't know well, even though I figure they'd fully understand.

After I've been quiet for a while, Steve clears his throat again. "Do you want to go on, Mike?"

Not really, no. But I decide to mention one more thing. "Like each of you, I've got my aches and pains. They can be constant, or variable, coming and going. Periods of unusual or excessive activity can bring on pain, or make it worse. But here's what I find curious: I'm just as likely to get pain from inactivity or non-movement—in other words, from *holding still*."

Others jump in. Minnie says, "Exactly! When I'm doing my calligraphy, if I keep my head and shoulders at a particular angle for too long, I get bad pain in those spots."

Dave Hawkins chimes in, too. "I notice if I sit in one position for a long time—like when I'm on a plane or doing my model-building—pain usually follows."

Steve says "Yup. I've found it's very important to change positions as frequently as possible. Even a slight change can help put the load on a different group of muscles or tendons."

The apparent eagerness of others to add to this point makes me think it's one they haven't talked about before. So, at least, I don't feel bad about bringing it up. Soon, others are talking about PPS complications that I haven't yet experienced and hope I don't—difficulty breathing and swallowing. It sounds scary. I can't imagine layering that on top of what I'm already dealing with. But it's obviously part of the struggle of daily life for some of these folks.

When the formal meeting finally breaks up a little earlier than normal, there's no rush for the exits. Perhaps the continuing rain makes everyone want to linger a bit. Small groups form as people share symptoms and swap stories. I hear occasional hoots of laughter, groans of sympathy, expressions of self-recognition through the experience of others. This, I think, *this* is what a group like this is meant to evoke.

I overhear other conversations, too. Steve tells David that he'd like to stop by the latter's house sometime and see his models of military equipment. Earl asks Sofia about her genealogical work and what ancestry websites she finds most useful. Minnie comes over to me to elaborate on her comment about the pains she sometimes gets when she's been doing her calligraphy.

Eventually, people start to take leave. I venture outside, too, and am soon back in the front seat of Hannah's car. The sky has lightened a bit and the rain is letting up. Hannah asks if I want to stop for lunch at a restaurant she'd read about this morning. I haven't been there before and quickly start going through all my tiring mental gymnastics: will it be easy to navigate my walker, will there be steps, etc. I consider whether I should be "brave" and agree to go, or practice my new mantra: *It's okay to say no.* I realize it probably doesn't matter to her. And I feel drained from this morning's meeting. It was exhausting but also cathartic. I feel foolish for having been dismissive of support groups for all these years. Turns out, the emotional release of talking about one's feeling and experience feels good. Maybe old crips can learn new tricks.

"No. If it's all the same to you, I'd rather go home. We've got plenty of food there."

She smiles. "Great."

Chapter 28

Jack

"I let my windbreaker hang open so he could see my weapon. I think that shook him up."

I'm describing my encounter with Marty Stauffer to Mike, who's even more aghast than he was over my confrontation with Danny Wilson.

"You flashed your Glock at him?!"

"I didn't say I flashed it. I said I let him see I had it. There's a difference."

"So, in your view, you weren't threatening him?"

"Absolutely not. I didn't say I was going to harm him."

"Jesus Christ! You guys …"

"We guys?"

"You cops. No wonder people call you pigs."

"Hey! Not nice! How is one supposed to deal with people like Marty Stauffer?"

"Whaddaya mean 'people like Marty Stauffer'? You said yourself that you found no evidence that he's involved in this intimidation campaign against Amy!"

"True. But I got the sense that the only thing that gets his attention is a gun."

"So, you agree you threatened him."

"No, I do not."

Mike rubs his palm down his face and looks across the kitchen table at Hannah. "Do you want to weigh in on this?"

She laughs. "No. I'm enjoying your whole conversation immensely. I don't want to interrupt."

I look at Mike. "So, what else do you want to know?"

"Why do you trust what he told you?"

"I didn't say I trust it. I said he gave me no reason to believe he's part of this whole thing."

Amy walks into the kitchen and bustles about, preparing to leave for work.

Mike sighs. "Okay. Where does this leave us?"

"It leaves us at square one. We have no idea who is doing this stuff. And that's embarrassing. Pathetic." I gesture toward Amy. "I told Amy that the people behind this aren't geniuses. But at this point, they're still outsmarting us."

"Do you want to summarize what we know so far?"

"Not particularly."

Mike says, "Okay, then I will. We *know* nothing. We *think* Danny Wilson is not involved. We *think* Becky Dubrovsky is an activist, a protester, but not a vandal. We *think* Marty Stauffer is not involved because he claims to have been in Texas for the past six weeks."

"You're on a roll, bro."

"We don't *know* who the hulking dark figure on the security tape is. The person who vandalized the garage. We don't even know what to *think* about him."

"True."

"Gee. No wonder the world still doesn't know who killed JonBenét Ramsey. You cops are incompetent."

"Again, I say, 'Not nice.' And that's a particularly low blow. No fair."

I look over at Hannah for some kind of support.

She smirks. "That's clearly a foul."

"Thanks, ref! Good call."

"I calls 'em as I sees 'em." She grins.

Mike scowls, then bows his head and shoulders toward me. "Okay. Apologies to my fraternal Hercule Poiroit. But this is your line of work, not mine. Could you tell us where we go from here?"

How the hell do I know? But I gotta say something. "I guess we ought to ramp up our inspection of social-media sites. That seems like the obvious next move. And, just so you know, I've been spreading my social-media wings, big bro. Little Jacky here is now on Instagram. I have aspirations to become an influencer. Maybe do some Insta-marketing for Speedo."

Hannah snorts. "Good lord. What a horrifying thought."

Amy grabs her keys. "I agree. And I'm outta here. See y'all later."

Ever mature, I stick out my tongue at Hannah.

"Okay," Mike says, "after Speedo pours its treasury into your bank account, what else do you hope to do on Instagram?"

"Find people who talk smack about Amy. I'm also on Facebook, Twitter, and TikTok, where I hope to do the same."

Mike grimaces. "And?"

I shake my head. "I'm sorry to say, from what I've seen so far, she's certainly not a popular gal in town. But we already knew that."

"So, you're coming up with lots of suspects?" Hannah asks.

"Not yet. No. But my instincts tell me these are fertile fields to plow. And I'm tuning up my tractor."

Chapter 29

Amy

I stayed around the house this morning a little longer than I should have, listening to Dad and Jack talk. It sounds like they're making no progress on finding out who's harassing and intimidating me. In any case, I'm now a bit late for my 9:00 AM appointment with Agnes Moore, the 84-year-old who's determined to stay in her own home.

Agnes opens the door and steps aside to let me in. I usually get a smile from my clients. But Agnes greets me with a frown. "You're late."

Good lord. What a bitch. I consult my watch. "Yup. I'm all of six minutes late, Agnes. Sorry. I hope that didn't inconvenience you too much." I'm certain good ol' Agnes won't catch my sarcasm. Too bad. I'd like her to catch it hard right between her pebbly little eyes. "How are you this morning?"

"Okay, I guess."

She leads me to the kitchen this time, not the living room. Her gait is slow and wobbly. I notice that her cane is the wrong height—too tall for her, so it isn't providing her with the support she needs when walking. Put that on the list.

"I had my son look you up, you know. I always have him check out people who are coming here to the house. He goes onto the internets. He told me all about you!"

"Is that right? Gee, that must have taken a while. There's a lot to know." Another fast ball, right to the bridge of her nose.

"He tells me you're that Wilson lady who's on the school board."

I smack my forehead. "Whoa! He must be some kind of super detective to find that out. I was sure I'd kept that hidden—that *nobody* knew about that!"

With great self-satisfaction, she sits back in her chair. "Well, my Raymond knows his way around the internets. He's a very capable person." She then rocks toward me and actually holds her palm up to the side of her face, preparing to confide a secret. "You should see the filth he's found about that Kamala Harris woman."

"Oh, I bet he has!" Agnes doesn't know it, but she has just told me everything I would ever need (or want) to know about her Raymond. Yessirree, I bet he shares lotsa filth about the Vice President. Lots! "Did he tell you she's *Black*? But maybe you already knew that!"

"I *did* know that! Why, I bet that's the first thing I knew about that woman."

I don't doubt it. "And?"

"I don't approve at all. Not at all. I keep asking Raymond, 'What is this world coming to? What is it coming to!'"

"I keep asking myself the same question, Agnes. The same question, indeed." I slap my hands down on my thighs to punctuate a change in topic. "Well, we should get started."

For the next hour, we slowly amble around her house, and I talk her through all the modifications she needs to make in order to stay in the home safely. The exterior stairs should be replaced with ramps. In the kitchen, the microwave (which she said is her 'most-used' appliance) should be moved from its current place in a raised cabinet to a floor stand. She should get rid of throw rugs in areas with hardwood or tile floors. And where there's older, shaggy carpeting, she should replace it with carpeting with a shorter nap. She should get a medical alert system with a wearable device like a necklace or bracelet. A smart-home device like Amazon's Echo could help her with automated lighting, reminders for medications and appointments, calling her friends, easily ordering groceries or household products. An electric lifting chair could help tilt her up to a standing position.

"I'll leave you a complete list, Agnes. And, if you like, I'd be happy to email it to Raymond. All this will cost money, of course. But it ultimately will be cheaper than moving to an assisted-living facility. And you'll be able to stay here in your home, which is what you want."

"You don't have to email it to Raymond. You can give it to him in person. He told me he wants to be here the next time you come. So, give me advance notice of your next visit so I can let him know." Then she peers at me, her eyes narrowed to tiny slits. "Are you a nasty and wicked person?"

"What would make you ask that?"

"Well, you're the woman who wants to smother school kids with masks!"

Oh, good Lord. I can't take any more today. I'm finished with this woman. "Agnes, you can't begin to imagine how many women want to smother school-aged kids. I bet if you lived with one, you'd want to smother 'em, too. See you next time." Again, I let myself out.

As I drive away from the Valley View neighborhood, I feel my pulse ease up and my blood pressure drop. *Christ! Don't let these ignorant old shits get under your skin! Life's too short!*

My cell phone rings and I answer.

"Is this Amy Wilson?"

"Yes."

"I'm Trudy Brown from the Mesa County Department of Human Services. We've received an anonymous tip on our hotline alleging that your son Matthew is the object of physical abuse in the home."

"Oh my god! Are you serious? Who would say such a thing! Why would anyone say that about me? That's absurd!" So much for the lower pulse and blood pressure.

"Mrs. Wilson, it's our responsibility to investigate all such claims. I'm calling to let you know that Matthew will be picked up at the end of school today by one of our protective-service officers. She'll interview him and take him home after that. We've already contacted the school to let them know an officer will be picking Matthew up today.

We, of course, have not said why. At some point, we'll want to talk with you, too—and any other adults in the home."

I know better than to be rude. I try to calm down, to quiet the pounding in my head. "Well, I think I know what this is about. I'm a member of the school board, and somebody is engaging in a campaign of harassment and intimidation against me. I suspect this is part of that." Maybe this is sounding defensive. May be best to shut up. "Okay, so someone will pick Matt up and then bring him home? And someone will be contacting me?"

"Yes."

"Soon?"

"Yes."

"Okay. Thank you."

I pull the car over to the side of the road. I lay my forehead against the steering wheel and begin to cry. I feel like I've been punched in the stomach. My heart aches. My thoughts swim. I call my dad in hysterics, trying to make sense of this assault on my very being. How much more of this shit can I take? This is really beyond the pale. But surely, it won't be a problem. Will it?

Chapter 30

Marty

The squad meets up in person for breakfast every other Tuesday. I'm not certain it's a good idea. In general, I think it's best that we not be seen together and keep our contact confined to Signal. But K3LVR argues that bimonthly, in-person meetings are good for squad morale. Maybe so. In any case, today is a rare occasion where K3LVR couldn't join us, so Ray and Dwayne and I decided to meet for lunch instead. Their tastes (and budgets) usually run toward Olive Garden or Applebee's—or, frankly, McDonald's. I'm not rich, but I'd rather choke to death than eat at any of those places. They're so depressing. So I suggested my favorite place in Mesa Vista, Bin 707. Dwayne and Ray complained about the expense. I said I'd pay for it.

I don't really care about the fancy items on their menu.

I mostly like the place because of its exceptionally attractive patio, which is where we're now seated. When it turns out our server is a gorgeous young blonde woman named Kelly, I notice Ray and Dwayne seem happier with the choice. They order draft beers. I order a vodka tonic. Each of us asks for a Binbuger, and we order a plate of nachos for an appetizer.

Dwayne says, "I got the GPS tracker. And it's already on her car." He pulls out his smartphone and opens an app. "See? It shows me in real time where her car is."

"Have you learned anything else useful from it yet?"

"Not really. I just got it on her car yesterday morning. I waited down the street from her house, then followed her to a shopping center. I put it on the inside of the front bumper when she was in a store."

"Good. It's bound to be useful over time. We can use it to fine-tune our harassment. And if we find patterns in her movements, we could share some of that information with the women at Moms for Liberty. They could stage little mini demonstrations against her at the hospital, or wherever she goes regularly."

Dwayne asks, "Any progress on the, uh, whaddaya call it —doxing?"

"K3LVR has been very effective at getting Wilson's personal information out there." I notice the server has arrived with the nachos and drinks. I wait for her to move away before I resume talking.

But when she does, it's Dwayne who speaks. "I'd like a big bite of that ass."

Jesus Christ. She turns around and fixes the three of us

with a glare, then says, "You want ketchup with that?" We laugh, but I'm angry. I don't know how many times I've warned Dwayne about this sort of thing. *We don't want to do anything when we're out together to call attention to ourselves or make people remember us.* A lot of good my sermons have done! Now, Kelly's not the only one glaring at Dwayne. I am, too.

Dwayne holds his hands up to me. "Sorry, sorry!"

"She's the one you should apologize to, not me," I say. The look he gives me in return suggests there's about as much likelihood of that as his voluntarily dunking his balls in a vat of boiling oil.

We're all silent for a moment, then I pick up where I left off. "Anyway, K3LVR's using his radio and various darknet forums and sites to post Wilson's personal information. I suppose we're not really going to know what effect it's having, but it's bound to lead to people leaving her abusive voicemails and emails. That sort of thing. Might even lead to some pop-up protests at her house. K3LVR is going to encourage people to keep him informed about ways they use the information, but he doesn't know if they will." I see Kelly leaning against a servers' counter nearby, still glaring at us.

Dwayne is puttin' away those nachos like he's one of ten hungry kids at a family dinner table. Ray and I are watching him. Ray shoots me a glance that seems to combine alarm, resentment, envy, and admiration — all simultaneously. I laugh, and Dwayne looks up, but not long enough to slow down. I figure it takes a lot of food to be as big as Dwayne. I don't begrudge him.

We talk for a while about the school board. I'm the only one of the three of us to make it to the most recent public meeting. "It's interesting. I sorta feel that COVID-related controversies are starting to wane."

Ray says, "Really? What do you mean?"

"Well, for the first time in months, more of the public discussion time was devoted to comments about critical race theory, equity, the divisiveness of the curriculum, parental exclusion — topics like that — than to masks, vaccinations, and the like."

Dwayne has just taken a big swig of his beer and he lets out a burp. "Why do you think that is?"

"Not sure. Maybe people have said all they have to say about masks and vaccinations. Maybe all the media attention to the current discussion in Virginia about CRT and race in the curriculum is starting to affect the discourse in the rest of the country, too. In any case, it'll be interesting to see how this develops. I don't know that it matters to us. It's just as easy for us to fan the flames on race as it is on vaccinations."

Ray has been nodding vigorously as I've been talking. Now he says, "Well, that's just fine with me. I personally care more about the race stuff than about the COVID stuff."

Duh. Ray is the most bigoted guy I know. He truly, genuinely, deeply hates all racial minorities, believes that White America is under siege by colored hordes. "I know you do, Ray. I know you do." I think about K3LVR and how his animating subject is vaccinations. "Different strokes for different folks. Right?"

Kelly brings us our burgers, we order another round of

drinks. Ray asks if we could also have ketchup for our burgers and fries.

I decide to change the subject. "Dwayne, what's the status of our effort to target Diana Tarrant?"

"All systems go. It's like everything I've done to Amy Wilson was a rehearsal, 'cuz doing it to Tarrant seems easy as pie." He laughs. "It feels like—what's that expression?— *deja vu* all over again."

Kelly shows up with the ketchup. She places a tiny dip bowl of it in front of me, then moves around the table toward Dwayne. She bobbles the tray and the two remaining bowls spill forward, slopping ketchup onto Dwayne's neck, tee shirt, and forearm. "Oh, what a shame. I'm so sorry to soil such an attractive shirt. Please forgive me!" She flashes a big smile and hands Dwayne a napkin she just happened to have with her.

When she comes back again a few minutes later with our second round of drinks, Ray doesn't see her and continues lobbing ridicule and laughter Dwayne's way. "If Amy Wilson ever finds out who you are, Dwayne, that'll be shit splattering on you, not ketchup." He slaps his thigh, happy with his joke. I see the startled look Kelly gives Ray and I wonder what it means. Goddamn it. I silently vow never to go out in public with either of them again.

Through the remainder of the meal, I notice Kelly lingering near us—filling salt and pepper shakers at nearby tables, refolding napkins, keeping our water glasses full. We're still talking about school boards, conservative agitators, Republican senators we admire. That sort of thing. I repeatedly urge Ray and Dwayne to keep their voices down. When it comes time to pay the bill, I decide not to use my credit card because I don't want Kelly to have any name she can link us to—just in case I'm right that we've set off alarm bells in her head. And I hurry the two of them out of there when she goes inside to drop off a nearby table's order. I don't want her checking any license plates.

Chapter 31

Amy

Of all the things they've done to me, this is the worst. This false claim of child abuse. Each incident of vandalism and personal harassment shook me up. But this allegation has rocked me to my core. When I finally felt I'd calmed down enough to drive safely, I pulled the car away from the curb and headed home. Fortunately, one of my clients had cancelled an appointment scheduled for this afternoon, so the only other item on my calendar for the day was a team meeting at St. Mary's Hospital. I called the office and said I was feeling ill and wouldn't be at the meeting.

Now, I park the car in the driveway and wearily get out. Dad greets me at the door with a hug. When he puts his arms around me, I begin to cry again, shaking like a leaf. Sobs pour out of me in great, soulful gulps. Tears and mucus streak my face and moisten the shoulder of dad's shirt. After a while, he lowers his arms. He'd been holding me for four or five minutes. It suddenly occurs to me his arms and shoulders must now hurt. I wipe my face with my sleeve. "Oh, Dad. I'm sorry. Come on, let's get you seated." I lead him to his chair and help him ease into it.

He looks up at me, his big brown eyes doleful. "Sweetheart, it'll be alright. They'll quickly determine that this was a false allegation, and it'll all go away."

I know he means well and is doing his best to comfort me. But I also know there's a chance this won't all just "go away" quickly. And, in any case, I know that the trauma I've already experienced because of this allegation will be with me for a long time.

"I'm going to take a valium and lie down, Dad." I go to my room, hoping I can fall asleep and block all this out for a couple of hours. Instead, I lay awake, despite my emotional exhaustion. I can't stop thinking about the unknown person who's done this to me. I simply don't understand how someone can be so awful. I've always believed that people are basically good. That, in general, people mean no harm to others. But everything that has been happening to me—and now, especially *this*—is changing my fundamental view of others.

Somehow, eventually, sleep envelops me. When I wake up and venture out of my room, I find a note from Dad, saying he's gone out with Jack on an errand. But the key part of his note is this:

While you were sleeping, a Trudy Brown from the child-welfare agency came to the house. I told her you had been traumatized by the news of the claim against you and that you were getting some rest. She said that was fine and asked if she could talk with me, since she would have to interview me at some point anyway, seeing as how I live with you and Matt. I can tell you more later about our conversation. The upshot: I allayed her concerns; said you're an excellent, loving mother; and explained more about how you've been harassed lately. I think it's all going to be okay.

I hope Dad's right. But as I sit with his note in my lap, I wonder for the tenth time how Matt will react to being picked up and interviewed by a protective-services officer. I know full well that I've never harmed him physically, never given him any reason at all to say to anyone that I mistreat him. But what if he has bruises that I don't know about? What if, under questioning, he appears anxious or depressed? What if the school reports that he has behavioral issues I don't know about? Any of those things might make them think the allegation is true. I grow more nervous and jittery. Tears again come to my eyes. I try my best to push these thoughts from my mind, but with limited success.

I decide to busy myself in the kitchen making Matt's favorite meal, meatloaf. I set about dicing the onions as finely as I can. I've learned over time that if the onions are cut small enough, they cook through during the baking process and don't need to be sautéed beforehand. I add dried bread crumbs and the diced onion to some lean ground beef in a large bowl. Then add milk, an egg, ketchup, and Worcestershire sauce, along with dried parsley, garlic powder, salt, and pepper. I mix it all together really well then spread it into a flat, even layer in a loaf pan. I make the sauce with ketchup, brown sugar, and red-wine vinegar and pour the glaze over the meatloaf, then cover the pan and put it in the refrigerator.

After what seems like days, the front door opens and Matt walks in, followed by a middle-aged woman who introduces herself as Helen Miller. I rush to hug Matt, who endures the public embrace, then immediately goes off to his room. I shake the woman's hand. "May I get you something to drink? Water? Tea?"

"No. Nothing. Thank you."

"Won't you please sit down?"

"No. I should be on my way. I understand from Trudy Brown that she was unable to interview you today, but did speak with your father, who also lives here. Is that correct?"

"Yes, I think she did, yes."

She turns to go. "Well, she'll need to speak with you, too, before this case can be resolved. I'm sure she'll try to get back to you in the next day or so."

When she's gone, I close the door behind her and press my back to it. Christ! I need a drink. I pour myself a gin and tonic, take a healthy gulp of it, then head to Matt's room to talk with him. I knock gingerly on his door. When he says I can enter, I find him sitting on his bed, earbuds in, watching something on his iPad.

He stops the video. "What was all that about?" he asks.

"I wish I knew, honey." I explain what I think has happened, as best I can.

"Why are these people doing this to you? To *us*?"

"My guess is that they hope to get me to resign from the school board."

"I wish you would."

This takes me aback. "You do? Why?"

He looks at me. Tears start to fill his eyes, then spill onto his cheeks. "Because this just sucks, that's why!"

"What does?"

"All of this!" he shouts. "The vandalism, the scary people showing up at school and here at the house. Now, this! That woman asked me all kinds of questions about you and Pops—how you treat me, whether either of you ever hurt me or yell at me. I didn't like it. Not one bit. And I didn't like being picked up at school like that by someone who suspects you of abuse ..."

"She—" I start to explain that she didn't 'suspect' me of abuse, but was just doing her job—investigating an allegation of abuse. But I realize he's shook up and wouldn't care about the distinction. So I change tack. "These people who—"

Matt interrupts me. "You think it's only you getting shit over your school-board decisions? I do, too. Kids at school harass and bully me all the time because of you and the stupid school board." He starts to cry again.

I'm nonplussed, speechless. It's never occurred to me that he might be taking flack at school because of me. What does that say about me as a mother that I never even considered that? I feel heartsick, filled with self-loathing. I wrap my arms around him and hold him tight. "I'm so, so sorry, Matty. I wish you'd told me. ... I wish I'd asked if you were experiencing anything like that. Please forgive me." But how can he? My neglect is unforgivable.

Chapter 32

Mike

Hannah is sleeping late. She's heading back to Denver this afternoon. Amy and I are having breakfast together, though not interacting. She has her laptop open, doing a little work before her first appointment of the day. I'm reading the *Daily Sentinel.* I'm a creature of habit, and when it comes to newspapers, I still prefer hard copies to digital versions, when I can get them. So, although I read the *New York Times* online, I get the *Sentinel* delivered to Amy's house every morning, even though it's not really worth the price of the subscription. Still, the paper helps me have a better sense of this community I now live in.

A page-two article jumps out at me. "Public Health Official Describes Intimidation Efforts." With growing fascination, I read that Diana Tarrant, the Deputy Director of the

Mesa County Department of Health, has become the target of an intensifying campaign of intimidation and harassment. "Whoever is behind this seems to be ramping up their efforts to menace and scare me," she told the reporter. The article describes some of the incidents that she now perceives to be part of a coordinated effort to frighten her, perhaps in the hope of driving her from office. Her car had been keyed, the word "EVIL" had been burned into her lawn, "Vax = Bad" had been spray painted on the side of her house, and she'd started receiving menacing emails and messages on her personal phone, leading her to believe she'd been doxed.

"Look at this!" I turn the paper and spread it out on the breakfast table, so Amy can read the article. When she finishes, she speaks with a wry tone in her voice, "So, I'm not the only one with a crosshairs on my forehead."

"It seems not. But I'd suspect it's still a pretty exclusive club you're in."

"Lucky me!"

"Looks like we can rule out any personal animus. Like from Danny."

"Good point. But I never really thought that's where all this was coming from, anyway."

"Nor did I."

She points to the photo accompanying the article. "You know, I've met this Diana Tarrant. She and Jeff Benson, the department's director, came to an executive meeting of the school board in the summer of 2020. They talked with us about masks, social distancing, the possibility of vaccines, and other related topics. She's a totally reasonable woman.

Not a zealot or a radical by any measure—at least, not that I saw. Benson seemed more hopped up in favor of mandates than she. I wonder why she's the one being targeted."

"My guess is that it's not just a coincidence that you're both female. Maybe whoever's behind all this crap thinks they can harass and intimidate female office holders more easily than males." I pause, considering the question I want to pose. "What do you think about contacting the reporter at the *Sentinel* …"—I look for the writer's name—"this, uh, Brad Johnson, and telling him your story? That you're experiencing essentially the exact same intimidation tactics that Diana Tarrant is."

She thinks for a moment. "I don't know. I see advantages to doing that, including increasing pressure on the police department to try to stop this stuff. But there are also disadvantages. It might draw even more of this activity my way. Encourage people who haven't thought of such behavior to get in on the act. And if I do decide to leave the Board because of all this, I'd just as soon the whole community didn't know it's because I'd been driven out of office. Those are my first thoughts. But I'll consider it some more." She looks at her watch. "But right now, I've gotta hustle outta here. I have an appointment in twenty minutes."

I watch her scurry about and eventually rush out the front door. I push myself out of my chair and carefully traverse the kitchen without my walker to refill my coffee mug. Stupid thing to do. Could easily fall. I think about Diana Tarrant. I can't remember anything like that ever happening to anyone I knew in public health. And it's not as if there weren't controversial matters that came up during all those years.

I pour the coffee and lean against the counter, considering the amazing period I've lived through. When I was a kid, vaccines quickly came to be accepted as normal and valuable by the vast majority of Americans—as normal a part of a healthy life as brushing one's teeth. Now, a significant portion of the population is opposed to them, or at least wary of them. That didn't happen overnight, of course. It was a devolution that occurred over decades. DPT vaccines took the hit in the '70s and '80s over rumors about neurological complications. The MMR vaccine got victimized in the late '90s by Andrew Wakefield's scurrilous suggestion that it was linked to autism.

With trepidation, I make my way back to the breakfast table. No falls, no injuries. Successful coffee resupply mission. I pick up the paper again and come across a feature article about the spread of conspiracy theories related to COVID. It mentions one about the virus being caused by 5G mobile phone technology. Good Lord. Couldn't these rumormongers come up with something new? I remember how in 2003 some people claimed that 3G technology caused SARS. I also recall a meeting that Hannah and I attended together in 2009 about the Swine Flu epidemic where someone reported a rumor circulating that it was caused by the upgraded 4G technology. It's amazing to me this idiocy persists despite common sense and the various pronouncements by national and international scientific organizations that viruses can't travel on radio waves and mobile networks. I mean, really, who believes this kind of stuff?

Earlier that morning, I'd been thinking about Hannah's comments about how there'd been a decline in the public's trust of government, science, and other institutions. Seems to me that's a huge part of the problem we face today. But another part of it is a sense of lost dignity on the part of people who feel they're herded like sheep, treated as if they're expected to follow without questioning, that they have no voice or choice. They feel excluded and ignored. Worse, they feel sneered at over their concerns. It's no wonder to me that a feeling of being unheard, not listened to, is fueling the rising volume of voices opposed to immunization campaigns and vaccine trials.

I read a little further in the article and come across a quote from a young man who said he wasn't going to get vaccinated because he didn't want to be "watched" or "spied on," counted or controlled by the government or other authorities. He didn't like being expected to "follow the herd" into the vaccination pens. It occurs to me then that the comments by Anthony Fauci and other public-health experts about the benefits of possibly reaching 'herd immunity,' while well-meaning, probably exacerbate the perception some people have—like this guy quoted in the article—of being herded like sheep, asked to assume an unquestioning herd mentality, lacking autonomy, and just doing what 'the system' dictates.

My thoughts are interrupted when Hannah comes into the kitchen, still sleepy-eyed and groggy. Annabelle trots over to her and nuzzles her crotch.

"Hey, hey, Annabelle. Come here," I say.

"She's okay. She's just sayin' *good morning,* aren't you, Bellie Belle?" She ruffles the thick fur on Annabelle's neck and scratches behind the dog's ears. Belle's magnificent tail wags with delight. Hannah looks around. "We alone?"

"Yup. Just us."

She smiles, then walks over to my chair, opens her robe, and pulls my face to the warmth of her body.

Chapter 33

Amy

Two long days pass before I have a chance to talk with Trudy Brown from the child services agency. She was out sick yesterday. But now she's at the house to interview me. The prospect of it has unnerved me. I don't know why. I guess my anxiety stems from knowing that the consequences would be unbearable if somehow, horribly and wrongly, the determination were to go against me.

Seated across from me in the living room, Ms. Brown interviews me for about an hour, covering topics ranging from how I discipline Matt when necessary to what family household routines are like. Finally, she closes her notebook and takes off her glasses. "Mrs. Wilson, as you know, our agency is required by law to investigate any allegation of child abuse or neglect. My colleague Helen Miller, who picked Matthew up at school and interviewed him, has reported that she found no reason at all to believe that Matt is being neglected or abused in any way. She said he seems like a happy, well-adjusted, truthful boy. And his reports of how you interact with him give Helen no reason for concern." She pauses. "Similarly, after speaking with you and your father and seeing your home, I find no reason to believe Matt is experiencing any neglect or abuse. You seem like a very good mother, and this seems to me to be a safe, loving home for Matt."

I hadn't realized I'd been holding my breath. But I suddenly exhale, the tension leaving my body as fast as my breath. She's still talking but I pick up on only occasional words and phrases. "… unsubstantiated … obviously not true … " I begin to cry, tears again streaming down my cheeks. She gets up, goes into the kitchen, and returns with a glass of water, which she hands to me.

She says, "Unfortunately, we get lots of anonymous tips that are false. Some of them presumably are well-intentioned. The caller actually believes a child is being harmed. But we know many allegations are born of malice. Often, there's a divorce or custody issue at hand. It's sad. A horrible thing to do to another person. And it's a shameful waste of our scarce resources at the agency. Looking into these things is time-intensive." I grab a tissue from a box on the coffee table and mop at my soggy face. She continues. "I understand that you suspect this allegation is part of a larger pattern of harassment you're enduring as a consequence of your position on the school board. Is that correct?"

Sniffling, I nod.

"We recently had a similar complaint lodged against

another public official in town. Totally unfounded. It's a shame there are such malevolent people out there willing to do this to others."

We talk for another ten minutes or so. Then she gathers her things and stands to leave. "I'm sorry for your troubles, Mrs. Wilson. I wish you only the best. And for what it's worth, I want you to know that I, for one, am a big fan of the way the school board has handled everything related to COVID." She clutches my wrist. "Be strong. Have courage."

I walk her to her car. When I head back toward the house, I feel all the anxiety and apprehension I've been holding since her initial phone call begin to dissipate. But then I look at the lawn. The word "EVIL" is still noticeable, despite Jack's efforts to fix it. I realize this isn't over. Not by a long shot. This nightmare won't end soon.

I call Will to tell him that the DCS investigation into the claim against me has been cleared. We talk for a while about the interview with Trudy Brown and about the relief I felt when she'd said there was obviously no legitimate case.

He says, "Let's celebrate. We haven't been out for dinner in a while. Are you free tonight?"

"Sure. Let's do it."

"*Spoons?*"

"Could we go to *Le Rouge* instead? I really need a treat."

"Sounds good. I'll call for a reservation and will pick you up about 7:15."

"No, you know what? I'll drive. I need gas and won't

have time to get it first thing in the morning. So I'll get it on the way to your place. I'll see you then. Love you."

Now, we're seated at a quiet table next to the window. We've forgone salads in favor of appetizers, which are out of this world at *Le Rouge*. Our server brings my prosciutto-wrapped asparagus and pears, both broiled to perfection, served warm with a balsamic reduction. In front of Will, he lays a plate of jumbo lump crab cakes on a bed of crostini, topped with smoked jalapeno remoulade.

I eye Will over the rim of the smoked Manhattan the same server had talked me into. "Why do you suppose people love the smell of smoke so much?"

A smile dances across his face. "Well, you see, Miss Amy, the sense of smell is lodged in an ancient part of the brain called the limbic system, which houses emotion and long-term memory. At one time in history, before gas and electric stoves, all cooked food would have had an element of smoke. Our brains now think of smoke as an important dimension of food."

"I'd have gotten even more dressed up if I'd known I'd be having dinner with Bill Nye the Science Guy. Thanks for the episode of mansplaining, Bill."

He laughs. "Guilty as charged. It just so happens that yesterday I read an article about how cooked food helped humans evolve because it took less time to digest, leaving more time for us to do other things, like invent fancy cock-tails or serve on the school board. There were a few para-graphs about the connections between humans and smoky food. I found it interesting. I tend to remember things I find interesting."

I sip my drink again and take in that ancient scent. "Your mind is underrated, you know."

"By whom?"

"By me. I don't like to think that I might have to change my estimation of you."

He laughs again. "Well, you're not the only one who might need to do some reassessing. I may have been *over-rating* you all this time." He deftly manages to get a precariously heaped forkful of crab to his mouth.

"What? How so?"

He swallows, then wipes the corner of his mouth with his napkin. "Choosing to run for re-election to the board might be a sign of mental imbalance."

I scrunch my nose at him. "Nice, supportive boyfriend you are!"

"I *do* support you! I just have a strong protective instinct toward you, and I don't like seeing you putting yourself in the line of fire from all the crazies out there."

"*They're* the crazy ones. Not me."

"But it's crazy for you to keep doing this when you don't have to."

I am so tired of this conversation, because it's the same one I've been having inside my own head for weeks. "Can we not do this right now?"

He gazes at me with those huge brown eyes, which were what first attracted me to him. "Of course. I'm really not trying to irritate you, Amy. I wish only to save you from yourself."

"Will!"

"Okay, okay." He runs the symbolic zipper across his lips.

A long silence ensues as each of us tucks into our appetizer and pretends our thoughts have moved on to something else. I sweep my eyes around the cozy dining room. The ambience is as sublime as the food. It still amazes me that there are places like this in Mesa Vista. I feel so lucky to live here. Lucky to be with this man who, despite his unease about my service on the school board, is so encouraging and caring in countless ways. Lucky to have a sweet son, kind father, and protective uncle. My eyes fill with tears of gratitude.

Then, these same tear-filled eyes register someone moving rapidly toward our table. A middle-aged man. Smallish. Tan skin. Nearly bald. What hair remains is cut very short. Droopy mustache. Looks like he might weigh 180, but the weight sits on a frame designed to support 140. He carries a glass of beer. Before I know what's happening, the amber liquid drenches my face, hair, and the top of my dress. The man shouts, "Aw. Maybe you should have been wearing a MASK!"

As I gasp from the surprise dousing, Will leaps to his feet and confronts my assailant. "What the hell?"

The bald fatty drops his beer glass on the floor and throws a long, looping right punch toward Will's head. I watch with admiration as Will blocks it with his left forearm. Then my porky assailant throws a left of the same awkwardness and velocity. To my amazement, Will dodges that, then uses the slow force of Porky's missed punch to twirl him around. Will puts his foot against the man's ass and shoves. Porky stumbles forward, loses his balance, and splays out on the floor between two tables.

By now, multiple diners and servers, having seen what's

happened, have rushed to the area and stand near me, apparently to protect me from any further assault. The hostess brings me a stack of napkins to dry myself. The manager hurries over to our table, promising to comp our meal, and offering to bring us whatever else we want.

"I just want to get out of here," I say to Will, who puts his arm around me and leads us through the dining room and out the front door, each of us striving for as much dignity as we can muster.

As we head across the parking lot toward my car, I hear footsteps behind us and turn to see a huge, barrel-chested man hurrying toward us. He grabs Will's shoulder and spins him around, hits him in the stomach. Will stumbles forward, then regains his balance. He appears to be assessing the situation. He moves slowly around the man. When he's within striking distance, Will unleashes a roundhouse kick, striking the outside of the guy's knee with his shin. The man howls and bends over. Will moves close again, preparing another blow. But the man springs up and clocks Will across the jaw with a hard right swing. Will goes down like a sack of potatoes.

I already had started moving back toward the restaurant door. Now I run toward it. As I draw near, the manager and a server appear outside, ushering out the bald fat man who'd thrown the beer on me. I scream, "Help" and point toward Will's inert figure on the pavement.

The big guy, already running toward a corner of the parking lot, yells "Run, Jerry! Let's go!" The short guy breaks away and joins his large partner in a sprint toward a white pickup truck. As they tear out of the parking lot, one of them yells out the window, "We'll get you, you evil bitch!" There's not enough light for me to read the license plate.

Will is still down on the pavement, but has managed to sit. With the manager's help, I get him up and we take him inside the restaurant. The server had called the police, and I already can hear a siren wail in the distance.

Chapter 34

Jack

I was one of the original investigators on the JonBenét Ramsey case. (My brother's assholish remark about the unsolved case wasn't random.) Let me tell you, seeing the body of a six-year-old girl who'd had her skull smashed in and been strangled with a garrote hardens a person. After that, few things rattled me. But this shit involving Amy is getting to me in a bad way.

I've spent much of the day talking with Mesa Vista police and with employees of the restaurant, trying to get a complete picture of what happened at *Le Rouge*—the sequence of events, what people saw. Nobody on the staff remembers ever having seen the men before. The two attackers—versions of Mutt and Jeff—had arrived moments after Amy and Will, according to the restaurant's computerized seating system. Amy and Will had a reservation;

Mutt and Jeff did not. The two men had swiftly gone through two rounds of beer and were on their third. They hadn't ordered appetizers or entrees. They'd told their server they were still deciding. The server said the two men got up from their table at the same time, the shorter one heading toward Amy's table with the glass of beer, the taller one heading out the front door.

All of this leads me to conclude that what happened last night wasn't just the result of fortuitous chance—Jeff looking up from his brewski and noticing Amy, whom he recognizes, so decides to go over and teach her a lesson. No. It wasn't a coincidence that these guys were there at the same time as Will and Amy. Mutt and Jeff followed them there, with the intention of harassing them.

There's no security camera on the premises—a breach the manager admits he needs to rectify immediately. But one of the diners had pulled out her cellphone after seeing Amy get doused. She captured video of the short guy getting kicked to the floor, getting up, and eventually being escorted out by the manager. Unfortunately, she only caught him from behind and from the rear left. No front view of his face. Still, having that video is better than nothing. And we also know his name is Jerry. So, we're not completely in the dark. But I know it's not going to be easy to find these guys.

On the plus side, this assault, on top of the various incidents of vandalism and harassment, means that we now have the full attention of the police. They've made a copy of our security system's video showing the person who vandalized the garage. Last night, Amy had been too shocked to notice whether the large man in the parking lot had the same stride. But he had a white pickup truck, like what she's seen before. Tiny links like that may eventually add up to something.

The police told me that they assume the person or persons who are harassing Amy are also responsible for the intimidation Diana Tarrant at the public health department is experiencing. "In a way," one detective said, "that's good. The more they're doing, the greater the chance they'll make a mistake, expose themselves, get caught. All we can do is be as vigilant as possible."

The police have a device they used to scan Amy's car for the presence of a tracker. They found one. They removed it for Amy's safety and planned to see if, working through the manufacturer, they could find out who purchased it and installed it. I convinced them to get the identifying information from the tracker but then to reinstall it in the car. That way, whoever put it there wouldn't know that it had been discovered. I've had a lot of experience with stakeouts and with following people, so I figured I could keep an eye on Amy when she's away from home. Maybe I'd be lucky and be able to spot someone following her or consistently showing up where her car's parked.

When I get home to Amy's house, at the end of a long day, I find Matt to enlist his help. I'd poked around on various social-media sites enough to get a sense of them— how they work, what kinds of things people post. That sort of thing. Even I'm smart enough to know that a 12-year-old boy could teach me what I need to know. I explained to him what I was trying to accomplish, and within a couple of hours, he had it all sorted. He showed me how to do effective searches on Twitter, Facebook, and TikTok. He'd nixed

Instagram. "Useless for this purpose," he'd said. He'd set up Google Alerts for his mother's name and for the Mesa Vista school board. And for convenience, he also got me set up with Social Mention, a popular social-media monitoring tool that constantly searches blogs, news sites, Twitter and Facebook for the names or topics you designate. Pretty nifty.

Now, it's after 10 PM, and I'm sifting through the initial results. I'd searched for "Amy Wilson," "Mesa Vista School Board," "District 51 School Board" and also paired each of those search terms with add-ons like "mask" and "vaccinations." Already, I'm inundated with items. Good lord, think of the volume of stuff there must be out there on more important people and topics. The results consist almost entirely of Twitter and Facebook posts critical of Amy and two other board members.

I come across doctored videos that make Amy appear to have said something I know she didn't. And I've come across lots of posts from some person whose Twitter handle is K3LVR, who keeps up a regular drumbeat against the school board and Amy in particular. The same handle shows up on Parler and Instagram, where the wrath he or she directs at Amy is just as bad. But I come up dry when I try to discover the identity of the person behind the account.

Chapter 35

Mike

We tell ourselves stories about our own lives. And when we've told the same stories often enough, they become immutable. They become our truth. That "truth" gets backed up by all sorts of things we curate and select as reinforcements—memories, cultural moments, media impressions, as well as the stories told by others close to us. That perception of the truth becomes sticky, tenacious in its endurance and its willingness to survive, persist.

The story I had come to tell myself about growing up in the 1950s might as well have come straight from an episode of *Ozzie and Harriet* or *Leave It To Beaver.* The society I grew up in seemed like a cleaner, easier, less complicated version of what it would later become. Obviously, it was the life of a boy growing up in a middle-class family in a safe, homogeneous community, free of the stresses, dangers, and hardships that many other American kids experienced in their own families, their own communities. But it was all I knew, growing up in Denver in the 1950s. Sure, I had polio. But my life—and the life around me — went on despite that.

In the story inside my head, the kind of thing that happened to Amy and Will at *Le Mirage* wouldn't have happened in the 1950s. Not to people of their social class at a nice restaurant. Not over something like a disagreement about face masks. Am I telling myself a true story? I don't know. The fifties and sixties were hardly a "golden age," especially for those Americans who were marginalized because of their race or gender or social class or sexual orientation. Segregation, by race legally and by gender socially, was the norm, and intolerance was rampant. But would people in those days attack a public official or vandalize their property over a school face-mask policy? I don't think so. Then again, I'm neither a historian nor a sociologist, so maybe I'm wrong.

But what I *do* know—because I've lived through it as an adult—is how much this country has gone downhill since I was a kid. We've experienced a dramatic decline in economic equality, basically recreating the socioeconomic chasm of the last Gilded Age. We've experienced the deterioration of compromise in the public square, replacing a spirit of cooperation with political polarization. We've allowed our community and family ties to unravel to a marked extent. And our culture has become far more focused on individualism (I'd even say narcissism) and less interested in the common good.

Remember how JFK, in his inaugural address, called for

Americans to put shared interest above self-interest? It seemed at the time, even to me as a young teenager, like a reveille for a new era of shared triumphs. He painted a picture of a country that could do anything it wanted if people cooperated and worked together toward the public interest. Beat polio? Sure we did, he seemed to say, and you ain't seen nuthin yet!

But when I look back at that period now, with the perspective of the sixty years since then, it seems to me he was unwittingly sounding taps for an era that was about to close. America has become demonstrably less of a "we" society and more of an "I" society. What a shame. Now we're reaping what we've sown. And we're choking on the chaff.

Chapter 36

Amy

Will suffered a concussion, either from the punch to his head or from his fall to the pavement. I feel terrible, knowing this happened because of me. At least he didn't get a broken jaw and need to have it wired shut. But he's been rebuking me relentlessly over the past few days about my continued intention to seek reelection to the Board, so I've begun to think a wired jaw might not be such a bad thing for him after all. Each time he's brought it up, I've done my best to steer the conversation quickly to another topic. Frankly, I don't need his tirades to encourage me to reconsider my position. I'm doing that on my own. Matty's obvious misery has had a huge effect on me. Maybe it's best I hang up my cleats. I have a full enough life without serving on the Board. And I certainly don't need this aggravation.

I mull all this over as I drove to Agnes Moore's house. I'd spent the previous afternoon working out the details of the plan I'd developed to keep Agnes in her home. I'd emailed it to her son Ray and told him I'd be visiting his mother today.

Agnes answers the doorbell but still has the security chain on and speaks to me through the gap of the cracked-open door. "My Ray isn't here yet." That charming breath again wheezes out at me.

"What's the problem, Agnes?"

"Problem?"

"Why aren't you opening the door?"

"I have opened the door."

"Enough to let a fly in. How about opening it enough to let *me* in?"

She wheezes again. "I don't know that I can trust you. You're that school-board woman." I now have a new take on the odor: bad fish or rancid cheese. Most unpleasant.

"Agnes, I'm your occupational therapist. I'm here to help you." A car pulls into the driveway behind mine. A tall, thin guy in his late forties emerges from a beat-up, sun-bleached Honda Civic. His hair is longish, a dull gray-brown. His clothing gives off the air of someone who's been down on his luck for a long time.

He comes up the walk and throws me a wave and a smile. "Ms. Wilson! Welcome!"

In light of Agnes's reaction to my school-board work — a reaction that, I assume, is tainted by what her son has told her — Ray's bonhomie seems misplaced, disingenuous. But I decide to take the high road. "Ray? I'm Amy Wilson, the OT. Nice to meet you." I extend my hand for a shake. He takes it. I say, "I'm glad you could join us today, because I want to move your mother further down the path of staying here in her beautiful home."

We're still standing on the front porch, with his mother behind the protective door chain. He looks up at the house. "It *is* a lovely house, isn't it?"

"It surely is."

"Mom," he says, peering through the crack of the door, "how about letting us in?"

"Raymond, are you sure we should let this evil woman in?"

He turns to me. "I don't know what's gotten into her. Sorry." Then, back to his mother. "Mom, yes, please open the door."

Agnes slowly pulls the chain to the side, then opens the door wider. Ray introduces himself and steps back, making way for me to enter the house ahead of him. "Please"

Inside, he says, "Thanks very much for the "Stay In Your Home" plan you emailed me, Ms. Wilson."

"Please call me 'Amy'. I'm glad you —"

Agnes interrupts me. "I bet you don't let them call you 'Amy' at those school-board meetings. I hear you think you're the Queen Bee."

"Mom, let's not be unkind."

"*You're* the one who —"

"You know what, Amy, let's go through the house together and discuss the various suggestions you've made in your plan, so I can be sure I have a clear sense of what you're thinking. Mom, you stay here. No need for you to traipse all over the house again." Agnes harrumphs and plops herself down at the kitchen table.

We walk around, talking about various ideas for making Agnes safe. Ray is alarmed by the cost, but says, "It's her money. She can decide how to spend it." And with more than a little bitterness, he mumbles, "God knows she doesn't share it!" At one point, he asks me how I like my OT work.

I give him the stock answer I usually issue in response to that question: "... fulfilling ... enjoy helping others ... blah, blah, blah ..."

He then asks me how I like serving on the school board.

"I liked it just fine until COVID came along and we were thrust into making decisions about things beyond budgets and personnel. None of us wants to be having to set policy about school closings, masks, or—God help us— vaccinations. I don't like knowing that so many people in the community are deeply unhappy with our decisions. The thing is, I'm not some crazy ideologue. I don't have some liberal agenda I'm trying to ram down the throats of people in Mesa Vista. I'm just a citizen, doing a job, and trying to make the best decisions I can with the information I have available at a given point in time."

I can't decipher the look he gives me. It' s some combi- nation of surprise and confusion. After a pause, he says, "You're right: there are a lot of angry people out there. That must scare you."

Something about the empathy in his voice—and, perhaps, the freshness of the attack against me and Will— breaks down a wall I'd normally maintain in a conversation with someone I don't know. I tell him about the harass- ment I'm enduring. "Honestly, it's pretty awful. I don't understand how people can do this to someone over a policy disagreement. It just seems crazy to me. Anyway, I'm sorry to go on about it."

"No, that's fine. I asked!" We're now in the living room, about to rejoin Agnes in the kitchen. Does all this make you feel like quitting? Make you want to just walk away from it all?"

I stop. I look at this man I don't even know. And I tell him what I haven't told even those closest to me. "Yeah. I'm seriously considering it. I'm thinking of quitting."

Chapter 37

Mike

Peggy is back as the PPS group's mediator. "Sorry I missed the last meeting. I understand it was excellent. Why don't we pick up where you all left off. Earl, let's hear from you."

Earl says, "At our last meeting, Mike talked about how dealing with the unexpected is part of a polio survivor's routine. I'm gonna tell you a story about this power chair of mine." He pats the armrest. "This was a couple years ago now. I'd just returned home from a couple of weeks at a rehab center where I'd been evaluated by a PT, an OT, and my personal physician — all of whom concluded that I needed a power chair. The longtime weakness in my legs makes it difficult for me to walk around the house. And increasingly this post-polio business has left me with arm weakness, too. So, a power chair is in order. The folks at the rehab center contacted a power-chair supplier and arranged for them to meet with me to figure out the right chair for me.

"So far, so good. After I was home and using the rented power chair, I engaged a home-health agency to send around a PT that the doctor had ordered. That's when the trouble started. This PT, seeing me only once, decided he'd be some sort of miracle worker. Without consulting anyone, he called the power-chair supplier and declared that only a manual chair was indicated for my level of arm weakness." Like he did on that first day he spoke, Earl looks around at each of us, seemingly daring anyone to challenge his story.

"I'm here to tell ya that we do not have to sit by passively and watch so-called experts take over our lives. I told that whippersnapper PT, 'Look, I'm in charge here. Not you.' I sent him packing and I fired the home health agency. Then I set about hiring a new one that would honor the perfectly acceptable evaluations I'd already received. What I'm getting at with this story is that we have to understand that our health-care decisions are up to *us*. We should not casually hand over our authority to every individual who stumbles into the picture." He folds his arms across his chest and releases a kind of "hmph."

Peggy says, "Well that's an interesting story, Earl, but it doesn't tell us how you *feel* about your post-polio syndrome. Can you reach a little deeper and tell us some of the emotions involved—like Mike apparently did at the last meeting?"

Earl glowers at her as if she's just asked him to pull down his pants and let us all have a good look at his genitals. "I just *did* tell you how I feel about it. I feel it's important we don't let so-called experts make personal decisions for us." He pauses. When he resumes, he does so with more volume and steam. "There's too damn much of that in this society. We've got that damn Dr. Fauci at the national level telling us to get vaccinated, and you have that damn Governor Polis closing restaurants and churches according to his whim. The county public-health department and the damn school board here in Mesa Vista order masks and social distancing and are considering a vaccine mandates. Where does it all end? This is America. We're supposed to be a free people. But then we let these public officials—nitwits, all one of them!—make decisions for us. It's appalling. Just appalling. It's got to stop."

My history with this group isn't long, but from what I can tell, the group isn't accustomed to this sort of diatribe. And, clearly, Earl doesn't know that I'm the father of a pro-mask member of the school board. Just as well. I'm not going to apprise him of that fact. But I feel obliged to speak up. "Earl, there are perfectly good reasons for all those public-health measures relating to COVID. What makes you think the officials behind them are intent on restricting your freedoms?"

"Because they don't care about normal citizens. All they care about is what they can do with whatever power they have. They're like a little boy with a hammer to whom everything looks like a nail. To people in government, everything looks like a problem that can only be solved by some cockamamie 'solution' they've devised. It's some sort of mental sickness they have! And we, the people, have let them get away with it for too long. If this country's gonna survive as a democracy, it's gonna require that the people stand up and take matters into our own hands and say, 'Enough! We're in charge here, not you!"

"How does wearing a mask restrict your freedom?"

"Cuz I *don't want* to wear a mask."

"Does it bother your face? Make your breathing difficult?"

"No."

"Then why? You don't want to wear one just because some so-called expert or person in power says you have to?"

He pauses and appears to think about it. "Well, yeah. That's right. Who are they to make personal decisions for me?"

"They're not. They're making decisions for society—for the good of all. That's their job! To look out for the public interest."

"Oh, bullshit. You've bought into the notion that those people can identify problems and solve them. I'm tellin' ya, they can't. They *are* the problem! And let me tell ya somethin' else. Sofia here steered me to some ancestry websites she finds useful. And I did some genealogical research on you and your family. I know who you are, Franklin. And I know about your daughter."

"Oh, really, Earl? And, pray tell, what amazing information have you uncovered?"

It would take a moron all of two minutes to find out about me and Amy.

"I know that your daughter is Amy Wilson, who has a seat on the school board here. She's one of the undesirables on the board, in my opinion. And I know about you. I know you were the head of the state's department of public health for some years."

Nobody reacts to the news about Amy. But heads turn about my own public service. Peggy says, "Is that so, Mike? And you didn't tell us? Why not? You were hiding your light under a bushel!"

I had anticipated that at some point, my service in state government might become known to the group. (I had figured that Sofia and Steve, seemingly the best informed of the group's members, might somehow know of me.) So, I'm prepared with an answer to Peggy's question."Well, it didn't seem appropriate to bring it up. I didn't want anyone to think I believed my opinions or views should carry any more weight than anyone else's just because of what my career was." Several people nodded.

Earl fixes me with a cold stare. "But telling us might have helped us understand why you're so hyped up about governmental power. And it would have been good to know that your opinions on things like vaccines and face masks reflect a professional bias."

I return his stare. "I don't see how it would have benefited you to know, Earl. You don't like my views anyway."

"You're right. I certainly don't."

Peggy had let us go on for quite a while, but she finally exercises her prerogative as moderator and intervenes. "Gentlemen, I think it's time to move on." Others appear to agree, for there are nods around the room.

I don't remember much of what happened at the meeting after that. I couldn't get Earl's words or the look on his face out of my head.

Chapter 38

Jack

Amy showed me the text message she received from her friend Kelly Albertson, who's a server at Bin 707: *Amy, get in touch with me when you can. I recently served three men who were talking about you in a way I didn't like. I want to tell you about it.*

I persuaded Amy to let me go with her to see Kelly. We'd waited until the lunchtime rush had subsided so she'd be more likely to have time to chat with us. I can see why Amy likes this place. But as I look over the menu while we wait for Kelly, I realize that any restaurant that's a semi-finalist for a James Beard Award is probably too sophisticated for my meatloaf-blighted palate.

We've taken a table at a sunny corner of the outdoor patio. Kelly joins us and brings margaritas for us and a lemonade for herself. Amy introduces me and explains why

I'm there with her. "So, we're eager to hear what information you have for us."

Kelly pulls her shoulder-length blonde hair into a pony tail and ties it with a turquoise elastic ribbon. She takes a sip of her lemonade. "I was serving a table of three guys yesterday at just about this time of day. One of them, a fairly smart dresser—not fancy, but neat, well put-together, you know? The other two looked less prosperous, In fact, one of them looked disreputable—a big guy, sort of sloppy, sort of thuggish looking. I didn't recognize any of them. Anyway, they each had a couple of drinks. So, I was coming to their table fairly regularly. They were talking about COVID, mask policies, Biden. That sort of thing. By the time I brought their food, they were pretty loose, you know? They were talking about the school board, and one of them said your name, Amy, which of course caught my attention." She takes another sip of her drink, then turns her face skyward and stretches her arms up behind her head. "God, the sun feels good out here today."

"What did he say about her?" I ask.

"He was saying she'd been doxed. That somebody had put all her information out on the internet—personal email, phone number, address, photos. That sort of thing, you know?"

"Did he say who did it? Or where this stuff was posted?"

"Not that I heard."

"What did the others say?"

"The others laughed. One said something like, 'That's gonna produce some incoming fire for her!' Then the other guy said, 'No kidding. She's about to get scorched.'"

Amy shifts in her chair and runs her fingers through her hair. The whole conversation obviously is making her uncomfortable.

"Anything else you remember?"

"Nothing coherent. There were lots of mentions of the Republicans and conservatives. They used words like 'agitation' and 'targets,' but I caught most of that in passing. I couldn't really hang out near them without being really obvious, you know?"

I thought back over what she'd told us. "You said one was a smart dresser. Any of them in Western wear?"

She considered that for a moment, then said, "No. The smart dresser wore chinos and a crisply pressed button-down shirt. He did have a big silver buckle on his belt, but no cowboy short, no boots, no hat."

"Close-cropped hair, ruddy cheeks?"

"Yes, actually."

"And what about the guy you described as 'a bit disreputable?' What do you mean?"

"He was a big guy — tall and brawny. Bald head. Flat nose. One ear, sort of deformed in some way. And he just was sort of sloppily dressed. Worn-out jeans and a tee shirt."

"Anything distinctive about the way he walked?"

"I didn't notice."

"And the third guy? Just 'less prosperous?' Anything else you can say about him?"

"He was about six feet, skinny. Long nose. Dark brown, unkempt hair. Looked depressed."

"You didn't by any chance see their license plates, did you?"

"No, they left when I was getting a drink order for a table of six."

"Well, you've been a big help, Kelly. Thank you." Another thought came to me. "How did they pay?"

"The short, sharp-looking guy paid the bill with cash. It was about a hundred and twenty dollars. He left me a twenty-five dollar tip."

I figure this was Marty Stauffer and a couple of his confederates. The big guy may well be the same man who's been stalking Amy. The same one caught on our home video. The same one in the parking lot at *Le Rouge*. But I have no proof and nothing really to take to the police.

Chapter 39

Ray

It's a Thursday evening, and we meet in person at Marty's apartment. K3LVR isn't here because Marty's apartment is on the second floor of a walk-up, and K3LVR has a hard time getting up the stairs. But he joins the three of us by phone. I start, excited to tell the others what I've learned—that our efforts with respect to Amy Wilson seem to be having an effect.

"What makes you say that?" Marty asks.

"Because she told me so herself."

"When was this?"

"A few days ago. I did what we discussed: I went to my mother's house when Wilson was there for an appointment."

"What, exactly, did she say?"

"Well, real casual like, I asked her about her work and

then about how she likes serving on the school board. She said she used to like the school board before COVID started. Then she talked about how many angry people there are out there and how she's being harassed. I asked something like 'does that make you feel like quitting?' And she said, 'Yeah. I'm seriously considering it. I'm thinking of quitting.' She seemed like she meant it. So, congrats to us!"

K3LVR says, "That's very good news. Very good."

I say, "Yeah, and I should thank you guys for suggesting that I not fire her but try to talk with her and see what I could learn. Turns out, that was a good idea!"

Marty says, "Do you think it would seem unusual if you were there again at some future appointment?"

"No, I don't think so."

"Good. This is great having a direct line into her head! What a lucky break!"

K3LVR asks, "What about you, Dwayne? Any news to report?"

Dwayne spills out a story about how he and a buddy of his followed Wilson's car to a restaurant and decided to go in and watch her. "So, we're sitting there, my buddy Jerry and me. We're having a couple of beers. And we can see Wilson and her companion across the dining room. Jerry says to me, he says, "You know what would be funny? How about I go toss a beer in her face? Well, we both start laughing about this, thinkin' about Wilson sputtering and blubbering after she's drenched with a beer. And, before I know it, Jerry is on his way across the dining room and, sure enough, throws a beer in her face. He yells somethin' like, 'Too bad you're not wearing a mask, bitch!,' which I thought was a nice touch."

Marty springs to his feet, his face beet red. He yells at Dwayne. "Jesus Christ, Fowler! You should have told us about this sooner! Nobody authorized you to personally accost Wilson. Throwing a beer on her is assault and battery. That's a crime, you idiot. It's not just some funny joke!"

Dwayne is looking confused, like he was expecting to be praised after telling this story, not scolded. "What's the problem? Isn't everything we're doing a crime?"

"None of it has been in person, you idiot. I assume there were other people in this restaurant?"

"Yeah."

"That means there are people who could identify you."

"I got out of there when Jerry threw the beer!"

"Okay, but you said you sat there long enough to have a couple of beers. That's plenty long enough for people to have taken notice of you. And let's just say you have a fairly memorable appearance."

Dwayne objects. "What's *that* supposed to mean?"

Marty apparently decides not to go there. "So, who is this *Jerry*?"

"Just a friend of mine."

"What happened after Jerry threw the beer on her?

"Her Black boyfriend got up and kicked Jerry to the floor."

I think I heard that wrong. "Did you say 'her Black boyfriend'?"

"Well, I assume he's her boyfriend."

"But you're saying the man she was with is a Black guy?!" I'm having a hard time processing this.

Marty says, "Then what happened?"

I don't understand how Marty is just pushing on without discussing this bombshell.

"I was out in the parking lot when Wilson and her date came out. I went up to him and hit him. Knocked him out. I didn't like him knocking Jerry down."

"Dwayne! Are you out of your fucking mind?" Marty puts his palms to his forehead. "What then?"

"The manager had escorted Jerry out the door, and I yelled to him to run. We both ran to my truck and got out of there."

"They see your truck?"

"Probably. But the parking lot was very dark, so I doubt they got a good look at it."

"Police?"

"Someone must have called them. We heard a siren in the distance."

K3LVR, who's been silent through all this, says, "This is most disconcerting. Dwayne, you can't go rogue like this. You can't just go around pulling a major stunt like this without discussing it with us first."

"Yeah, yeah. Okay, I get it. Okay?"

K3LVR asks, "Has your GPS tracker placed her anywhere unusual since . . . when was it this happened?"

"Tuesday night."

"Since then?"

"Not that I've noticed."

"Not the police? Not the *Sentinel's* office?"

"No."

Marty says, "The tracker's working normally? No sign that they found it and removed it?"

"Nope. It's working fine."

"Jesus. Okay. Well, as K3LVR says, don't do anything to Wilson except track her, unless you clear it with the squad first. Okay?"

"I *said*, okay!"

We're all quiet for a moment, then Marty says, "Anybody else have anything to report? Any questions?"

The meeting breaks up soon after that. During the twenty minute drive back to my trailer in Loma, I can't help thinking about what I heard tonight about Amy Wilson. A Black boyfriend! Goddamn! That just blows me away. I'd softened up a bit toward her when I met her in person and she didn't seem like the left-wing zealot I'd always thought her to be. But this news throws me for a loop. It really does. It confirms that she's even worse than I thought! More dangerous than I knew. If anyone needs any more proof that there are people trying to pull off a "Great Replacement," they needn't look any further than Amy Wilson. She embraces vaccines *and* minorities. That's not a coincidence, I'm tellin' you. She's out to get us Whites. What a shit show. This is bad. Maybe we're wrong to rein in Dwayne. Maybe we should just let him do what comes naturally to him.

Chapter 40

Amy

I'd told Dad I'd go to the grocery store on my way home from work, so I stop at Sprouts after I leave Agnes's Valley View neighborhood. I've been cruising the aisles for about six or seven minutes now. My cellphone rings. The screen says "Private Number." I answer anyway.

"I'm watching you." A male voice.

A shiver runs through me. "Who is this? What do you want?"

"I just want to watch you. You're in the baking and spices aisle at Sprouts. You're wearing dark jeans and a light blue sweater. Looks like soft cashmere. Very nice, Amy. I bet you'd be huggable—maybe even fuckable—if you weren't such a bitch."

As he's speaking, I scan in every direction for someone looking my way. Nothing. In fact, I only see two males, both busily working behind the meat counter. I shut down the call, grab a few more grocery items, hurry through the check-out process and out to my car, then drive home— wary that someone might be following me. I see no one.

Home, I get the groceries put away, pour myself a glass of wine, and put a bag of Blount Clam Shack Gumbo in a pot of boiling water on the stove to heat up. At the kitchen table, I pull up my personal email on my laptop. A dozen or more new emails since I checked this morning. Very unusual. While I may get this many messages each day on my work account or at my school-board email address, I seldom got more than a few on my personal email.

The messages are all in the same vein. Some wish for me to be raped. Others, for me to die. One grammatically flawed email reads, "Your lucky someone hasn't killed you and your whole family. It'll probably happen. Save us the trouble. Buy a gun and a bullet. Put the barrel into your mouth and pull the trigger. I guarantee not one person on plant earth will miss you."

The subject line of another declares, "Your about to get ruined." The contents read in part, "Get ready. We are coming for you. Your a hateful, evil monster. I hope this is a nightmare to you're life." Different email address, but the same impressive mastery of grammar. Probably the same person, using alias email addresses.

I've forgotten about the gumbo. Damn! Water now roils over the sides of the pot, hitting the stovetop with dramatic hisses that bring me out of the shock the emails have induced. I cut a corner of the bag and slosh half the gumbo into a soup bowl, pour another glass of wine, and return to the table. Annabelle pokes her nose under my forearm to see if there's something I'd share with her. "Not yet, girl. Too hot still." She knows the meaning of *not yet* and settles to the floor with her head on her crossed paws.

I pull my cellphone out of my purse. In the 45 minutes since I'd last held it in Sprouts, six text messages and five voicemails have come in, all of them vile and full of hate. One is a photo of one of my campaign's lawn signs — "Re-elect Wilson"—riddled with bullet holes.

Tears rush to my eyes as my legs give out from under me. I sink to the floor next to Annabelle, who lays her paw on me, as if to try to stop my body from shaking.

At the dinner table that evening, I clink my fork against my water glass and stand up. "I have an announcement to make." I pause. Then decide I need a sip of water. "I'm done. I quit. I resigned from the school board this afternoon. Effective immediately." I look around the table. Every head has snapped up, eyes wide, some mouths agape. Dad seems particularly surprised.

I'd made sure each had a drink (Matty had a root-beer float). And I'd already done one round of refills. I'd waited about a half hour into the festivities to make my announcement to make sure the alcohol had worked its sedative effect. Booze or no booze, I have their attention.

"Well, don't be so surprised. More than one of you has expressed hope that I'd do this!" I look around, holding each with my eyes. "It's time. Past the right time to do it! I'm sorry it took me so long. Sorry I've subjected all of you to this craziness. Each of you has suffered in some way—

big or small—from my being on the board. I know you know that was never my intention! This world just has become a crazier place in the past couple of years! And I no longer want to do this. I'll no longer subject my family to this craziness."

Amidst the murmurs of "No, no, don't blame yourself," and "Oh, wow, what a big decision," I watch my Dad struggle to his feet and move toward me. He lifts his arms to hug me, and I know that's painful for him to do. But it feels so good to have his arms around me. He turns his head to my right ear and whispers, "You're my hero, Amy. You'll always be my hero." He drops his arms, turns to the others, and lifts his glass. "To Amy, who served her community well, giving it far more than it deserved."

Jack and Matty look at each other, perhaps confused as to their appropriate response, then join in the toast. Jack says, "Congrats, Amy, on your good service to the community. And congrats on coming to grips with this hard decision."

"Proud of you, Mom!"

All the excitement stirs Annabelle, who moves to the center of the circle and cranes her neck around to each of us, as if wondering which of us she should bless with a lick. She picks Dad, and bathes the back of his outstretched hand.

Chapter 41

Mike

Two days later, the *Daily Sentinel* carries a front-page story about Amy's decision to resign from the school board—and the reasons behind it. "Wilson Driven Off Board by Aggressive Harassment and Intimidation," the headline declares. I know Amy doesn't like having the public know why she resigned, but Jack and I had convinced her there was no shame in it—and that the public deserved to know that this sort of thing was a real problem in town, stretching beyond the previously reported harassment of Diana Tarrant, the public-health official.

Brad Johnson, the *Sentinel* reporter who had written the earlier article about Tarrant, has done a skillful job of laying out the campaign of intimidation against Amy and linking it to a broad pattern of such behavior emerging across the nation.

What happened to Amy Wilson is among many examples of how twin national crises — a pandemic and mass misinformation — have combined with polarization to create a toxic political atmosphere. As politics grow increasingly acrimonious, threats against and harassment of public officials also seem to be on the rise, according to Michael Kleinfeld, a senior fellow at the Carnegie Endowment for International Peace.

"We are facing a pretty unusual uptick in violence and threats and intimidation against public officials across the range, from the really hyper-local people who are serving on school boards or in public health departments, all the way to members of Congress," he said.

More than 80% of local government officials have experienced some form of harassment, abuse or violence, according to a report released last week by the National League of Cities (NLC). The findings are based on a survey of 112 local officials and nine interviews.

`Among the incidents that local officials reported were death threats, vandalized homes, intimidating phone calls and outrage in public meetings. The trend has only accelerated during the COVID-19 pandemic, the report found, and has been fueled by the spread of misinformation on social media.

Brooks Drinkwater, Director of NLC's Center for City Solutions and a co-author of the report, notes that the harassment is disproportionately targeting women, people of color and LGBTQ+ officials, which can impact representation in local government. "It's an incredible challenge to continue to diversify our elected officials when this level of vitriol is targeted at them."

The harassment, NLC found, can have a range of effects on the functioning of government. Early retirements or officials choosing to leave can drain institutional knowledge and damage diversity efforts. There can even be a budgetary impact because of the need for additional security both at public events and officials' homes. "What's at stake is the continuation of our local democracy as it has functioned for centuries," NLC's Drinkwater said.

Here in Mesa Vista, Amy Wilson is not the only public official to have been the object of menace. The Daily Sentinel previously has reported that Diana Tarrant, the deputy director of the county department of public health, also has been on the receiving end of alarming intimidation. Contacted for a comment about Amy Wilson's experience, Tarrant said, "I feel for her, and I know exactly what she's been going through."

Tarrant noted that she has had groups of protesters outside her home on numerous occasions. "One night, they had a bullhorn and were yelling into that and then running sirens, and they were banging on some kind of drums outside. They were playing the soundtrack from *Scarface*," Tarrant said.

Protesters showed up the next night as well,

upsetting her 8-year-old son, who slept on the floor of her bedroom because he was afraid of the protesters.

"I am just very sad that a decision that I made to serve in public office has resulted in my kids feeling unsafe in our own home," Tarrant said, echoing comments that Wilson also made about her own son. "He was home alone when our garage was vandalized. He was followed and harassed outside his school by a woman yelling, 'Your mother is an evil bitch. She hurts little kids.' And he's been the target of abuse and bullying at school by kids whose parents tell them his mother is an awful person."

Wilson said, "I am a vociferous advocate for the right and importance of peaceful protest as enshrined in the United States Constitution. But having people intimidate you at your home, send you text messages threatening your life, or harass your children at their school is crossing a line.

"When your life can be threatened just for doing your job, you can't blame people who just want to walk away." She paused, shook her head, and with a plaintive tone, asked, "What kind of system is it where people are asked to accept martyrdom as the price of doing their job?"

As we sit at the breakfast table and talk about the Sentinel's article, Amy tells me that the last straw for her was the recent sudden onslaught of messages threatening physical harm to her and family members. Putting her hand on my forearm, Amy says, "I could never forgive myself if somebody hurt you or Matty." She pauses to take a sip of her coffee. "And the whole thing has spilled over into my day job, too. I lost a client this week. She called me 'that awful school-board woman" and said she couldn't trust me. As I drove home that day, I just knew I had to quit. I couldn't do it any more."

"I know how hard this decision must be for you, Amy. But you were suffering real emotional harm. You've made the right choice."

"Yeah. I know. But the whole thing just makes me incredibly sad. People are choosing emotional and mental health and wellbeing over staying in public service. What a choice to have to make! And what a pathetic and dangerous point for us to be in as a country."

"It *is* sad. It's happening in public health, too. And at election agencies. The departures are coming at a time when it's brutally hard to backfill positions, leaving leadership gaps in communities across the country. People who leave take with them institutional knowledge and memory that we won't have as we continue to fight the pandemic or face the next crisis."

Amy takes her empty coffee mug to the sink. She turns around and crosses her arms. She looks tired, drained.

I decide to finish my thought. "The result is the increasing decay of the American state's ability to perform its basic functions — running free and fair elections, protecting public health, educating children. These are essential functions of any democratic government. But our polarization crisis, accelerated by Trump and his allies, is making those tasks harder and harder to carry out."

Amy nods. "The MAGA people say the system is broken. But they're the ones breaking it."

I give a wan smile. "No 'both sides' bullshit from you!"

"Not a chance."

Chapter 42

Amy

I was the talk of the town for three whole days. But now an even more sensational story has broken. The *Daily Sentinel* devotes much of today's front page to the news item, which continues on page three:

TARRANT INJURED IN CRASH WHILE EVADING PURSUERS

ONE MAN KILLED, OTHER BADLY HURT

Diane Tarrant, the deputy director of the Mesa County Public Health Department, was severely injured in a three-vehicle crash Thursday night at the intersection of North Avenue and 1st Street in downtown Mesa Vista. Her husband was driving their Ford Fusion when it collided at a high speed with a Honda Civic. Police say the Tarrants were being followed by two men in a pickup truck who had harassed them earlier in the evening at a restaurant east of where the crash occurred.

A Mesa Vista police officer happened upon the scene only seconds after the crash occurred. As he pulled over to assist, two men fled the pickup truck and ran across highway lanes. They were struck by a Chevrolet SUV, whose driver and passenger were not injured. One man died there, and the other, badly injured, was taken to St. Mary's Medical Center, where Diane Tarrant is also being treated for injuries. Her condition is reported to be serious. David Tarrant was not injured in the crash.

Police say the incident began to unfold moments earlier. The Tarrants had dined at The Winery at Main and 7th streets. When they were walking across the restaurant's parking lot to their car, they were assaulted by two men who got out of a white pickup truck. The men started hurling insults at Diane Tarrant and one used a Nerf "Super Soaker" water gun to spray liquid at the couple. The liquid turned out to be urine. The Tarrants managed to reach their car and lock the doors before their assailants could do more harm.

David Tarrant raced out of the parking lot and headed north on 7th Street. As he approached North Avenue, Tarrant noticed the pickup truck fast approaching from behind. Tarrant ran a red light and turned left onto North Avenue. The pickup truck followed suit and soon was on Tarrant's tail, repeatedly smashing into his rear bumper. As Tarrant neared the intersection with 1st Street, the pickup truck rammed him again, sending his car out of control and into a collision with a Honda Civic that was entering North Avenue eastbound from the highway. The pickup truck smashed into the other two cars. The driver and the passenger in the Honda Civic suffered only minor injuries.

At this point, the police officer, who also was coming off the highway eastbound onto North Avenue, arrived on the scene. He turned on his flashing lights and pulled over to assist. As he did so, two men leaped out of the pickup truck and ran across all four lanes, apparently hoping to flee into nearby Lilac Park. They were struck by an SUV that was coming off of Highway 50. One of the men died at the scene, the other was taken to the hospital and not expected to survive his injuries.

The Daily Sentinel previously has reported that Diane Tarrant has been the target of an intense campaign of harassment and intimidation from people opposed to policy decisions she has made about COVID mitigation protocols. A police spokesperson says this incident likely is related to the earlier events, and a full investigation is already underway.

I don't know how to begin to process the mix of emotions I feel after reading this article. First, of course, I feel anguish for Diane Williams and her family. How awful for them. If anyone in town could genuinely understand what they'd been going through, it's I. On the other hand, I also have a whole but-for-the-grace-of-God feeling going, knowing how easily it could have been I who ended up in a hospital bed at St. Mary's.

But I also feel a little sorry for myself. Why? If my timing had been different—if I'd just waited a few more days before announcing my resignation—maybe I wouldn't have had to leave the board. Assuming the two men who'd been chasing the Tarrants were the same men who'd been harassing me, my antagonists are now neutralized. But Dad and Jack pointed out earlier this morning that the number of people who hate me and wanted me out of office far exceeds two men, so the menacing wrath aimed at me wasn't likely to subside, even if the ringleaders were no longer active.

They're no doubt correct about that. And I've done the wise thing, taken the right step to protect myself and my family.

Chapter 43

Jack

As a former cop, I'm familiar with the dark side of human nature. There are a lot of fucked-up people out there, warped by their anger, their fear, their hatred. Why some people act on those emotions and others don't is a question beyond my capacity to answer. But I'm used to dealing with the mess caused by people who can't cope, who give in to their emotions, their base instincts. The ones who do harm. I'm used to finding out what I can about them.

Over the couple of weeks following the horrific Tarrant incident, we got more information about the two men involved in the assault. Some details came out in newspaper articles, some from friendly sources I milked within the police department. One of the dead men was Dwayne Fowler, a former professional wrestler, who was apparently a well-known fixture of the local conservative protest community. He often showed up at public-agency meetings and made a ruckus. He was said to be more interested in the ruckus itself than in the policy controversies.

The other deceased man was Jerry Sanford. A police source told me that Sanford was a local ne'er-do-well with no known employment history. He had appeared on police radar in the past for his virulent anti-government attitudes. He was charged with vandalizing a local judge's home, but the "timid-shit district attorney" (a source's words) declined to prosecute, believing the evidence against Sanford wasn't strong enough to win a conviction.

I was able to learn from my sources that the police found a tracking device in Fowler's truck. And hidden in the back right wheel well of the Tarrants' Ford was a transponder linked to Fowler's device. It took only a little cajoling and some light palm greasing to get my source to confirm my suspicion that Amy's car also was linked to Fowler's device.

When I showed Amy photos of both Fowler and Sanford, she confirmed that they were the two men who had assaulted her and Will at *Le Rouge*. Moreover, she recognized Fowler as the man she had seen at numerous school-board meetings and, alarmingly, at too many places around town for his presence to be merely coincidental. It seemed pretty clear that Fowler and Sanford were the ones responsible for the vandalism Amy had experienced and, probably, for the doxing as well. But the police were unable to provide any proof of that.

Fowler's mobile phone had the encrypted Signal app, but of course the police weren't able to get any information from that. They found nothing in the browser, email, or text messages referring to Amy or Diane Tarrant. And there were no exchanges about either woman with other persons, so my hopes were dashed that Fowler's phone (or a search of his apartment) would lead us to others involved in harassing Amy.

It seemed like the trail was ending with Fowler and Sanford. Maybe that was it: just two dumb lummoxes who indulged their worst, hateful instincts. But I suspected not. Clearly, Fowler was one of the men whom Kelly Albertson had served at Bin 707. Neither of the other two men was Sanford. (I'd stopped by and shown her a photo of him, and she'd confirmed that he hadn't been at the table.) To my mind, that meant there were still at least two men out there who had something to do with tormenting Amy—and probably Diane Tarrant, too.

Chapter 44

Marty

What a clusterfuck! That idiot Dwayne was bound to screw up in a major way at some point. And he finally did. At his own expense, obviously. But maybe at our expense, too. That's what Ray, K3LVR and I have been trying to assess: whether we're in jeopardy because of Dwayne's actions. K3LVR thinks not. He points out that we've always been careful to use Signal for all communications. None of the three of us ever exchanged regular phone calls, emails, or text messages with Dwayne. And at the beginning we discussed not having any contact information for the others on our devices. We think—we hope!—Dwayne followed the protocol, but who knows? It wasn't even two weeks ago that we read him the riot act about accosting Amy Wilson at *Le Rouge*! He swore he wouldn't do anything like it again. And then he went out and did something similar to Diane

Tarrant. So, in my view, it's hard to be confident that we're not at risk. We don't really know what sort of trail Dwayne has left behind.

The good news, though, is that we achieved our goals. We managed to drive both Amy Wilson and Diane Tarrant out of office. (Just this morning, the *Sentinel* reported that Tarrant would not be returning to her job.) It wasn't what you'd call a tidy process. But, hey, you've got to break some eggs to make an omelet. Right?

So, we decided we'll shut this operation down for now. Let the heat die down. We can gear back up when we have to. And we know we'll have to. The libtards aren't going to stop trying to take away our liberties. If we don't stop them, who will?

Chapter 45

Mike

You'd think that when you reach your eighth decade you'd stop being surprised by what life throws your way. Well, not I. In fact, I'm bowled over. Blown away. Knocked for six. However you want to put it. You're wondering to what I'm referring. Let me tell you. Pull up a chair, friend. You'll want to be seated when you hear this.

Remember that morning Hannah came into the kitchen and opened her robe to me? That in itself was surprising, to say the least. Even more startling is that she cancelled her plans to return to Denver that afternoon. Instead, she stayed for a few more days, each of which began with the same robe opening, leading each day to a variety of pleasurable activities that I had thought were long since behind me. And once she was back in Denver, we spoke by phone several times a day, and she came out for long-weekend visits twice in five weeks.

Even more astonishing is what happened yesterday. Hannah called with news that truly floored me. Apparently, last week she had lunch with Jeff Benson, the executive director of the Mesa County public-health department. He was in Denver for a meeting of the state's county health executives. She and Jeff have known each other for years through public-health circles. Hannah initiated the lunch. She told me she wanted to find out how Jeff's been coping with the vacancy in his deputy position, and otherwise catch up on public-health gossip. I guess they had a grand old time.

Obviously, that's not the news that left me gobsmacked. This did: Jeff called Hannah the next day and asked her if she would accept the deputy position here in Mesa County. She said she would, pending my approval. So, she called to ask for my assent.

"You'd give up your job as deputy of the state agency to become deputy of a county agency?" I asked.

"Sure. Why not? I've held the state job for plenty long. The county job would be fun, like returning to my roots."

"Well, I don't know about 'fun.' You might—"

"Anyway, dopey, the job is just a pretext. What I really want is to move out there permanently with you."

"You do?"

"I do."

"Why?"

"You really want me to answer that?"

"I do."

"Okay. ... Because I like Amy. And Jack. And Matt. And Annabelle. Because I like Mesa Vista ..." She paused. "And because I love you. Always have, always will."

Part Two

A Year Later - 2022

Chapter 46

Amy

Life is funny. You never know what twists and turns it will take. A year ago, I gave up my position on the school board because the political climate surrounding school policies had become too toxic, and people who opposed my views had made my life miserable. Now, Hannah is living with us and is eight months into her new job as the deputy director of the Mesa County Department of Public Health. I had tried to talk her out of it. Not out of moving to Mesa Vista. I'm ecstatic about that. But about taking the new job. What was she thinking? Did the harassment of me and the near-fatal hounding of Diane Tarrant mean nothing to her? Did she not realize that, if anything, the top jobs in public health these days are even more difficult and stressful than the ones in education? What made her think she's impervious to the pressures, insulated from the scourges?

"Look," she'd said at the time she accepted the job, "I'm not a newbie, not a spring chicken. I can take whatever they throw at me. And if I can't—or if the seat gets too hot or too dangerous—I'll quit. Easy, peasy. I'm close to retiring anyway. But I think I can do this for a few years. And, besides, I think the worst of the COVID conflicts are over. They're behind us. And it's not like there's a steep learning curve for me with this. I could do this job in my sleep."

What does one say in response to that level of self-confidence? Not much. Or, at least, I didn't.

But now things are taking another twist, and I don't know how I feel about it. The county public health department is managed by its executive director and deputy. But it is overseen, and its policies actually are set, by a five-member volunteer board—the Board of Public Health, whose members serve five-year terms and are appointed by the county board of commissioners. Hannah and her boss, Jeff Benson, have persuaded the county commissioners to appoint Dad to a vacancy on the health board.

"There isn't a better person in the whole state—much less in Mesa County—to serve in that position," Hannah says, pushing back at my opposition.

"But he's 75!"

"So what? He still has all his marbles. And it's really not a position that requires heavy lifting. The other board members all have demanding, full-time jobs in addition to this volunteer service. Besides, he wants to do it."

I turn to Dad. "Do you?"

"Oh, how nice that somebody has decided to involve me in this delightful conversation! Thank you! And, yes, I would like to do it. I agree with Hannah that it wouldn't be arduous, and I think it would be interesting. Plus, I feel I still have something to offer."

I know I'm unlikely to be able to derail this runaway train. But I decide to make the conductor feel bad. Raising my eyebrow, I turn to Hannah. "Don't you think it will be unseemly — and potentially scandalous — that there's a close personal relationship between the agency's second-in-command and its new supervisory board member? The public may not like the whiff of that!"

"Oh, please," Hannah says. "One in four Americans can't name a single branch of the national government. They certainly aren't going to be attuned to the personnel details at DPH."

"They will if the *Sentinel* decides to make an issue of it."

"Let them try. Your Dad and I have already talked to the county attorney's office about it. They had no concerns, since your father won't be my direct superior and will share general supervisory responsibilities with four other people. Plus, he can recuse himself from any decisions specific to my position, such as salary increases." She pauses. "Look, Amy. Your Dad has a wealth of expertise to share. If he wants to do it, we shouldn't stand in his way."

I look at Dad. He has an eager expression on his face, reminding me of Annabelle as a puppy. "Okay. Public service is a noble calling. Go for it. Just don't come whining to me if they key your car or throw a beer in your face at a restaurant."

Chapter 47

Mike

Today's *Daily Sentinel* carries a small page-three news item (and photo) about me and my appointment to the Board of Public Health. It notes that I had a long career at the state's public-health department and had led that agency for eight years. To my surprise and delight, the paper also has a short editorial, applauding the county commissioners for appointing a man of my experience to the board and commending me for taking the position. I don't know why, but I hadn't expected the appointment to be announced so publicly.

At a meeting of the post-polio support group this morning, I'm the last to show up. When I enter the room, some members of the group start clapping. Peggy says, "In case any of you don't know, that applause for Mike is in response to the news that he will be serving on the county board of health. Congratulations, Mike!" Another round of applause. "Why don't you tell us what you see as some of the agency's immediate challenges."

Earl releases a sigh of frustration. "Must he?"

Several people shush Earl, so I feel emboldened to say a few words, but know I'd best keep it brief. "I think what the pandemic has shown is that our nation's local health departments play a critical role in protecting the public's health. But, decades of under-funding and under-staffing have stretched local public-health infrastructures to their limits. So, in order to deal with the COVID crisis, agencies have been forced to de-prioritize essential services such as environmental-health programs and maternal and child-health programs, exacerbating already existing health inequities. The same with substance-abuse disorders. We saw epidemics like the overdose crisis quietly escalate during the pandemic. So, the funding problem is a serious one."

Earl groans dramatically.

Undeterred, I continue. "Also, the rampant politicization of COVID-19 protection measures implemented by local health departments has made the local public-health response challenging. Local public-health workers on the front line of the pandemic response experienced widespread harassment and threats from within their own communities. We witnessed that vividly right here in Mesa Vista with the horrific intimidation campaign against Diana Tarrant, the former deputy director of the agency. That may be an even bigger problem than the funding issue, and even harder to solve."

Earl crosses his arms and harrumphs. "So, let me get

this straight. Peggy asked you about 'immediate challenges' the agency faces. And you've replied exactly as I would expect you to. First, you whined about not having enough money, enough taxpayer dollars to spend as you like. Second, you whined about having critics, fellow citizens who exercise their constitutional right to disagree with what you're doing. How precious! Jesus, you people really are something."

I consider how hard to come back at him. "Earl, conservatives have been trying to starve all levels of government of needed resources ever since the Reagan era. You've done a good job of it. Too good. It's pound foolish not to be investing heavily in our public-health infrastructure. We're not going to have the capacity to deal effectively with public-health threats to come."

Then I decide to lower the boom on him. I lean forward in my chair and point at him. "And it's appalling that you sit there and describe the near-fatal harassment of a public official as a form of 'disagreeing' that is protected by the Constitution. Appalling, sick, and ignorant."

The folks around the circle again applaud and offer me murmurs of approval. Nobody comes to Earl's defense. His face is bright red. The man is clearly apoplectic—breathing heavily, perspiring, eyes darting all around the room.

Sofia eventually breaks the silence. "Mike, your comment about the weakness of our public-health infrastructure raises a question I've been wondering about. From what I can see, the governmental responses to COVID—federal and state—are *ad hoc*, tuned to this particular pandemic. Am I correct in thinking that nothing's really being done to prepare us for the next one?"

"Yes, unfortunately, you're right, Sofia. And it concerns me greatly." I look around at the group. "I've already talked too much this morning, and I don't mean to hog the floor. But I wonder how many of you have read or heard the news that cases of monkeypox recently have been reported in places like the UK, where the disease is not endemic."

Steve, Sofia, and Minnie all raise their hands. "You read my mind, Mike. I was thinking of monkeypox when I asked my question."

I smile at her. "Well, first of all, it's important to know that there's no reason for great alarm. Yet. We're pretty sure this monkeypox is being spread through sexual activity. That makes it different from—and I think less scary than—something like COVID, which is primarily spread by inhalation of very fine respiratory droplets and aerosol particles. But if that were to change—if, for example, monkeypox were to be spread simply by touching surfaces that have the virus on them—then we would be in a new world of hurt. And so, your question is appropriate, Sofia, because this is the first time that many monkeypox cases and clusters have been reported concurrently in non-endemic and endemic countries in widely disparate geographical areas."

Minnie is passing her iPhone around the circle. Apparently, she has pulled up photos of the horrific skin eruptions on people who've contracted monkeypox. Each passing of the phone elicits new gasps.

"Again, my point is that it's so important that we as a society invest in public-health agencies and activities. It's absolutely imperative that we have the capacity, regardless of what kind of disease outbreak we're dealing with, to work with other countries on surveillance, laboratory work, clinical care, infection prevention and control, as well as risk communication and community engagement to inform communities at risk and the broader general public."

The conversation continues in this vein for a while, with Steve making the apt comment about how short-sighted Americans are, perhaps especially our politicians and policy-makers. "We seem incapable of thinking beyond the current crisis. And once the crisis is over, we act as If another one will never occur. The lessons of the current crisis are soon lost on us. And we soon forget about its victims."

People sit with this observation for a moment. Then, David, the Vietnam veteran whose hobby is making models of military weapons, sums up, bringing the focus back to what brings this group together. "For a while, the fight against polio brought out many of the best qualities of American society. Then the vaccines were developed, and not only did polio disappear in America, but the war against polio seemed to be forgotten—along with the survivors. We were once held up as examples of heroic human fortitude. But now, tens of thousands of us polio survivors who continue to need medical and financial help are largely ignored by the public." He pauses and seems to choke up. "As veterans of other wars have discovered, the public doesn't like to be reminded of the wounded and the dead after the war is over."

There's a stunned silence in the room. The sheer force of David's observation—and the surprise that it has come from one who so rarely talks—seems to have rendered us speechless. Finally, Steve says, "Amen, brother."

Gradually, people take their leave. Sofia and I stay to pick up some of the conversational threads we pursued during the meeting. When everyone else is gone, she says, "Mike, I have something to tell you. I probably should have shared this with you long ago. I'm sorry I didn't. But I was reminded of it again today when Earl unleashed some of his animus against you."

Curious, I smile and say, "What is it, Sofia?"

"Well, I'm sure you remember some months ago when Earl revealed that he had done genealogical research on you and discovered that Amy Wilson is your daughter and that you had led the state's public health department."

"Yes,"

"A few weeks later, he told me after one of our group meetings that he had done some more research on you and had discovered that your father-in-law was Walter Ward, whom Earl holds directly responsible for his having contracted the polio virus through the vaccine."

"What?"

"That's what he said."

"But I don't understand."

"Was your late wife's name Laura Ward?"

"Yes."

"Was her father's name Walter?"

"Yes."

"Did her family live in California when Laura was a child?"

"Yes."

"Are you aware that her father worked for Cutter Laboratories?"

"Well, I know he had a doctorate in microbiology as

well as a medical degree. But I'm only aware of his years as a professor at Stanford Medical School. By the time Laura and I met, both her parents had died."

"Well, apparently Mr. Ward was the director of medical research at Cutter Laboratories in California in 1954, and it was from a Cutter vaccine that Earl got polio."

I am truly flummoxed. "I … I don't … I … I've never heard anything about Walter being at Cutter."

"Look, the only reason I'm bringing it up is that—between you and me—I'd say Earl has a few screws loose, and I'm uncomfortable seeing the intensity of his hostility toward you. I wanted to make sure you're aware that he knows of your family connection to Walter Ward." She hands me a set of documents. "Here. This will tell you what I've been able to find out about Walter Ward. Sounds like you'll find it surprising and enlightening."

Chapter 18

Earl

Good lord. That man drives me absolutely crazy. He sits there, all high and mighty, pontificating about government and public health. He wants more of the taxpayers' money. He wants more power. He wants to be able to tell people what they can and can't do. How they must behave. What unreliable chemicals they must allow to be injected into their bodies. If we left things to the likes of Mike Franklin and his daughter Amy Wilson, this country—and certainly Mesa County would go all to hell.

And don't get me started on Amy Wilson's maternal grandfather, Walter Ward. Believe me, I've done a lot of research over the years—read everything I can get my hands on about how Walter Ward, Cutter Pharmaceuticals, and the federal government together screwed up and shot live polio virus into the bodies of children throughout the

American West. How they managed to leave people like me with lifelong paralysis. How they fucked us over. You feel like knowing the story? Not your choice. I'm gonna tell you.

In April of 1954, the largest human clinical test in the history of medical science got underway as the National Foundation for Infantile Paralysis started its field trials of Jonas Salk's polio vaccine. More than 1,800,000 children in the U.S. participated. A year later, on April 12, 1955, the safety of the vaccine was "powerfully affirmed," and distribution of shots began almost immediately. Two weeks later, five cases of paralytic polio were reported among children who had just received the vaccine. All five victims, it was found, had received vaccine produced by Cutter Laboratories in California. When the government requested that Cutter recall all its vaccine pending an investigation, Cutter complied. But by then the damage was done. The so-called "Cutter Incident" eventually encompassed 25 states, 260 cases of paralytic polio (one of those, me), and 11 deaths.

Why did I say earlier that Amy Wilson's grandfather, Walter Ward, was directly responsible for this debacle? Let me explain. As the director of medical research for all human products at Cutter, Ward oversaw all aspects of the company's polio virus manufacturing process: he reviewed all protocols detailing how polio virus was grown; he reviewed all graphs showing how polio virus was inactivated; and he viewed all vaccine safety tests. He was responsible for signing off on every lot of vaccine and for submitting protocols for approval to the U.S. government's Laboratory of Biologics Control. In the end, Walter Ward was the only person at Cutter Laboratories who knew exactly what was happening with the polio vaccine at every stage of processing, developing, and testing.

He *knew* that Cutter's processes showed a disregard for Jonas Salk's protocols for inactivating the polio virus in the vaccine. He *knew* that Cutter's success at killing the polio virus in its vaccine lots was inconsistent (nine of twenty-seven lots failed safety tests). He *knew* that Cutter had taken no steps to solve the problem. Yet he did not inform executives at Cutter of the problem, nor did he inform federal regulators of the manufacturing difficulties Cutter faced. So, yeah, I hold him responsible.

If I were to be fair—something I find very difficult to do when thinking of Ward—I'd have to say that there were other people around the country who committed acts of omission that contributed mightily to the Cutter disaster. Consider William Workman, for instance. He was the director of the U.S. government's Laboratory of Biologics Control inside the Public Health Service in the 1950s. He suspected that the testing protocols set up by the manufacturers to detect live virus in the vaccine might be inadequate. Worse yet, he failed to act on information that had been passed to him by a subordinate that there might be a critical flaw in Cutter's manufacturing process. So, there's plenty of blame to go around. That's for sure. But I still hold Walter Ward primarily responsible.

I remember when I told Marty about the Wilson connection with Ward back when we were trying to drive Wilson from the school board.

"I don't see how it has any relevance to our concerns about Amy Wilson." I remember that I had just pulled into my driveway when Marty said that. I turned off the engine and stared at my phone. No relevance? No fucking relevance! It's not relevant to "our concerns about Amy Wilson" that she's directly, linearly related to the man who caused my paralysis? What the actual fuck?! I lost it and ripped into him. "Marty, I've long thought Dwayne is the stupidest member of this squad. But you've just taken the trophy from him." I stabbed at the red button to end the call and stewed in the van for a good twenty minutes. That's how long it took for me to feel my heart rate and blood pressure returning to normal.

The power of that moment still sits with me. It's when I realized that Marty didn't give a shit about my polio. I wonder if he ever really cared even about vaccines. Maybe he only cared about pushing conservative causes and fucking around with the libs. In any case, I may need to get in touch with him. Now that Mike Franklin is on the county health board, I may need Marty's help to get him off it. I can't abide Walter Ward's son-in-law having a say about the health policies of Mesa County.

Chapter 49

Amy

We're sitting on the patio, having a drink before dinner. Jack has barbecued some spareribs, and Hannah has made a potato salad. I've baked a lemon meringue pie with a crust of crushed vanilla wafers—one of Dad's and Matty's favorite desserts. We've been talking about this crazy news regarding my grandfather Walter and looking at some of the documents Dad's friend gave him.

"Do you think Mom knew about this?" I ask him.

"I assume not. If she had, I'm sure she would've shared that information with me. I can't imagine she'd keep that to herself."

"Unless she just found it too embarrassing to deal with."

"I suppose that's possible."

"How do you feel about this? Are you upset?"

Am I? I consider. "No, I don't think I'd say I'm upset about it. I just find it peculiar and awkward to have this remote association with someone involved with the polio vaccine."

"I also feel at some sort of disadvantage vis-a-vis Earl, the guy in my PPS group who got polio through the Cutter vaccine and who knows of our family connection to that. He and I are always clashing, and sometimes his hostility toward me has felt quite personal without my understanding why."

"He knows about Walter?" Jack asks.

"Yeah, but his animus was obvious before he found out about Walter. And it has increased over time. He's a very bitter guy. Angry at government, at the political system, at scientists, at pharmaceutical companies. And at me."

Hannah says, "You know I'm the last person who'd be sympathetic to someone who is virulently anti-government. But I find myself wondering how I'd feel if I got polio because somebody messed up and distributed vaccines containing live virus. I think I'd be pretty bitter."

Dad's face is rigid. "More bitter than if you got polio because some infected kid at your school sneezed or coughed and you got droplets on your hands and then touched your mouth or breathed in the droplets. More reason to be bitter?"

I look at Dad. He doesn't seem annoyed, but I've been around him long enough to know both from the tone of his voice and the manner of his response that Hannah's comment ticked him off.

"More of a *right* to be bitter?" he asks, pushing the issue.

Hannah puts down her drink. "Michael, it's not a contest. I have led a charmed life, so what the hell do I know! I can't fathom how *anyone* afflicted with a dread disease doesn't become bitter and angry. But *you* didn't. And that's greatly to your credit. I guess all I'm saying is that maybe people who know exactly how they got some horrible virus react differently to their predicament from people who got the same virus but don't know how they contracted it. Maybe the former are more prone to anger and bitterness. Possible?"

I watch Dad. Some of the starch has leached from him. He grins at Hannah and says, "I see what you're saying. And, yes, I suppose that's possible."

I step in. "They say knowledge is power. And they say power corrupts. So, by some mathematical property I no longer can name, you could say knowledge can corrupt. In this case, Earl's knowledge of how he contracted polio has really warped or twisted his brain. He's become corrupted — infected, contaminated—by his knowledge."

Dad smiles and points at me. To the others, he says, "That's my smart baby girl talkin' right there."

Jack raises his glass to me. "Are you a beaver? Because, dam!"

Hannah snorts. "Oh, good god, Jack. I bet that's a pickup line you've used on women for years."

Jack stands up in mock anger. "I was just trying to compliment my amazing niece. And I don't need pickup lines, Hannah. I'm naturally charismatic and alluring. But I do have a repertoire of put-downs I've used for years on judgmental people like you. Want to hear some of them?"

Laughing, Hannah replies, "Hit me with 'em, you sleazy geezer."

"Try these on for size, Miss Deputy Director."

Dad groans and wipes his palm down his face. "No, please, Jack, no. For the love of god, no."

To increase the comical effect of what he's doing, Jack holds his hands up to his chest like he's grasping lapels. He tilts his head up and closes his eyes, as if searching his brain for the card containing his favorite insults. "How's this: 'Are you always such an idiot, or do you just show off when I'm around?'"

"Ooooohhhh," Matt says, appreciatively.

Jack winks at his nephew. "Or, 'Sorry, I don't understand what you're saying. I don't speak bullshit.'"

Matt guffaws. So does Dad, who tries to suppress it.

"The Jerk Store called. They said they're all out of...*you*!' Snorts, guffaws. Now, Hannah and I are laughing too.

"If ignorance is bliss, you must be the happiest person on the planet." Matty's laughing even harder.

Dad is starting to look alarmed. "Oh, my god, Jack. Just stop!"

"Just one more, dear brother." Now, he turns to Matt. "Drum roll, please, my good man."

Matt, who can produce a mean drum-roll sound from his mouth, obliges.

Jack clears his throat ostentatiously, then says, "Look, if I wanted to hear from an asshole, all I had to do was fart.'"

And now, Matty is again incapacitated with laughter. And my dad—my solid, intellectual, cultured dad—is also laughing so hard that no noise is coming out of him, but his shoulders are bouncing up and down and he's clapping like a retarded seal.

Chapter 50

Hannah

The day starts out bad. Then it gets worse.

I'm in my office for all of two minutes before Jeff Benson comes in and closes the door behind him. No introductory greeting. "Somebody tipped off Gloria Snyder at *The Sentinel* about you and Mike. They're running the story tomorrow and want the agency's comment."

I'd prepared myself for this moment. As I'd told Amy, I'm not some naive rookie. I figured this would happen eventually. Some people are bored and easily titillated by the slightest whisper of scandal. (Please! Scandal? *What* scandal?) And there's a Venn overlap between them and others who delight in stirring up trouble. So, here we are, thanks to some mischievous moron.

"We already talked about this, Jeff. Just tell the *Sentinel* what we worked up in advance: nothing improper; no supervisory or direct work relationship; it's a nothing-burger"

"I know. And that's what we'll do. Look, I'm not worried or upset about this. I'm only here to let you know that it will be in the paper. Didn't want you to be taken by surprise."

"Thanks. That's considerate of you. I appreciate it."

"That's not really why I'm here anyway."

Detecting concern in his voice, I look up.

"Did you see the *New York Times* this morning?"

"Not yet. Why?"

"Apparently, a couple of months ago, a young man in Rockland County outside New York City went to the hospital complaining of a stiff neck, pain in his back and abdomen, and a gradual weakening of his leg muscles. Lab tests at the hospital revealed a shocking diagnosis: the culprit was the polio virus."

"Really? That's highly unlikely." I happen to know that in the past twenty years there've been just three known instances of polio in the U.S—all thought to be imported—affecting a total of ten people.

"I know. But when alerted by the hospital about the man's diagnosis, public health experts from the CDC, the New York health department, and Rockland County sprang into action. Through wastewater testing, they discovered that the poliovirus had been circulating in Rockland County since May. They also found it in wastewater from neighboring Orange County and New York City."

"Oh, god," I say. I know what that means—that there are probably thousands of people in the NY metro area who are infected with the polio virus but don't know it because they have no symptoms. Fortunately, most of them aren't at risk of paralysis because they've been vaccinated against polio. But the unvaccinated stand a real chance of contracting the virus, and as many as one in two hundred of those people could become paralyzed.

And I'm certainly alarmed to hear that this has happened in Rockland county. Anyone who's been in public health as long as I have knows that many towns in Rockland county are notable for having two things: large populations of ultra-Orthodox Jews and extraordinarily low vaccination rates. You might think those two things are unrelated, but they're not.

And now you might think Orthodox Jews have a thing against vaccination. In fact, most of them don't. Vaccine hesitancy isn't characteristic of Orthodox Judaism generally. In most Orthodox Jewish neighborhoods, vaccination rates are close to 100 percent. The vast majority of rabbis and Jewish scholars interpret several passages in the Torah and other Jewish texts as being supportive of vaccines. So, why do we see low vaccination rates in many Orthodox communities across New York? It's the result of an organized campaign waged by national anti-vaccine groups for years.

These groups targeted communities that share several common traits, such as having strong values of purity (either secular or religious) and liberty–a combination of "my body is a temple" and "you can't tell me what to do." So, we see these anti-vaccine pockets not just in many Orthodox Jewish communities but in Amish communities in Ohio and Pennsylvania and among Somali refugees in Minnesota. Weirdly, you also see it in some wealthy, liberal enclaves in Marin county, California; Portland, Oregon; and Clark county, Washington.

In all these places, questions about vaccines started to emerge in the early 2000s with a new generation of parents who had no first-hand knowledge of vaccine-controlled diseases such as measles and polio. In the minds of successive cohorts of parents, the salience of real or perceived side effects went up compared to the salience of actual disease. To put that in more normal language, what I mean is that people became more afraid of the vaccines than of the diseases. And that happened over several decades because vaccines were so successful. People not well connected to accurate information are easily preyed upon by groups who know exactly how to take advantage of them. And, unfortunately, you find such people across all ethnic groups, all religions, and all economic classes.

But my concern now isn't just about vulnerable unvaccinated people. I fear how this might feed anti-vax mania. I turn to my computer, intending to pull up the *Times* article, but the damn machine is going through some reboot sequence. Looking back to Jeff, I say, "Those cases detected earlier this year in Jerusalem and London were vaccine-derived. Do they know about this one in New York?"

"Yeah. Genetic testing shows this one is vaccine-derived, too. So, this originated in another country and was unwittingly brought into the U.S. by a person who didn't know they were infected."

"I worry about how the media are going to play this. Christ! We don't need to give people more reason to be skeptical of vaccines. But that's what's gonna happen!"

Jeff looks miserable. His shoulders stoop, as if the

mantle of leadership weighs heavily upon him. He probably wonders how he has the bad luck to be a county public-health director at the time when all hell seems to have broken loose: COVID is still active; monkeypox is on the loose; and now, we may have to worry about a polio epidemic among the unvaccinated. I feel for him. My title, after all, is deputy. He's the director. The buck doesn't stop with me. It pauses and looks at me, then hurries on to Jeff.

"I'm sorry to lay yet another one on you, Hannah. But I have more bad news."

I'm beginning to wonder if I was wise to take this job. "What's up?" I ask, trying to project an upbeat spirit I certainly didn't feel.

"The CDPHE just sent us the latest monkeypox data. The number of human cases in the state hit 157 in August."

The CDPHE is my former employer, the state public-health department. I pay close attention to the good data they produce. I know the number of such cases was 2 in May, 6 in June, and 66 last month. The fact that the number is still going up so precipitously isn't good at all. I know that, as before, the great majority of these cases in Colorado are likely to be in the counties around Denver. But I know the data show that every county that has college or university has more cases than those that don't. Because Mesa County has Colorado Mesa University, I'm afraid to ask what I need to know. "Oooph. Bad. What's the damage here in Mesa County?"

He winces. "Eight."

I was expecting perhaps three, so this is much worse.

"All eight right here in Mesa Vista. And seven of them at CMU," he says.

No wonder he looks distressed. The new semester is just two weeks from starting at CMU and monkeypox is on the loose on campus. This could be a nightmare. "Good lord, Jeff. We'd better act fast."

"You're not kidding."

The rest of the day is taken up by doing the sort of thing county health agencies excel at: arranging for testing and conducting contact tracing for cases; ensuring that high-risk individuals have easy access to vaccination; and communicating with the public. Because most of the monkeypox cases in the U.S. (and, from what we can tell, all of the cases in Mesa County) have occurred in social networks of men who have sex with men and among individuals with multiple or anonymous sex partners, I spend much of the afternoon engaged in outreach with gay organizations on the CMU campus and in the community.

Now, I'm home. I've already spoken with Mike a couple of times today, so he's clued in to what I've been dealing with all day. When I walk through the door, he greets me with a warm hug and a cold martini. "God. I need a little more of both."

He laughs. "Neither is in short supply."

"Praise the Lord." I collapse into my favorite armchair. Annabelle arrives within a nanosecond of my subsidence. She shoves her velvety muzzle under my arm, spilling some of my precious martini onto my lap. I'm too tired to chastise her. Instead, I rub her behind her ears and coo. "Bellie wants some Tanqueray. Bellie's a gin girl. Yes, she is. Yes, she is. A good gin girl. Bellie, Bellie, Bellie!"

Mike shoos Annabelle away and slowly eases himself onto the couch to my right. "There's no point in talking about the coming Sentinel article. I want to hear what else you know about the polio situation."

Chapter 51

Marty

I don't claim any great powers of foresight. But when I saw the two articles in this morning's *Sentinel*—about Mike Franklin and about the discovery of the polio virus in New York City—I had an inkling that I might hear from K3LVR for the first time in months. And now, here I am on the phone with him. I've heard K3LVR in an agitated state plenty of times. The subject of vaccinations really riles him up, and vaccinations have been a ubiquitous topic the past couple of years. But right now he's at a level of distress I've never before witnessed. Holy cow, the guy is shaken.

"It's a vaccine-derived outbreak, Marty! The vaccine is the culprit!"

I have to hold my phone away from my ear. K3LVR has a big, rich baritone voice, and when raised to a holler, it's enough to hurt one's ears. "I know, Clever. I know! I read that."

"They're even admitting it this time! They're saying it straight up!"

"Okay. So, they are. Isn't that a good thing? They're finally being honest about it?"

"Goddammit, Marty! That's not the point!"

Fuck my life. "Well, what's the point, then, Clever?"

"The point is that they're going to keep distributing these vaccines that kill and cripple people!"

"And you're calling me about this, why?"

"Because Mesa County's health policies are in the hands of lunatics, Marty, and we have to do something about it!"

I feel like screaming, *I've kinda got my hands full helping Tina Peters fight off her election-fraud charges, Clever!! Are you aware that there are bigger fish frying around here than your fucking vaccines?!* Instead, I swallow hard, take a few deep breaths, and say, "What do you want me to do about it?"

"We need to do to Hannah Matthews and Mike Franklin what we did to Amy Wilson and Diana Tarrant—drive them out of office!"

"Really, Clever? This is a high priority?" I ask. I hope the derision drips from my voice.

"Marty!! Have you been drinking? What's wrong with you?! You used to be the front line of defense against these statist assholes!"

"I still am, Clever. I am." Can he hear the dissimulation in my voice? "I just have a lot on my plate at the moment. Even so, I'm here for you, buddy." Good lord, listen to me.

"The thing is, without Dwayne, who's gonna do the dirty work?"

"I don't think we bother with vandalism. We go straight to doxing them. I think the thing that drove Wilson out was the threatening emails, texts, and phone calls. Maybe the same thing will work on these two."

"So, what do you want me to do?"

"Nothing at the moment, I guess. But I'll find the information we need and then I'll want you to be ready to help me disseminate it."

"Aye, aye, cap'n!" Oh, for chrissake! There's really something wrong with me. Why am I blithering like an idiot to K3LVR? I don't owe him anything! Absolutely nothing. If the tables were turned and I wanted his help for something, would he oblige? I doubt it.

Chapter 52

Mike

I really don't have the time or inclination any more to attend these PPS meetings, but I think I'd feel bad if I just stopped showing up. And I've genuinely come to like and respect some of these people—and am particularly beholden to Sofia for all the useful information she's given me. Today, I'm the last to arrive. My car wouldn't start this morning, and I had to call Jack for a ride, so I'm a bit late. But now here I am, sitting in the same talk circle. Our topic this morning is mitigating the effects of PPS.

Minnie has been talking for a while about the importance of energy conservation. "We have to pace our physical activity and rest frequently to reduce muscle fatigue. And if you can get physical therapy, that's great. It's important to find exercises you can do to strengthen your muscles without fatiguing them." She beams at the group.

"I consider myself really lucky that I can still swim and do water aerobics."

We somehow get into a discussion of pain relievers, weighing the relative merits of aspirin, acetaminophen, ibuprofen and others. Several people sing the praises of gabapentin, a prescription medicine that's often used to treat nerve pain and also has some anti-depressant effects.

Then the conversation veers off. I knew it was gonna happen. Just a matter of time. People are bemoaning the polio outbreak in New York and getting agitated. Peggy says, "I just don't see how this can happen in this day and age with the availability of vaccines."

Earl pounces, like a coyote on an unsuspecting rabbit. "It's the damn vaccines that are responsible!"

Peggy draws back as if she's been slapped. "What do you mean, Earl? What are you talking about?"

Earl rolls his eyes in the dramatic fashion of an aggrieved teenage girl — and accompanies the eye roll with an indignant upper-body squirm. "Jesus Christ, Peggy! Do you ever read beyond the headlines? If you did, you'd know that the original source of the virus that's spreading in New York—and in London and Jerusalem—is the oral vaccine itself!"

Sally gives Earl a look like she just smelled some unfortunate excretion on her shoe. "What are you saying, Earl"? She draws out his name as if it nauseates her.

"I'm saying the viruses detected in all three countries are 'vaccine-derived,' meaning that they're mutated versions of a virus that originated in the oral vaccine. It's basically what happened to me. People have been given a form of the live virus and now they're dying or suffering paralysis," he says, gesturing to his chair-bound legs. "It's confirmation of what I've been trying to tell you people all along: vaccines are dangerous!"

Steve says, "Earl, I think that's not the right lesson to take from this outbreak."

"Oh, really, why not?"

"First of all, the polio vaccines used in the U.S. and most other countries are injectable vaccines containing a killed virus. It's not dangerous at all. By contrast, the form of the vaccine responsible for this outbreak is the oral vaccine, which—you're right—contains a weakened form of the live virus and has been used around much of the world since the late 1980s. Why? Because it's cheap and easy to administer (two drops directly into children's mouths) and better at protecting entire populations where polio is still spreading—Pakistan and Afghanistan, for example. In very rare cases, the oral vaccine can lead to children being paralyzed by the virus or dying from it."

"There. What'd I tell you?!"

I'm about to speak in order to shut down Earl's idiocy. But Steve quickly persists.

"What has happened in this case is that the weakened virus has mutated into a more dangerous form and sparked outbreaks, especially in places with poor sanitation and low vaccination levels."

"Okay, smart guy. Then how does it end up in the United States?"

Now, when Steve replies, there's a level of contempt in his voice that matches Earl's. "If *you* read beyond the headlines, you'd know that the kind of outbreak that has occurred in New York typically begins when people who've been vaccinated shed live virus from the vaccine in their feces. From there, the virus can spread within the community and, over time, turn into a form that can paralyze people and start new epidemics. That's why public-health officials are alarmed about this." Steve turns to me. "Am I correct in what I've said, Mike?"

I smile at him. "You gave a perfect summary of the situation, Steve."

"Oh, god, now Mr. Let's-Vaccinate-Everyone-For-Everything is entering the discussion."

David and Sonia, who've been quiet this whole time, now explode in unison, addressing Earl and talking over each other.

"Oh, be quiet, Earl. You're—"

"Earl, you are so ill-mannered!"

"—a real pain in the ass. You don't have a decent bone in your body. I, for one—"

"You don't know how to engage in civil conversation."

"—don't want to hear another word from you."

When their outburst subsides, I try to speak in a measured tone. "Earl, it is you—not I—who has positioned himself as a vaccine expert. And, unfortunately for you, the facts of this case belie your beliefs about vaccines. The area of New York that's in jeopardy from this outbreak is in danger precisely because the people in those communities have refused to get their children vaccinated against polio. In areas with high vaccination rates, there's no danger at all."

Minnie—dear, sweet, diminutive Minnie—punctuates my statement. "Earl, I'd urge you to take in those facts Mike just offered you. But I think you'll have to shove them up your ass, because your brain is clearly already full of shit."

Everyone looks around first with shock, then delight, and breaks into laughter. All but Earl. He crosses his arms and slowly looks around the circle as ridicule rains down upon him. His face grows red, contorts, and reddens further. He angrily switches on his mobility scooter and flees the room. The rest of us watch him leave. When the door closes behind him, Minnie says, "My goodness, I don't know what came over me. I don't think I've ever spoken to someone like that in my life."

Steve laughs and says, "Well, Minnie, I'm glad I was here to witness it when it happened. You were fabulous."

Peggy says, "Do you think we were too hard on him?"

"Not hard enough, in my opinion," Sofia says.

"I agree," says Steve. "From the day he joined this group, he has presented us with nothing but an endless stream of bitterness. I get it. He experienced real misfortune. But so did we all. Each of us could go around moaning about how unfair it is that the polio vaccine didn't come out five years earlier than it did. But we don't—at least, none of us does that here in this room. I fail to see why he should get a be-an-asshole-for-free pass just because of the particular way he contracted polio."

Sofia runs her hand through her salt-and-pepper mane. "Well said, Steve. I also don't like the way he's downright disrespectful and rude to everyone—much less the way he actively denigrates the importance to the country of a good public-health infrastructure, including vaccines. And if that galls me, I can only imagine how *you* feel about it, Mike."

I appreciate her comment. I throw her what I imagine to

be my most responsive and appealing smile. I probably look developmentally challenged. "Thank you, Sofia. Yeah, actually, it's hard to take. But there are lots of people like Earl out there, and I try not to let them drain my spirit." People nod with thoughtful expressions as if the Buddha himself had just spoken. Peggy uses the opportunity to suggest an adjournment.

Outside, I wait for Jack to pick me up. Everyone else has left and the parking lot is empty. Jack roars in, driving his 2018 Mustang like a teenage boy on testosterone boosters. On the bit of loose gravel near the door, he executes a sliding 180-degree turn that could easily have taken me out. He pops the trunk so I can throw my walker in. When I open the door and peer in, he grins and says. "I've still got it, eh? A far better driver than you."

"We'll never know. I don't compete in the "Dumb Asshole" division."

"Is that any way to greet your chauffeur?"

"I don't know how you've lived as long as you have. Between the way you drive and your propensity for Laphroaig, you should have been dead years ago."

"Laphroaig is the only thing that has kept me alive. And you're not exactly Mr. Carrie Nation yourself."

"True, dat. In fact, I could use a drink and a sandwich right now. You have time?"

"Yup."

"Let's go to Toby's."

On the way into town, Jack asks how the meeting went. I tell him about the brouhaha with Earl and about sweet Minnie's deft and hilarious putdown. "And then he actually stormed out of the meeting. I'd be surprised, frankly, if he ever comes back. It was so clear that he's universally disliked by the group."

"He left the meeting early?" Jack asks.

"Yeah, he was really pissed."

"Do you know what kind of car he drives?"

"Yeah. A dark blue, side-entry wheelchair van. A Ford Explorer, I think. Why do you ask?"

"When I was driving out of the parking lot this morning after dropping you off, I noticed that van. It has the license plate 'KL3VR.' The van wasn't there when I came back to get you at the end of the meeting. I figured it was probably somebody from your group. But realized it could be someone else visiting the church."

"Definitely a member of the group. My least favorite member. What would make you notice that license plate?"

"It rang a bell. I went home and looked through my notes. Just as I thought, someone with the handle K3LVR was one of the people who was posting lots of shit about Amy during the height of the intimidation campaign against her. I suspected him at the time of being one of the ringleaders behind the doxing, but I couldn't find a way to discover who the person was. It was a lead that went cold."

I stare at him. "Well, I'd say it's not cold any more. As I say, his first name is Earl.

I don't even know his last name. We don't use last names at the PPS group."

Jack says, "I'll call one of my friends in the state patrol. He'll run the license plate. We'll get Earl's full name and address. And then we should be able to get other information about him, too. It was a lucky break that your car didn't work this morning and you needed me to take you to the meeting. We might never have put two and two together otherwise."

As we pull up to Toby's, Jack adds: "Is there anything else you can tell me about this guy?"

"At one meeting, people talked about what their hobbies are. If I remember correctly, Earl said he uses the internet, especially social media, to educate people about their oppressors in government who are guilty of overreach. And, oh, he runs a ham radio station where he does the same thing."

"Really?" Jack says. "I wonder if K3LVR is his ham-radio call sign. I bet it is. If so, we'll have to figure out how to tune in to find out the kind of thing he says."

"I have a pretty good sense of the kind of thing he says. But I agree. We should do that. Right now, though, I need that Laphroaig."

Chapter 53

Jack

My friend who's a state cop got back to me with information about the K3LVR license plate. It's registered to Earl Gottsdanker, age 73. Today, I spent four or five hours scouring the internet again to see what I could find about him. Interestingly, a search of his real name revealed very little. I was able to learn that he had been an accountant. But I guess your typical accountant doesn't leave much of an internet trail. Earl certainly didn't. "K3LVR," on the other hand, has left nasty slime trails everywhere he's appeared on the internet. I refresh my memory about the sort of bile he's posted on Instagram, Parler, and Twitter. I've already seen a lot of the older stuff, but there's almost a year's worth of new posts from him that I wade through. And with the instructional help of another cop friend, I explore the darknet, where the the shit flows strong and deep. By the time I'm done, I feel a need for a cleansing shower — and a stiff drink.

There's no doubt that K3LVR was instrumental in doxing Amy. Was he the ringleader? Not clear. But his digital fingerprints are all over it. I'm not a prosecutor, but I've been in the going-after-bad-guys business long enough to have a good sense of the sort of evidence the state needs to charge someone successfully with a crime. I think there's close to enough there. So, yes, I'm pleased by what I've been able to unearth.

But I'm also alarmed, uneasy about the most recent internet activity I'm seeing from K3LVR. He's started railing against Mike. Here are the headings of some of his recent posts that are filled with vitriol. "Longtime Bureaucrat Noses Into County's Health." "Mike Franklin, Father of Former School-Board Nazi, Wants to Control Your Body." "Beware of New County Health Board Despot." Going after my niece put him at one level of despicability. But if he goes after my brother, he'll be elevating matters to DEFCON 2. And things aren't going to turn out well for him. Not well at all.

Chapter 54

Hannah

Both Mike and I have been getting angry and abusive text messages, phone calls, nasty letters, and emails. They began as a trickle, then became a torrent. I, for one, have not been eager to share this news with Amy. This is exactly what she cautioned me about when I took this job at the health department. And I remember puffing out my chest and dismissing her words of warning, boasting that I'm no spring chicken and could handle whatever shit the assholes of the world throw at me. Mighty brave words for someone who never had to face any of this before. I admit I don't feel so intrepid and courageous any more.

Mike and I, of course, have been talking about it between ourselves—comparing messages, threats, wording, timing. It's clear we've been doxed, but we're not sure how or where. We've brought Jack into our discussions. Right now, the three of us are sitting at the breakfast table, pulling apart the threads of what feels like a tightening noose. Jack is telling us what he discovered when he went back and took a deeper dive into online doings of K3LVR.

Mike looks at him hard. "So, you're pretty sure all this is connected? You think Earl is responsible for what happened to Amy and Diana Tarrant—and what's now happening to Hannah, and me?"

"I do. Not Earl alone. It seems clear to me that he must have been working with others. But as of now, I don't know who," Jack says.

"So, what do we do?" Mike asks him.

"You do nothing at the moment. Just try to stay strong and ignore the incoming shit. These people are vile, but I'm guessing they're not a physical threat to you," Jack says. "So, for the moment, leave things to me. I'm going to do this right. Gather our evidence before we take this to Mesa Vista's finest men in blue. We don't want those hapless idiots going in first and fucking things up."

Chapter 55

Jack

I'm a total doofus when it comes to things like ham radio. Fortunately, I have a buddy I could ask. I have buddies I can consult about almost anything. Would they pay for my dinner? No. Would they answer my question about something like ham-radio reception? Yes. I may not be the most likable guy around. But as Obama said about Hillary, I'm "likable enough." Just likable enough.

The used ham-radio receiver I bought at my buddy's suggestion only cost me about $200. He showed me how to tune in to K3LVR's broadcasts. He also told me that K3LVR's call sign was probably a cutesie way of signaling his devotion to a "K3" high-performance transceiver manufactured by Elecraft. And in the short time I've been listening in, I've learned something interesting: amateur radio can be at least as wild and toxic as the darknet. At least, that's so in this case. Maybe not every ham operator is like Earl, who vomits his bile out onto the airwaves around Mesa Vista for hours each day and night. He has opinions about everything. College football, the space program, Chinese food, you name it. But he focuses most of his time and attention on politics and government—especially public health.

To hear him talk, you'd think vaccinations are the worst scourge ever visited upon humankind. His ramblings aren't always coherent. It's not always clear, for example, what Earl thinks is the purpose behind "the great vaccine con," as he often calls it. Or exactly who is behind it. But a con, it is. A massive, evil deception. He's sure of that. And wants his listeners to know it, too. And he wants them to act on that knowledge. Rise up. Oppose the evil government bureaucrats trying to "push the needles into your body, like the Roman bureaucrats who pressed that crown of thorns down on the brow of Jesus Christ." Yup. That's the gist of it.

Sometimes, he brings in a guest. In the short time I've been listening, I've twice heard a fellow named Raymond carry on at length about how vaccines are part of the "Great Replacement" plot to systematically substitute the white race in this country with non-white, minority cultures. He thinks vaccines are being used to move this replacement along. Last night, I heard this Raymond say that vaccines contain antigens that impact fertility. "White women are being sterilized through vaccines, and white men are being injected with carcinogens that will lead to death. Anyone who agrees to be vaccinated is an idiot."

Earl laid in right on top of this: "And now, right as their

government-hyped COVID hysteria is dying down, they find a couple more reasons to vaccinate you: polio and monkeypox! Don't fall for it, people. Don't fall for their great, evil hoax! They'll *always* have some made-up reasons to pump harmful substances into your veins!

"And who do I mean by *'they'*? You know who. Government bureaucrats. The Dr. Anthony Faucis of this world. But don't think for a moment the worrisome ones are only in Washington, DC. No, folks. They're everywhere. Right here in Mesa County, we have to worry about Hannah Matthews, the deputy director of the county health department. And, of course, her loverboy, Mike Franklin, whom she managed to get appointed to the county board of health that's supposed to oversee her office! These two are dangerous. They're pro-vaccine liberals that want to vaccinate you and your children. Their latest crusade is about the polio vaccine. DO NOT FALL FOR IT, people! You're more likely to get polio from the vaccine than from not being vaccinated. Don't listen to their vile lies.

"And if, like me, you want to tell these evil people what you think of them, you call them or text them. Here are their personal cellphone numbers. The Matthews woman's is 303-555-1212. That's 303-555-1212. And the number for Mike Franklin—oh, wait. Have I told you lately that he's the father of Amy Wilson, that odious former member of the county school board? Yes, he is! Daughter and father are cut from the same pro-government, anti-liberty mold. Tell him what you think of him. Tell him how you'd like to rip his shriveled old balls off. Tell him how you'd like to pour some molten lead up that bureaucratic butt of his. The number is 303-296-8743. That's 303-296-8743."

I listened for a while longer as Earl also told his listeners the email addresses for Hannah and Mike. I hadn't seen him dox these two online. Maybe Earl feels his radio broadcasts are somehow a safer setting for him to engage in this illegal activity. No written record on the airwaves, unlike online.

And maybe until now, he's never had someone in his audience interested in taking him down. But now he does. Someone with a tape recorder.

Still, it would be good to have more evidence than just his villainous voice on the recorder. And I figure I can find more. I decide to put a GPS tracker on Earl's van. So, at dusk, I take a drive to Earl's house, which is out on Canyon Creek Drive, west of town, in the hilly neighborhood of Redlands. Even before I see his house number, I know which house must be his when I spot a radio tower, which looks to me about 70 feet tall. Adding that tower to the location of his property—at the crest of a hill—I figure he must have damn good transmission power. His signal can reach a lot of like-minded assholes.

Fitting the transponder onto his van is easy. Now it's just a matter of seeing where he leads me.

Chapter 56

Mike

I'm not a wimp. Far from it. Or so I've always thought. But the kind of crap Hannah and I have been dealing with for the past week or two is truly scary. And frankly incredible. I headed the state health agency for eight years and never was subjected to the level of abuse that's now become part of our daily life. Although she's putting up a brave front, I know it's bothering her. I can see the worry lines deepening on her face.

As I've told you, I've had an aversion to leaving the house for a long time now. It's just too psychologically exhausting for me to think in advance about all the physical hurdles I'm going to encounter, all the ways it's going to be difficult for me to navigate my walker, to find good hand-holds, to deal with people.

And now, the people I might encounter may not be just

the usual sort one would want to avoid—normal, everyday, tiresome people—but actual hostiles, people who want to do me harm. Needless to say, that reality has elevated my disinclination to leave the house. I try to urge Hannah to work from home. Sometimes, I succeed, and she works from the dining-room table. Other times, she pats me on the cheek, and says, "I have to go in, Mike. I'll be fine." I spend those days nursing nervous bowels.

Chapter 56

Jack

As it turns out, Earl doesn't go out and about much. From what I've seen so far, he mostly just goes to the grocery store or drug store. But right now I'm a few cars behind him as he winds his way out of the hills and onto Rt. 6. He pulls into the parking lot at the IHOP, and I follow suit a moment later. I watch as the van's automated wheelchair lift lowers the scooter to the pavement. Earl makes his way around the vehicle, onto the scooter, and heads into IHOP.

An aging, skeletal woman directs him to a table not far from the door and shows him where he can park his scooter. She then returns for me. I ask her for a booth a bit deeper into the restaurant and I sit on the bench facing Earl's table, so I can keep him in sight. I've only been there a minute or so, when a voice greets me.

"I've been standing over there trying to remember how

I know you. Finally, it came to me: you're that fella from Texas who came in here back during COVID wearing a "Grandpas for Liberty" teeshirt. You was with a handsome guy who had a walker." Becky Dubrovsky picks up my coffee mug, fills it to the brim, and sets it back in front of me, sloshing a bit of it on the table in the process.

"Why, you sure are right about that, Miss, ah, Miss … Becky! That's it. Miss Becky! I told you I'd never forget that pretty face of yours, and dang it, I didn't."

She giggles and jiggles. But there's a lot less jiggling than the last time I saw her. She's lost a ton of weight. "You sure didn't," she says. "And I didn't forget your name either. It's Jack! I remembered that because it was the name of my first boyfriend." She actually bats her eyebrows at me. Good lord. "And I even remember what we talked about—that awful Amy Wilson woman and who might have been vandalizing her property. Right?"

"Why, I reckon you're correct about that, Miss Becky. You're right as rain!"

"It's good to see you, Jack. What can I get for you this morning?"

"I'll have the Denver omelet and a small glass of orange juice, Miss Becky. Thanks."

She leaves to hand in my order. When I return my gaze to Earl, I see that another man is now at the table. His back is to me, so I can't see who it is. Becky pours coffee for the newcomer, warms Earl's cup, and takes their order. Soon, she's back at my side. She freshens my cup, too, and says, "Remember when you was here I mentioned a fella named Marty Stauffer as someone who likes to kick up a ruckus at meetings of local public boards?"

"I do remember that, Miss Becky. I surely do."

"Well, that's him sitting at that table over there with Mr. Grumps." She tosses her glance toward Earl.

I take another look at the guy with Earl. Of course! Marty Stauffer. I thought there was something familiar about the back of that guy's head. Incredible! I try to refocus on what Becky has been saying. "Mr. Grumps?"

"That's what me and the other servers call the old guy. He's one of the crabbiest people I've ever waited on. And the pair of 'em are in here every other Tuesday, so we have to put up with Grumps more often than I'd like. Our other name for Mr. Grumps is Grabby Paws, because he's a big-time fondler."

I'm processing all this as I try to smile and nod at Miss Becky. Marty Stauffer and Earl Gottsdanker. Together.And the two of them come here together every other week? Now, that's a fascinating piece of information. Thank you, my dear Miss Becky. You just unintentionally provided some important testimony. "So, that younger fella is Marty Stauffer, eh? Do you know him pretty well?"

"Nah. I don't really know him personally. I just know who he is."

"You say the pair of 'em come in here every other week. Is it always just the two of 'em?" I ask, with the innocence of a child.

"Mostly so, these days. Sometimes there's a third guy. Used to be a fourth, but that one just stopped coming all of a sudden over a year ago. Never seen him again."

I have a thought about that, but decide to return to it later.

"The third guy, the one who still sometimes comes. Do you know him?"

With a coquettish sway, she says, "Jack, I don't make a point of getting to know every man who comes in here. Just a few."

"Well, Miss Becky, I'm guessin' most men who come in here want to get to know *you*! How do you choose?"

"I only encourage the handsome ones." She smiles at me and puts her hand on my shoulder. "And I'm tellin' ya: the fella who sometimes turns that deuce into a three-top is *not* good-looking! Tall and skinny. Long nose. Dark brown, unkempt hair. Greasy. Looks depressed all the time."

"Do you know his name?"

"Actually, I do."

I give her an ah-ha look, like I've just caught her out. "Miss Becky, I'm suddenly not feeling so special!"

"No, no. You got the wrong idea. It's just that the scooter guy says things like, 'Bring my friend Ray some orange juice,' or 'Ray needs his coffee refreshed.'"

"Ray can't speak for himself?"

"He can. I think the scooter guy just likes to be in charge. He seems pretty full of himself."

"Yup. I know people like that myself."

A young couple has taken a booth behind me. Becky leaves me to tend to them. When she returns after several minutes, I say, "Forgive me for asking you more questions about those fellas over there. As someone who's pretty much a loner, I find it fascinating when I see men hanging out together. Most of us old guys suffer from what them coastal intellectuals call 'social isolation.' Fancy way of sayin' 'no friends!'"

Her eyes fill with sympathy. "Well, you was in here with another fella that time we met!"

"Yeah, but that was my brother. Doesn't count." A bell rings at the counter. She leaves and then returns with my omelet. I adopt a more intimate tone, like I'm askin' for her help solving the complicated formula of male friendships. "I'm intrigued. You say there used to be four of 'em, but one fella just stopped coming all of a sudden. That fourth guy: what did he look like?"

She matches my demeanor and leans close to me. "That's an interesting question, Jack. I always thought that guy didn't fit with the group." She glances toward Earl and Marty. "Not that those two are exactly normal, but that fourth guy was even weirder. Huge. Bald head. Flat nose. An ear that had been damaged somehow. Sloppy dresser. A real mess of a human being."

"Ah, now—"

"Well, he *was*! And I don't know what it means when the weirdest of the group takes off and never returns, leaving behind a lecherous cripple, a gay, and a spooky creep. Maybe the other three voted him out of the club or he said to himself, 'These guys are too normal for me! I'm outta here.'"

I laugh obligingly. Then, I fully track what she said. "Wait. A gay? Who's the gay?"

"Marty!"

"What makes you say that?"

"Oh, well, I don't know for sure, of course. But when you

spend enough time in this job, you get pretty good at readin' people. Me and the other servers all think Marty's a faggot. He's a smart dresser, and he just carries himself in a certain telltale way. You know what I mean." She makes her wrist go limp. "And he walks fast, taking little steps like he has his butt cheeks clenched. I'd show you, but with this butt of mine, you'd have a hard time detecting a clench." She laughs and wiggles her bottom, which frankly doesn't look so bad.

I flap my hand at her as if what she just said about herself is the most ridiculous sentence ever uttered. "Miss Becky, you continue to amaze me. You are a true observer of humanity! And a person of rare beauty."

She giggles and sashays away, her retreating hips offering me a lascivious wink. I can't believe I was able to grill her about that table of men without raising her curiosity about why I wanted to know. I attribute my good fortune to a history of clean living. And my killer smile. Or maybe Becky's just not the suspicious sort.

I dig into my omelet and watch Earl and Marty. They're deeply involved in whatever they're discussing. They don't notice Becky taking a photo of them with her iPhone. When she returns to me, she holds her phone toward me and says, "Punch your number in here, Jackie, and I'll send you that photo I just took of those two."

"I'm mighty happy to have your phone number, Miss Becky, but what makes you think I'd want a photo of them?"

"'Cuz you are super interested in them for some reason. And I like you, Jack. So I want to help you out, whatever it is you're up to."

"Well, now, can't a fella just be curious?"

"Oh, you're way beyond curious, my Texas friend. Way beyond. And just so you know, I think you're some kinda cop. But I'm happy to help you anyway, 'cuz I've never liked that group of men."

Uh-oh. Becky's more street-smart than I suspected. How to play this? "Busted. I'm a Texas Ranger, and those guys are drug lords we've been after for years."

She crosses her arms and rolls her eyes. "Uh, huh."

"Okay, I'm FBI, and we think those guys are part of Hillary Clinton's ring of pedophiles."

She grins. "A bit closer to believable."

"Okay, okay. I'm a Mesa County undercover detective. Those guys have been taking two samples from the cheese counter at Sprouts, when the sign clearly says, *ONLY ONE*."

Now, she giggles. "Look. I don't really care what it's about. I just don't want you thinking I'm some sort of clueless moron, too stupid to see what you're doing."

"Becky, I never—"

"Shhhh." She presses her index finger to my lips. "Don't ruin it, Jack. Now, if you sit there a minute, I'll be right back with something I know you'll like."

I finish my omelet and drain my coffee mug. Becky returns with a polaroid photo, which she snaps down on the table in front of me. "That's a picture of the four of 'em."

"Wow. How do you have this?"

"As we were talking, I remembered that this photo was among many on a bulletin board in the employee break room. We used to offer all-you-can-eat pancake breakfasts and took photos of anyone who ate more than twenty-five." She flips the polaroid over and points to "29" written on the back. "The big goon ate a mountain of 'em." At the bottom, I notice a date: February 25, 2020. The four of 'em. Together. In 2020.

I grab Becky's forearm and draw the back of her hand to my lips. "Miss Becky, you are a force for good in this world. How can I ever repay you?"

She considers this. "Take me out for a drink sometime, Jack. You have my number."

I decide right here and now that I'll marry Miss Becky and worship her body for the rest of my life if her actions help me put away these nasty fucks seated across the room.

Chapter 57

Amy

I don't know why Dad and Hannah have tried to hide all this, pretend it's not happening. Are they afraid I'll say, 'I told you so'? Are they trying to protect me and Matty from worry? Not sure. But it's ridiculous. One would have to be pretty oblivious not to notice the signs. Suddenly, the mailbox is full of letters addressed to each of them, penmanship scratchy and wild. There's chatter in local social-media groups, griping about why the county is spending money to test Mesa Vista wastewater for the polio virus or staff a monkeypox screening center. And almost every time I go into town I have to pass by the DPH building, where at least half the time there are a few demonstrators out there hoisting anti-vax placards. So, yeah, the waters are roiling around Dad and Hannah, and I'm feeling the ripples.

A really big wave washes up on my doorstep this evening in the form of my ex-husband, Danny. He's here to pick up Matty for an overnight. Danny tells him to wait in the car for a minute while he talks to me.

"What's up?" I ask, wondering what fresh hell he has in store for me.

"I want to tell you about something I overheard last night at a bar in town."

Well, this isn't what I expected. "Oh, okay. What was it?"

"Next to the table where I was sitting was a guy about our age who seemed really drunk—loud and talkative, you know? He was telling a younger companion all about himself, said he's a 'prominent anti-government activist' in town. Claimed to be partly responsible for 'taking down' a school-board member and a public-health official."

Woah! Danny certainly has my attention in a way he hasn't for years. "And?"

"His companion found all this intriguing and was asking all kinds of questions, like how he'd done that. He said, 'We vandalized their property. I keyed her car myself! We doxed them and encouraged harassment. Finally, they buckled when they realized this storm of shit wasn't going to stop until they left office.'"

"This is incredible. What did you do?"

"Nothing, except move a bit closer and listen even more intently. At one point, this guy said something like, 'Now, we're targeting a couple of crazy, pro-vax health officials, trying to drive them out of office, too.'"

"Do you know who this guy is?"

"I'd seen him in this place before. I didn't know him,

but I asked around and found out that his name is Marty Stauffer. People said he's a wingnut on the far right."

"Do you know who his 'companion' is?"

Danny actually blushes. "I do. He's a CMU student. Lucas Murdoch."

"Where was this?"

"Charlie Dwellington's."

A gay bar. I'm not surprised. I know Danny's gay. That's why we divorced. "I thought you usually hang out at Quincy's."

He grins. "I do." Shrugs. "Just mixing it up."

"Well, Danny, this is huge. Um, I'm surprised you'd tell me all this. We haven't exactly been on friendly terms."

"I always liked your dad, Amy. He's a good man and was always good to me. I wouldn't want to see anything bad happen to him. If this guy Marty was actually involved in what happened to you, I'd hate to think he's going to do the same awful shit to your dad."

For the first time in years, my heart warms a degree toward Danny. "Thanks."

———

Now, the four of us—Dad, Hannah, Jack, and I—are at the table, having coffee (and stiffer libations) after dinner. We've been here for several hours. Listening to Jack's recordings of Earl's heinous broadcasts. Hearing about what Becky Dubrovsky told him at IHOP. Marveling that Agnes Moore's son Ray is involved in all this. Dissecting what Danny told me about the conversation he overheard.

Dad says, "My butt and hips are sore from sitting in the same chair. Could we move to the living room?"

As we do, Jack says to me, "Maybe the craziest coincidence of all is that you've met this guy Ray!"

I take the polaroid he's holding and say, "*Met* Ray and *encountered* the big guy. Two out of four!"

Hannah looks to Jack. "What do we do now?"

He says, "I think we take what we know to Tom Duffy, the police chief. It's more than enough for his department to put together a case and arrest Earl. Getting Marty will be a bit tougher and will depend on the willingness of Danny and this CMU kid to testify in court. Getting Ray will be the toughest of all. Unless . . ."

"Unless what? I ask.

"Unless Earl flips."

Chapter 58

Earl

I know there'll be people—including some of my own friends and relatives—who say that Donna wouldn't have died of COVID earlier this week if she'd been vaccinated. They can believe that, if they want. I don't. I think she'd have died of it, regardless. Or maybe died *because* of the vaccine. That's more likely. In any case, my wife of 54 years is gone. Probably just as well, because if she were around now, seeing what's about to come down on me would probably be the thing to kill her.

I was no sooner home from Elsie's private burial yesterday than a Mesa Vista detective showed up at the house. At first, I thought he was a well-wisher—perhaps a neighbor (I make a point of not knowing any of them) or a former work associate of Donna's, here to express his condolences. But he'd only been here a few minutes before it was apparent to me that Donna's death wasn't the most consequential thing I'd be dealing with this week. Consequential for me, at least, if not for Donna.

It's strange how we process our own behavior. After one has engaged in wrongdoing for a while and suffered no punishment for it, one begins to believe the behavior is okay—or, at least, that one can engage in it with impunity. Yes, yes, of course I knew it was wrong to target, harass, vandalize, scare, dox, and otherwise violate Wilson and Tarrant, and then Franklin and Matthews. But one of the things we all learn as kids is that lots of bad deeds go unpunished. Of course, the corollary lesson is that our wrongdoing eventually catches up with us, even if we don't know quite how.

And that's the case here. I don't know quite how the MVPD put all these pieces together. But Detective Falk (I kid you not) had recordings of some of my broadcasts and printouts of many of my internet and darknet posts. Even I could see that it was pretty incriminating. Then he began to spool out evidence that Marty, Ray, and I know each other—and (dear god) were regularly in contact with Dwayne until his death.

I watch enough tv to have known not to say anything to Falk without my lawyer present. But after he arrested me, Mirandized me, and managed to get my paretic body into the back seat of his car, he turned around and looked over the seat at me. "Forgive me, Mr. Gottsdanker. Just one more thing . . ."

"What is it, detective?"

"Do you know a Becky Dubrovsky?

"I don't think so, no."

"She's employed as a waitress at the IHOP in town."

"Oh, Becky at IHOP. I know who she is, yes. Why?"

"She claims you sexually assaulted her last year by placing your hand on her bottom and cupping her cheek. Says other servers saw it happen and are willing to testify to it. I'm just wondering, Mr. Gottsdanker, sir, if any of that rings a bell."

I was gagging on the bile that had surged up my esophagus, but I managed to croak, "That fucking cunt."

Chapter 59

Mike

I have no interest in going out for dinner. I told you earlier about my aversion to outings in general. I can no longer abide the sheer physical challenge of it, navigating a walker through a restaurant full of tables, chairs, and inconsiderate people. But everyone else wants to go out to celebrate, so I don't feel comfortable being the party pooper by saying no. I feel obligated to go along, even though it's exhausting. I wish we could just stay home.

But now here we are—Hannah, Amy, Matty, Jack, and I — at a pushed-together table for six at Spoons Bistro. I have the extra place at the end. My walker and I sit across from each other. It's a reliable companion, if not particularly loquacious. The group conversation, which started in the car on the way over, is still focused on the news that the police have arrested Earl Gottsdanker, Marty Stauffer, and Ray Moore.

Jack has put on his "aw, shucks" face as the others act as if he's just brought down Jack the Ripper, the Zodiac Killer, or (forgive me, Jack) the murderer of JonBenét Ramsey.

"No, no, no," he says, turning aside their praise. It's not brilliant detective work at all. I'm telling you, 90 percent of the time, solving a crime comes down to blind chance or dumb luck. Like in this case! Someone sees something that's seemingly insignificant and barely registers in their memory. Someone overhears a conversation that catches their attention because of a name or a place mentioned. A disabled car leads to someone observing a peculiar license plate. A restaurant manager photographs a quartet of men because one of them downed 29 pancakes. A flirtatious waitress decides to open up to a customer who's clearly misrepresenting himself."

"Oh, come on, Jack. You're too modest," Amy says.

"No, I'm tellin' ya: people talking; others listening and sharing what they've heard or seen. That's what it often comes down to." Now, he turns to Matty. Leans into him and gives him a long, earnest look. "Little buddy, remember when I told you the superhero I'm most like is Captain America, able to bring down bad guys without super powers?"

Matt nods amiably.

"My power—my ordinary, everyday power—is listening and observing. If you ever want to be a cop, that's all you need to be good at what you do."

Without hesitation, Matt says, "I don't want to be a cop.

Most cops are assholes. Sorry. Not you, Uncle Jack. But most of 'em."

Jack laughs and says, "Can't argue with that, my man."

Matt—my wise, smart, precocious grandson—says, "But I'd guess being observant and a good listener are good traits to have for almost any line of work."

His mom is impressed. She ruffles his hair and says, "Yup, buddy. Even better than math skills."

He squirms away from her. "Personal foul!"

Hannah says, "Jack, help me with this. I see what the police had on Earl: the evidence you handed over to them. But how did they get Marty Stauffer?"

"Earl flipped on Marty like an egg going over easy."

Matt looks confused. "Flipped?"

Jack says, "It basically means Earl told the police some things—or gave them some physical evidence — that will help them indict Marty. Probably in exchange for a promise of some lesser charge against himself."

"Does that happen a lot?"

"More common if you're dealing with people who aren't part of the mafia or some other organized group with a code of silence. Why? Because most asshats, once criminally exposed and vulnerable, want to protect themselves in any way they can. And the best way often is to turn on some other asshat."

I pat Jack on the shoulder as I say to Matt, "That's a highly sophisticated analysis by one of America's leading law-enforcement experts."

"Eat my shorts, Mikey. Eat my shorts."

Matt guffaws.

Amy smiles indulgently, then asks, "Did Earl turn on Ray, too?"

Jack says, "Yes, from what I understand. But I heard from somebody I know in the county prosecutor's office that Ray's facing even more serious legal problems."

All heads turn to Jack.

"Apparently, he's about to be charged with the murder of a black man a year ago out in Loma, where he lives in a trailer park. The evidence Earl gave them about Ray's racist attitudes spurred the cops to take a closer look at him for that crime. And I guess they found some physical evidence in Moore's trailer that links him to the crime."

Hannah says, "Good lord. These are truly awful people."

Amy releases a big sigh. "That's for sure. But they're all getting their comeuppance, big time. Earl loses his wife and gets indicted for criminal harassment. Ray is going to be indicted for both criminal harassment and possibly, from what you say, Jack, murder." She pauses to consider. "Seems like only Marty Stauffer is going to skate by without getting hit with a double whammy."

Jack smiles. "Oh, I'm happy to assure you that's not true."

Amy's face is earnest. "Really? Tell us!"

Jack can barely contain his glee. "Marty has monkeypox."

Chapter 60

Amy

Dad has been waiting for this titanium wheelchair for months. Goddamned Kaiser Permanente has been yanking him around about it forever. But he got it today, and he's a happy camper. Instead of manipulating that awkward walker, he now zips around like a border collie on cocaine. It's a little unnerving to me when he suddenly announces he's "going for a spin" and zooms across the whole first floor of the house, Annabelle madly barking behind him. But, what the hell. He deserves whatever delights he can find. *You go, geezer!*

He told me yesterday that he's somewhat conscience-stricken about feeling a frisson of *schadenfreude* over the extra problems each of our nemeses is now facing. "I'm glad they'll be held to justice for what they did to all of us. But I shouldn't be feeling this delight about the additional awful things each of them is now dealing with—well, except for Ray, of course."

"Look," I say, rubbing his forearm. "It's not like you're finding joy in the misfortune of *good* people. You're having a perfectly healthy, normal reaction about people who are genuinely awful human beings—people who, in my view, deserve whatever horrible things come their way. Besides, you can't control your feelings. You feel what you feel!"

He gives me one of those slow, tender smiles of his. "I guess you're right. Thanks." We sit quietly for a moment. Then he asks, "Where's Matty? I haven't seen him today."

"He's working on his Halloween costume. He says this may be the last year he goes out and he wants to make it especially good."

"Do you know what he's going as?"

"Nope. He's being secretive about it. Yesterday, he asked Jack to take him to Petsmart. Jack just laughed when I asked him what Matty bought. He wouldn't spill the beans. … May I make you some lunch?"

"No, thanks. I'll get something in a bit. … Do you still have the stuffed animals Matt had when he was younger?"

"Yup. They're in a bag in the attic."

"Would you bring it down here for me when you get a chance?"

"Sure. Anything specific you want?"

"Yup, but I'm not gonna tell you. It's part of my costume."

We'd all decided that this year we'd all dress up for Halloween in honor of Matt's decision that this will be the end of his trick-and-treating. The plan is to meet in the dining room at 6:00pm sharp, costumed and ready to consume a light dinner before Matt goes out with his friends.

At the appointed hour, I'm the first to show up, in order to pull salads out of the fridge. It was a busy week for me, and I had little bandwidth to think about a homemade Halloween costume. So, my get-up is pathetic. I'm wearing black leggings and a black teeshirt that reads "I was going to be a REPUBLICAN for Halloween, but my head wouldn't fit up my ass."

Hannah walks in and we both start laughing. It's clear we were on the same wavelength for this occasion. She's wearing a brassy-yellow shoulder-length wig. Her face is expertly made up as a clown, and she has an "MTG" brooch on her shirt. I say, "Marjorie, darling, how nice of you to pull your head out of your ass for the dinner hour!" I offer to get her a drink.

"Good lord, yes. Impersonating this twat is too painful to endure without some alcohol."

Jack arrives at the front door. Hannah, laughing much harder now, ushers him into the kitchen. He's wearing a ridiculous "Captain America" costume, the polyester blue tights proving a bit more revealing than he probably likes.

I size him up in my iPhone lens. "Oh, my god, Jack! You went all out. How much did this cost you? Whatever it was, it was too much for a one-off joke."

"Just so you know, I intend to get five or six years of use out of this. And let's just say it wasn't cheap." He brandishes the two-foot-wide shield on his left arm. "This alone cost $40."

A door opens at the back of the house and the clickety-clack sound of Annabelle's nails on the hardwood floor precedes her arrival in the room. She stops at the entrance to the kitchen, like a debutante awaiting her formal introduction to society. When we all laugh and applaud, she wags her tail and enters the room. She's wearing an "Underdog" costume for dogs — a red teeshirt, emblazoned with a white "U" and a royal-blue cape.

I say to Jack, "I'm guessing this was your doing?"

"Matty's idea. My purchase. But a necessary one. Superheroes need allies."

Now Dad arrives in his wheelchair. His hair is gelled or sprayed to look like it's blown straight back by the wind. He's wearing thick-framed sunglasses and has something in his lap. Jack, Hannah, and I are looking at each other, shrugging, unable to identify who or what he's supposed to be.

"Does this help?" Dad asks. He flips the object in his lap. It's a plush animal—the penguin "Opus" from the comic strip "Bloom County."

Jack now laughs so hard that he has to bend over, causing his tights to rip in the back. "OMG, that's perfect, Mikey. You're, uh, uh, what's his name? Oh, it's coming to me. Wait . . . Cutter John!! You're Cutter John!"

"I am, good sir. I am." Now he looks around, faking bewilderment. "I'm looking for my raven-haired girlfriend, Bobbi Harlow." He rolls over to Hannah. "How about you, blondie? You seen my Bobbi?"

Hannah grabs his chin and pulls his face toward hers for a kiss. "I'll make you forget all about Bobbi, buster. You're all mine now."

A kazoo plays a flourish. Matty enters the room. He's wearing a "Central High School" baseball cap. Some writing on a white bib around his neck reads: "Pee and Poo Here," with an arrow pointing down. Around his neck hangs a belt or leash, attached to a flat tray that sticks out in front of him, like one of those "cigarette girls" who plied their wares in restaurants in the 1940s. Glued to the tray is about a one-inch layer of kitty litter. The front of the box reads: "For Furry Use Only."

When Dad stops laughing, he asks, "What are you going to do if someone hops up onto your litter box and makes use of it."

"Hmmm. Hadn't considered that."

Jack says, "Maybe you should take Underdog with you. Keep other furries away." He holds his fist out to Jack in approval. "Chops, man."

Hannah inspects Jack's creation more carefully. "It's amazingly creative, Matt. Do you think people will get it?"

"I figure it's like most good costumes: lots of people won't get it, but those who do will think it's hysterical. That's the audience I'm aiming for."

The doorbell rings. Matt says, "Oh, hey, I'm sorry. I can't stay to eat. Amber and Jason decided to come early. I gotta go."

We all follow him to the door to see his friends' costumes. Amber is unmistakable as Lauren Boebert. She's wearing a slutty-looking black latex bodysuit, probably a repurposed "Cat Woman" costume. She has a Glock (fake, I hope) holstered on her hip. And a red MAGA baseball cap. Eyeglasses and hoop earrings. She chews gum. The perfect package.

Jason is ... what? His back is to us. He's wearing a baroque Marie Antoinette ball gown and a tall, platinum-blonde, French-style aristocratic wig with cascading ringlets. When he turns around, we see his cheeks are heavily rouged, his lips scorched with bright-red lipstick, his eyebrows dramatically penciled. His neck choker reads "Dr. Oz." He holds a piece of broccoli by the stem and flourishes its large floret toward us. "Crudite, anyone?"

The early evening brings to our door the customary witches, fairies, superheroes, pirates, and vampires. As the evening wears on and the tots turn to teens, we get a parade of seductive Taylor Swifts and a plethora of naughty nurses, cowgirls, Playboy bunnies, maids, and Hooters waitresses.

I snarf down a miniature Milky Way and summon my inner scold. "What's with teenage girls these days? Why must they idolize skanks?"

Jack says, "Oh, c'mon, Amy. Don't be such a prude. Inside every madonna is a whore, waiting to burst out."

Hannah and I hurl handfuls of candy at him. She says, "Take that back, caveman!" She looks to Dad for support. "Can you rein in this Neanderthal?"

Dad laughs and says, "I suspect not. We all know that Jack is beyond redemption."

Hannah says, "Some of the political costumes tonight gave me hope. Maybe this town isn't hopeless after all."

"What are you thinking of?" I ask. "Matty and his friends?"

Hannah hiccups. "Well, yes, but there were the two girls who were Serena and Venus!"

Dad, realizing that perhaps Hannah is pretty far along in her cups, says gently, "I'm not sure that wearing blackface is a liberal statement, Shar. Besides, didn't you notice all the bumbling Joe Bidens, the evil Dr. Faucis and Nancy Pelosis, the 'kneeling NFL player,' and all the triumphant-looking Donald Trumps?"

The doorbell rings again. I say, "Good lord. It's getting late. The kids have to wrap it up and go home!"

Jack looks at his watch. "No, I think that's my date." He goes to the door.

Hannah straightens her back in an effort to signal her indignation at Dad's challenge. The effect is somewhat hilarious, given how her head is wobbling atop her neck. "Well. There were some *negative* Donald Trumps! And there was that one kid dressed as a gravestone that read "GOP R.I.P."

Dad laughs. "So, apart from Matty and his friends, we saw three or four political costumes the entire evening that were 'liberal'" I think it's fair to say this city is a Republican cesspool."

Jack comes back in the room with his arm slung over the shoulder of a short, plump woman. Her red baseball cap says, "Let's Go, Brandon!" She's wearing red leggings and a red tee-shirt that reads,"Forget dogs and cats! Spay and Neuter LIBERALS."

"Hi, y'all. I'm Becky!"

Afterword

Thank you for reading *Jesus Is My Vaccine*.

Reviews and ratings are absolutely crucial for authors these days. If you enjoyed this book and have a few moments to spare, please furnish a rating and brief comment on Amazon. That would be enormously helpful to me in connecting this novel with more readers.

— M.N.

About the Author

Raised in Colorado and educated at Johns Hopkins and Harvard, Mila Norquist writes in various fiction genres.

Made in the USA
Las Vegas, NV
23 December 2024

15270467R10197